She wa___
to get involved...

And he was nothing but trouble. She was
crazy to resist him, for he was the sexiest
thing she'd ever seen in her entire life.
She was simply crazy.

His eyes stared down into hers. "One last
chance," he whispered, but he lied. It
wasn't a chance at all, not with his long
fingers cupping her neck, not with his
mouth so close to hers, not with the
drugging sensuality of his golden eyes
burning into hers.

Slowly, hesitantly, she pressed her mouth
against his. Her lips were trembling,
her hands were shaking and he was
holding himself very still, giving her no
assistance, almost savoring her suddenly
clumsy efforts. His mouth was soft and
responsive against hers. Very shyly she
touched the tip of her tongue to his lips.
They parted instantly, and the taste of
cognac swirled around them, cognac
and passion.

AUTHOR'S CHRISTMAS MESSAGE

I always get disgustingly sentimental when it comes to Christmas, and this year won't be any different. It'll be our first Christmas in our new house, we're awaiting the birth of our second child and we're finding that life is worth celebrating. I hope all of you have yourselves a merry little Christmas and that your new year is as splendid as ours will be.

Love,

Anne Stuart

Books by Anne Stuart

HARLEQUIN AMERICAN ROMANCE

30–CHAIN OF LOVE
39–HEART'S EASE
52–MUSEUM PIECE
93–HOUSEBOUND
126–ROCKY ROAD

HARLEQUIN INTRIGUE

5–TANGLED LIES
9–CATSPAW

Bewitching Hour
Anne Stuart

Harlequin Books

TORONTO • NEW YORK • LONDON
AMSTERDAM • PARIS • SYDNEY • HAMBURG
STOCKHOLM • ATHENS • TOKYO • MILAN

For Lorelei Wheeler and Bev Young—
I couldn't have done it without you.

Published December 1986

First printing October 1986

ISBN 0-373-16177-8

Chapter One

"Something's coming." Sybil Richardson stared down at the tarot cards covering her already littered desk, and her high forehead wrinkled in confusion. "I can't tell whether it's something nasty or not. But it's powerful."

"Did you try the I Ching?" Leona looked up from her position on the floor beside the rack of dowsing pendulums. The front rooms of the old house on Water Street in Danbury, Vermont, held the business offices of the Society of Water Witches, better known as SOWW. The back room held Sybil Richardson's occult bookstore, and Leona was in the midst of unpacking the latest stock of psychic and dowsing paraphernalia. "You know you do best with Eastern forms of mysticism."

"The I Ching was even more confusing," Sybil said gloomily. "Why don't you do a tarot card reading? You have more talent than I have."

Leona rose to her full five feet, and her round face wrinkled in disapproval. "You know there's no such thing, Sybil. We all have psychic ability; some of us are just more in touch with it."

"I'm not within screaming distance today," Sybil said, pushing back in her chair and running a hand over her coil of dark blond braids that were, as usual, giving her a headache. "I just have this premonition."

"Then you should pay attention to it," Leona said firmly. She was a slightly comical figure, like a cross between Yoda and Mrs. Santa Claus, with a round plump body, a round plump face, small dark eyes that looked like raisins in a suet pudding and a halo of untidy white hair. She never told her age, but Sybil suspected that she was somewhere on the shady side of seventy, despite her limitless energy. "Premonitions have a purpose, and it's risking all sorts of danger to ignore them. You should go upstairs and meditate. I can watch the office."

"Can't do it," Sybil said with a sigh, shuffling the malevolent-looking cards back into an untidy pile. "The newsletter has to be typed; it's already three weeks late. And That Man's coming."

"What man?" Leona sank down onto a straight chair, her short little legs dangling like those of a child.

"Nicholas Wyndham Fitzsimmons." Her voice sounded as if she were naming a snake. "The one who writes all those snotty books, ridiculing everything he doesn't happen to believe in. Which ends up being almost everything that matters to us."

"Oh, dear," Leona said faintly. "If he doesn't believe in anything, why is he coming here? Not to write an exposé, I hope."

"Apparently the great man believes in dowsing. Real dowsing, as he puts it. The ability to find water using a divining rod or pendulum, and that's all there is to it. Just like the trustees."

"Oh, dear," Leona said again.

"Exactly. He thinks the be-all and end-all of dowsing consists of old men finding wells. And he's coming to do research on them."

"Well, we certainly have enough of them. As long as he leaves the rest of us alone."

"Hah," Sybil said. "I'm sure he's as obnoxious as his books. He'll be snooping around, looking down his aristocratic nose at us, and sooner or later I'll be driven to murder."

"Does he have an aristocratic nose?" Leona asked in her most prosaic voice.

"I wouldn't know. He doesn't have his picture on the cover of his books. But he teaches at Harvard; I imagine he's extremely aristocratic."

Leona rose. "Do you have any of his books in the shop? I don't remember seeing them."

"I keep them under the counter." Sybil began shuffling the cards again, frowning once more. "I have to have them in case some poor misguided fool wants to read his venom-dipped prose. But I don't have to advertise them." She turned over the Queen of Cups, moaned and flipped all the cards over.

Leona was looking at her oddly. "The Queen of Cups usually means romance for you. Just how old a man is this Nicholas Fitzsimmons?"

"Ancient," Sybil said. "All you have to do is read his books to know. He's a reactionary old poop, a narrow-minded fossil like most of the trustees. He'll feel right at home with them."

Leona breathed an audible sigh of relief. "Good," she said. "You know how I feel about romance."

Sybil grinned, and the smile lighted up her plain face and turned it into something close to beauty. "I know how you feel. You have your reactionary moments, too."

"If you wish to expand your horizons, to get in touch with the infinite inner and outer reaches, then you can't diffuse your energy with sex," Leona announced.

"I know, you've told me that a million times," Sybil said in a cheerful voice. "Personally I wouldn't mind a little healthy diffusion. It's just that everyone here is married, senile or just reaching puberty."

"And it's a good thing," Leona said sternly. "I'll take these pendulums back to the shop, and then you can sit still and I'll do a reading for you."

"Give me one first." Sybil held out her hand, and Leona dropped a metal, bullet-shaped object into her palm.

"I thought you didn't like dowsing."

"Only because I have such lousy results. Every time I try to dowse for what kind of baby someone's going to have it always comes up with the opposite. But nothing else is giving me any results today. Maybe for once the pendulum will work."

"It will work if you let it," Leona intoned. "You mustn't get distracted by simple bodily urges. Rise above them."

Sybil watched her sturdy little figure toddle away. "God, would I love to get distracted," she said mournfully. She shoved the cards into her desk drawer with a blatant disrespect for their antiquity, slammed it shut and lifted the small pendulum by its metal chain. She held it up, and it began twirling in concentric circles. "Clockwise for yes, counterclockwise for no," she informed it. It just kept spinning.

"Okay, pendulum," she said. "Is something going to happen?" It spun around in wildly clockwise circles. "All right. Is it something good?" The pendulum halted for a moment as if confused, then continued its aimless spin. "Will I like it?" Still clockwise. "So far so good," she muttered. "Does it involve a man?" The pendulum got quite excited at this point, spinning in an arc that was almost parallel to the ground.

Sybil stared at the exuberant pendulum. "Okay, okay," she said. "Here's the hard part. Are my eyes brown?"

The pendulum dropped down, stopping, and then began a slow, counterclockwise motion. Sybil stared at it from her warm brown eyes and cursed. She dropped it into her desk drawer along with the much abused tarot cards. "So much for dowsing." And she turned to her long-neglected typewriter.

It was just an all-round bad day, she thought four hours later when she finally pushed her rolling chair away from the aging Selectric. She cast a cursory glance around the deserted office for the plastic cover, but as usual it was missing. She shivered as she looked out of the multipaned window to the snow-covered road. It was early December, dark at four-thirty, and it snowed or sleeted almost every day. November averaged less sunshine than any other month, but this December was giving gloomy November a run for its money. They'd had thirteen days without sunshine, ending with freezing rain last weekend, making travel impossible. The road still had a solid coating of ice beneath the fresh snow, and Sybil had every expectation of sliding home, even with the blessed amenity of four-wheel drive.

Still and all, the weather had its compensations. The roads were too bad for her to drive to the Burlington airport and fly down to see her family in Princeton. She could spend a few more weeks without the doubtful pleasure of her family's disappointment and well-hidden disapproval. Now if the fates could only come up with a blizzard on Christmas she'd be safe until one of her overwhelming family risked allergy and asthma to visit her. She might even make it till spring.

Not that she didn't love her family. Her father was bluff, kind and tactless. He was also the president of a bank. Her mother was clever, loving and concerned. She was a corporate vice-president. Her older sister, Hattie, was a gynecologist, with a solid-gold practice of rich, grateful patients and a national reputation; her middle sister, Emmie, was a lawyer in one of Philadelphia's most prestigious law firms; and her baby sister, Allison, was a career diplomat, on special assignment for the State Department. They were all very bright, very accomplished, very competent, astonishingly attractive and very kind. And then there was Sybil.

She couldn't be around them without feeling like a changeling. Their determined kindness only made it worse. Because Sybil had no great gift, no great talent, no frightening intellect that made strong men weep. She was just an ordinary sort of woman, with an ordinary amount of brain power that carried her through Bennington College with acceptable grades. She was passably attractive, with thick brownish blond hair, warm brown eyes and regular features that were pleasant enough. Her body was average height, average size, with an inch too much around the hips, but then, who didn't have that? Not her family, of course, but most mortals.

In any other family she would have been a more than acceptable member. But in the Richardsons, women conquered empires, ruled worlds; they didn't like to bake bread. In the Richardsons, women gathered advanced degrees as if they were collecting china figurines; they didn't have gardens and bumper zucchini crops. In the Richardsons, you strove until you dropped and the honors were piled at your feet. You didn't make a disastrous marriage to an unimaginative banker, leave him instead of having children and run away to Vermont, of all places. And you certainly didn't get involved in flaky organizations like the Society of Water Witches.

But thank God, all Richardsons had money. Their maternal grandmother had been the first female self-made millionaire in the New York stock market, and she'd left all her money to her granddaughters. When Sybil could finally take no more of her rigid married life in Scarsdale, she had packed her clothes, left Colin an apologetic note and taken off for the family home in Vermont. Her first act had been to acquire two springer spaniels, which quickly became six.

The dogs had kept the Richardsons at bay. Along with all their other qualities, all the Richardsons, except Sybil, suffered from intense allergies. They couldn't be in the same room with a dog without wheezing and coughing and resorting to inhalants. It had worked out beautifully.

And she didn't have to feel guilty. They hadn't used the house in Vermont for years anyway; it was only opened on an occasional Labor Day weekend, and even then half of the family couldn't make it. So it was Sybil's and she reveled in it, with her six dogs and her solitude and her fresh-baked bread that was directly responsible for that extra inch around her hips. Fortunately the zucchini crop helped to take it off.

No, if it weren't for the lack of eligible men, her life in Danbury, Vermont, would have been absolutely splendid. And she didn't really know if she wanted a man, she just wished she had the option of turning one down. But she had a job she enjoyed, friends and creative outlets that turned her family pale with horror. She was blissfully content, even on such a dark, gloomy, snowy day. If it weren't for this premonition.

Leona hadn't been able to come up with much in her tarot reading. The ancient fortune-telling cards were obscure, offering more vague warnings about diffusing her energies, warnings Sybil took with a grain of salt. It had been three years since her divorce, three years of celibacy, and her psychic powers didn't seem to be increasing. If Prince Charming happened to show up, it might be worth trying a new tack.

But it was Nicholas Wyndham Fitzsimmons who was going to show up. He had to be seventy if he was a day; the board of trustees didn't trust anyone under sixty-five. The last thing she needed was a gold-plated academic. Her ex-husband had been aristocratic enough. No, what she needed was some earthy, sweating hunk to warm her through the long winter nights. Or failing that, at least someone who didn't make her feel as inadequate as her family did.

But all her partially formed instincts and psychic powers told her it was going to be a completely uneventful winter, with no more passionate diffusing than went on in a convent. With her usual good humor she banished the incipient depression that crowded around her at the thought. There was a great deal to be said for peace, even at her miserably advanced age of thirty.

Her only problem right now was having to wait for the old man. The snow was coming down with more enthusiasm than she cared for, there was the monthly meeting of the psychic group to contend with, and by the time they were finished it would take her ages to get down the narrow road to her cottage. Damn the man, why couldn't he be there on time? If he didn't arrive by six, she'd leave him a note and he could find his own way around. Flicking off the desk light, she headed for the small bookshop at the back of the building.

Nicholas Wyndham Fitzsimmons's dark green Jaguar XJ6 slipped sideways on the snow-packed road. With deft precision he turned into the spin, gently tapping with responsive brakes, and felt the tires regain their traction and their forward momentum down the deceptively icy road. It was the fourth time he'd nearly lost it in the last half hour, creeping over the secondary roads from St. Johnsbury and I-91. Despite the loose clasp of his leather-gloved hands on the steering wheel, he was in the worst mood he'd ever been in. He'd been cursing steadily for the last ten miles, peering through the whirling, blowing snow for signs of his destination. It was with only a faint lessening of temper that his headlights illuminated a white painted sign that announced he was now entering Danbury, Vermont, established in 1793, home of the Society of Water Witches. Nick's lip curled as he slowly, carefully negotiated the left hand turn onto Water Street. It had been a stupid time of year to come up for research, but he hadn't had much choice in the matter. He was due in England by the end of January, and he had to have his information well in hand before he went. But damn, he wished he were back in his cozy little apartment in Cambridge.

Even through the blowing and drifting snow he didn't have any trouble finding the old white farmhouse that held the society's headquarters. A single light was burning in the front of the building, with more in the back, and one snow-covered station wagon was parked out front. At least the secretary had stayed to welcome him. What was her name—Sybil something? He knew just what to expect. Some wispy spinster in her fifties, with filmy trailing garments, vague eyes and the IQ of a toaster. He pulled the Jaguar to a stop and had the distinctly unpleasant experience of having it slide two feet more until it bumped gently against the snowy retaining wall. With a savage curse, he turned off the key and bounded out into the night air.

The door was unlocked. For a moment he just stood inside the hall, letting the heat and light surround him. There

was no one in the darkened office, but he could hear music from the back of the building. Or at least, he thought
it might be music. Shaking the snow off his head, he
ducked under the low doorway and headed toward the
noise.

SYBIL SAT BACK on her heels, surveying the display of
dowsing rods with a critical air. She liked the small brass
ones best—they could fit in one's purse and be ready for
any likely occurrence. But they didn't fit the rack she'd
built for the longer, L-shaped rods, and she didn't like
them just huddled together on the counter. She picked up
a pair, hefting them lightly in her hands. She had somewhat better luck with rods than with pendulums, but not
much.

With a sudden, uncanny movement the twin rods shifted
to the right, moving with precision and coming to a full
stop. Sybil's brown eyes followed their path to discover
they were pointing at a pair of snowy feet standing in the
doorway. Slowly her eyes moved upward, way upward,
past long, jeans-clad legs, past a fisherman knit sweater
with melting snow glistening on it, way up to a face. She
uttered a tiny sound of complete panic. She felt as if she
were looking into the face of the devil himself.

He was standing motionless, watching her, and the eerie stillness of his long, lean body added to the sensation.
She stared back, mesmerized, unable to move. He had a
narrow, dangerously beautiful face, with a strong blade of
a nose, a thin, sensual mouth and the most disturbing eyes
she'd ever seen. They were a golden sort of topaz that
seemed to glow with an unearthly light as they stared down
at her. His hair was black, unfashionably long, and he had
a widow's peak in front. His eyebrows were equally black
and sharply defined, emphasizing those strange, other-

worldly eyes. He stood there without saying a word, and those eyes seemed to hypnotize her.

Sybil stared up at him, unmoving, and gulped.

"I suppose you're Sybil." The vision shimmered, altered, moved and dissolved. The man standing in the doorway walked into the room, and she could see that he was only a man after all, albeit a good-looking one. Also an extremely bad-tempered one. "Don't they ever salt the roads around here? I've been sliding on sheer ice for the last thirty miles."

"Salt is bad for the environment," she said absently. "Yes, I'm Sybil Richardson. Who are you?" It was a stupid question. She didn't need psychic powers to guess, and to know that all her previous suppositions had been dead wrong.

"Nicholas Fitzsimmons. You were expecting someone else on a night like this?" he snapped. Even in temper it was a charming voice, she had to admit that. Low-pitched, musical, as mesmerizing as his golden eyes had been. Except those eyes were so bad-tempered and blazing they no longer had any effect on her except irritation.

"Hope springs eternal," she said cheerfully, dropping the brass rods back onto the shelf and rising to her full height. On top of everything else her entire family was taller than she was, most of them topping five feet ten, and the lean giant in front of her brought out her usual feelings of inadequacy. A short, sweating hunk was what she wanted, she added to herself. "I'm sorry about the roads, but as I expect you'll realize, they're not my fault."

For a moment he seemed to collect himself. "No, you're right," he said grudgingly. "They're not your fault."

"Besides," she added with a trace of mischief, "they're not really that bad."

"When were you last out, Miss Richardson?" he demanded in a voice as icy as Route 15.

"An hour ago," Sybil lied blithely.

"Then why were there no tire tracks in the snow?"

She grinned. "I did what I always do in bad weather, Mr. Fitzsimmons. I levitated."

"Very funny," he said sourly.

Finally Sybil took pity on him. "You'll get used to them sooner or later," she said, flicking off the lights and moving toward him, forcing herself not to react to his intimidating height. "And you'll feel better after you've eaten."

He was still watching her warily. "Deke Appleton said you'd make arrangements for me?"

She smiled, only a twinge of guilt marring her composure. "And I have. First you're coming to a meeting of our psychic group. It's the best way for you to meet everyone, and we're having a potluck supper so you'll be well fed. You'll be spending the night at Deke's, and tomorrow we'll get you settled into the old Black Farm."

"What's wrong with the old Black Farm?"

She looked up at him. She was sure her voice had sounded completely normal when she'd mentioned it. "Why, nothing at all. It's got all the amenities, including electric heat if you get tired of dealing with the wood stoves. You'll be very comfortable."

He just looked at her, and those topaz eyes glowed slightly in the dimly lit room. "Maybe," he said. His voice sounded low, sexy and very skeptical.

Sybil, remembering the Black Farm's history, merely smiled.

Chapter Two

The temperature had dropped drastically since earlier in the day, and Sybil shivered as she pulled her down coat closer around her, ducking her head as she stepped outside. It had to be down in the teens, and the snow was falling at an unpleasantly enthusiastic rate. She looked at the sleek, beautiful lines of the Jaguar sedan and gave an audible sniff.

"No wonder you slid all the way," she said. "You need something a little more prosaic on these roads."

"Like that?" His tone of voice as he gestured to her aging Subaru was as contemptuous as hers had been.

"It'll get you where you want to go," she replied, sweeping the drifts of snow off the windshield. "Which is more than I can say of yours."

With an effort her unwelcome visitor controlled his temper, but she could see the irritation sweep across his handsome face. Good, she thought, ignoring her spasm of guilt. If he could be argumentative and bad-tempered, so could she.

"Would you care to place a small bet on it?" he said evenly.

"Nope. Deke lives on a back road and I don't want to spend hours digging you out of whatever snowdrift your elegant car chooses to slide into. You'll have to drive with me. We're late anyway, and the group likes to get started promptly during the winter months so everyone can get home early."

"Then you admit the roads are bad."

"Of course I do. We treat the weather and the roads with the respect they're due. We don't try to drive too fast in cars that are unequipped for the weather. I bet you don't even have snow tires."

"All-weather radials."

She shook her head. "Not good enough. Steve at the garage can fix you up with studded snows. That is, if you're still planning to stay for a while."

"I'm planning to stay," he said in a deceptively even voice. "Sorry to disappoint you."

She gave him her dazzling smile, and for a second he looked startled, blinking those extraordinary eyes of his. "Oh, I'm not disappointed," she said. "I think you'll end up being quite entertaining. The cat among the pigeons, and all that."

"I aim to please," he said.

"I find that very unlikely," she said frankly. "I happen to have read your books, and your reactionary views aren't going to be very welcome. But winters are long and boring around here, and you'll provide fodder for some good arguments if nothing else."

"I'm glad I have my uses."

"Get in the car," she said, scraping the ice off the windshield. "Just dump the papers in the back seat."

He opened the door. "What about the Tab cans littering the floor?" he demanded.

"Kick 'em out of the way. Deke's farm is only three miles away—you won't even notice them."

"Don't you want to start warming up the car?"

"It wastes gas. We try to be energy-conscious around here." He was shivering slightly as he slid into the front seat, and for a moment Sybil took pity on him. With an effort she hardened her heart. Nicholas Fitzsimmons mocked everything she held dear; she was damned if she was going to welcome him into her world just because he was the best-looking man she'd ever seen in her life.

Besides, it wouldn't matter. The moment he set those wonderful topaz eyes on Dulcy he'd be lost, and Sybil Richardson would be relegated to the status of a sexless maiden aunt. She'd seen it happen too many times, and it failed to disturb her. It wouldn't bother her this time, either. Dulcy would know just how to handle him; she wasn't sure that she could.

She climbed into the driver's seat, turned the frozen key that she'd left in the ignition and listened to the engine's customary whine of protest. Nicholas's tall, lean body was shivering beside her, his long arms were wrapped around his torso and his teeth were clenched. She turned the key again, and once more the engine chugged, sputtered and died.

"Third time's the trick," she said, turning it again. It caught, rumbled ominously and died.

"Why don't you dowse it and find out what's wrong?" Nicholas said cynically, the effect ruined by his chattering teeth.

"Good idea," Sybil said, whipping off her glove and running her fingers on the dashboard.

"What in God's name are you doing besides courting frostbite?"

"Dowsing. You can find all sorts of things besides water, you know. I run my fingers over any smooth surface and if it sticks the answer's yes."

"Or else your fingers have frozen to the dashboard," he snapped.

She ignored him. "Nope, the car's okay," she said, putting her glove back on. She turned the key once more and the engine zoomed into life. They sat there for a long moment, both of them listening intently. "What did I tell you?" she said proudly.

"Where's the heat?"

"It won't do any good to turn it on yet. It'll just blast cold air on your feet."

"Cold air is already blasting on my feet," Nicholas said. "Turn the damned thing on."

"It's your funeral." She turned the blower on high, shoved the stubborn gear into reverse and backed out onto the icy road.

They drove in a silence only marred by the sound of Nicholas's chattering teeth. Sybil's guilt finally got the better of her. "I have a blanket in the back," she offered.

"No, thanks. I like freezing to death," he said with mock politeness. "Did you say you were taking me to Deke's?"

"Only for the night. He and Margaret are leaving for Europe tomorrow. It's a shame, too. Besides being the president of the SOWWs..."

"Sows?"

"Society of Water Witches. SOWWs for short. Anyway, Deke's a water dowser, or water witch—right up your alley. You'll just have to find your own partisans."

"So what's this psychic group we're going to? Is it part of the SOWWs?"

"Yes and no. All the members of the group are members of the SOWWs, and they all believe in dowsing. But half of the society doesn't believe the stuff we're into. New

Age stuff, like earth energies, sacred geometry, past-life regressions, trance mediums, nature religions.''

"Nature religions like witchcraft?" he asked.

She steeled herself for his disapproval. "White witchcraft," she corrected. "And Native American religions. That sort of thing."

"You're a bunch of dangerous idiots," he said calmly enough.

The red haze of fury that formed in front of Sybil's eyes almost obscured the icy road. "And you're an opinionated turkey."

She felt rather than saw the meditative smile that lighted up his dark face. "As long as we have that clear in our minds."

"Quite clear."

"You do realize that I find you as infuriating as you find me?" he inquired as Sybil slid to a stop in the crowded driveway of the brightly lighted house.

"That's some consolation," she said sweetly, turning off the car. She turned to face him in the darkness, about to order him out into the cold, when she stopped, motionless, astonished. The heat had never come on during the short ride, and her breath was a billow of icy vapor that rose and met his, mingling with it in the confines of the old Subaru. She stared at the clouds of breath in front of her, watching them entwine and tangle like two lovers, and a frisson of premonition ran over her backbone.

She met his eyes. They looked almost as startled as hers did, and his breath, his mouth, moved suddenly closer.

"What are you doing?" she whispered, not moving, not backing away.

He stopped within millimeters of her, and she could feel the warmth of his breath in the cold car. "I'm not sure," he said in an equally soft voice. "I'm either making a pass at you or trying to intimidate you. Maybe both."

"Either way it's a lost cause," she said, her startled eyes looking into his.

"Oh, I'm not so sure...." He moved closer, but this time she did move, ducking out of his reach and out of the door before he could make contact.

"Bring those papers with you, will you?" Her voice sounded admirably calm. She kept her pace modest, decorous, as she headed for the front door, and he caught up with her before she made it.

"I don't suppose there'll be something hot and strong in there?" he asked, and the moment in the car might never have existed.

"Herb tea or hot cider."

"I was thinking more along the lines of coffee and whiskey."

"Drugs cloud the mind and affect your psychic concentration," she said.

"I have no psychic concentration. I just have a frozen body."

"I'm sure Deke will take pity on you."

"I don't know if there's any pity in the entire state of Vermont," he said morosely, following her into the light and warmth of the crowded old farmhouse. Sybil made no reply.

Sybil could never enter Deke and Margaret Appleton's place without a sense of disorientation. On the outside it was the perfect, rustic Vermont farmhouse, with narrow, white-painted clapboards and green shutters, a tin roof to repel the snow and cozy little dormer windows placed at haphazard angles. Inside it was pure Scarsdale, imported by the Appletons when they retired from their suburban New York home. From the baby-blue wall-to-wall carpeting that always got tracked with mud, salt and snow, to the beige chintz sofas that always picked up every trace of dog hair clinging to Sybil's clothing, to the spindly little Chippendale bamboo chairs that looked as if they wouldn't safely hold anyone over forty-five pounds and were now obscured beneath several two-hundred-pound-plus Vermonters, it was elegant, downstate and impractical.

Margaret Appleton had resisted the impulse to put up her Christmas tree the day after Thanksgiving, as far too many Vermonters had begun doing, but there were a few tasteful touches—a papier-mâché reindeer and sleigh on the mantel, some artfully arranged evergreens in a copper vase. Cat spruce, Sybil thought, wrinkling her nose at the litter-box smell. Trust a flatlander not to know the difference between balsam and its smelly cousin.

There was a good crowd tonight, despite the weather, she realized with a start of nervousness. The smells that filled the house were wonderfully down-home in contrast with the upscale luxury—the baked beans that were de rigueur for any potluck dinner, spicy chili and Leona's latest concoction, which always tasted of rosemary no matter what she cooked. The scent of the mulled cider mingled with the wood smoke and the faint, lingering trace of wet wool slowly drying in the warmth of the overheated house. She gave Nicholas a glance in time to see him wrinkle the nose that was just as aristocratic as she had imagined. Maybe she had more psychic ability than she thought. She certainly knew he'd have that disdainful nose. She just hadn't realized it would be surrounded by such a handsome face.

"Too many people," she muttered to a surprisingly patient Nicholas. "Let's find the kitchen." Without thinking she took his hand to pull him from the crowded, noisy room. It was a mistake—she wasn't used to touching men, and his hand was cool and strong beneath hers. But not for anything would she back off. She pulled him into the gleaming modern kitchen, shut the door behind them and leaned against the chrome and Formica countertop with a sigh of relief.

"They're a wonderful bunch of people," she said, pushing at the wisps of hair that were escaping her coronet of braids. "But in large doses they can be overwhelming."

"Why are we hiding in the kitchen?" he inquired. "Have you developed a sudden taste for my company?"

He was still looking a little blue around the edges, and Sybil no longer fought the guilt that she'd been flirting with. "I thought you might like a moment or two to warm up before you had to cope with the full force of the Danbury Seekers of Enlightenment."

"Oh, God," Nicholas moaned. "Who thought of that repulsive name?"

"I did. And I have someone I want you to meet. She'll be here sooner or later—she always ends up in the kitchen." She smiled, very pleased with herself. "I think you two will make a wonderful couple."

She'd startled him out of his bad temper. "Are you matchmaking?"

"Why not? It keeps me entertained."

"And my intended is some woman who always ends up in kitchens? I presume she weighs about three hundred pounds."

Sybil smiled. "You're a big man, Nicholas. You'll manage."

She'd pushed him too far. "Listen, I don't need matchmaking, I don't need the Danbury Seekers of Enlightenment and I don't need your wonderfully solicitous care. I need—"

The door opened at that moment, and Dulcy walked through, letting it swing shut behind her. "Hi, Sybil," she said with real warmth. "I wondered where you were hiding. I've been hearing about your contribution to our little gathering. Is this the Grinch That Stole Christmas?" She gestured toward Nicholas's suddenly still figure.

Sybil nodded. "Nicholas Fitzsimmons, Dulcy Badenham. Make him welcome, Dulcy." And she slipped from the kitchen before anyone could stop her.

Nicholas watched her go with mixed emotions. No, they weren't mixed at all—they were pure regret. He turned back to the paragon who had entered the kitchen and allowed himself a long, leisurely look. One that Dulcy permitted with a faint smile of amusement.

She was quite a sight, he had to grant Sybil that. She must have been close to six feet tall, with a long, willowy body with just the right amount of graceful curves. Her hair was white-blond, and hung straight and thick to her tiny waist. Her eyes were a hazy, mystical blue, her skin was a flawless porcelain, her mouth a sensual rosebud. She was a perfect, untouched beauty, with even the amazing asset of clear intelligence and humor shining from those eyes that watched him watching her. And she moved him not one tiny bit.

Sybil had presented her friend with the air of one offering a great treat. The expression on her plain, dark face had been one of smug pleasure, certain that her matchmaking had succeeded. And all he wanted to do was chase after her and argue some more.

"Finished looking?" Dulcy had a deep, beautiful voice to match her appearance. With an effort Nicholas dragged his attention back from Sybil's dubious charms.

"Very nice," he said absently. "Where did Sybil disappear to?"

"Probably to get something to eat. Welcome to Danbury, Nicholas Fitzsimmons. Are you going to make fools of us in your next book?" She sounded no more than vaguely interested, and he smiled a distant smile.

"I doubt it. I don't think the Seekers of Truth are worthy of that much print space. There are any number of crackpot psychic groups all over the country—I doubt you have anything special to offer."

"You might be surprised," she said tranquilly. "And we're the Seekers of Enlightenment. Better known as the Spook Group."

"Who came up with that one?"

"Sybil, of course. She doesn't take herself nearly as seriously as you seem to."

Score another point for Sybil, he thought. He looked at the glorious Dulcy, wondering why she left him so entirely unmoved. "Who are you, the resident familiar?"

"I'm a lawyer in St. Johnsbury. I have a fairly good-size practice in criminal law." She moved closer to him. "I'm also a white witch."

"Sure you are." He was getting bored now, along with being cold and hungry. Dulcy might be a smart lady, but she had the same bizarre fantasies everyone else did. "What's on the agenda for tonight?"

"I think Leona is planning a presentation, with Sybil's help."

"A presentation?"

The door opened, and Sybil reappeared, divested of her down coat, her knee-length felt-lined boots, her three scarves, her heavy sweater and her mittens. She looked like a thin brown elf, and her braids were sagging ominously around her small face.

"Past-life regression," she announced in answer to his overheard question. In her hands she held a plate heaped

high with food, and she presented it like a sacrificial offering. "Leona's going to take me back to a previous in-
carnation. It's a fairly common technique. Leona will lead
me back through time in a guided meditation and we'll see
if we can pick up a past life." She shoved the plate into his
hands. "Eat something." She looked back and forth with
a hopeful expression between Dulcy's tall, elegant body
and his own, and once more he was reminded of a spar-
row in search of a juicy worm.

It wasn't forthcoming. "Matchmaking again?" Dulcy
inquired, not in the slightest bit embarrassed. "You've
struck out. I'm not Nicholas's type."

"Did she tell you she was a lawyer?" Sybil hadn't given
up yet.

"She did," he replied.

"Still no go, eh? I'll keep looking."

"No, thank you. I can take care of my own sexual
needs."

She grinned. "To each his own."

"I didn't mean that," he began.

"Listen, you don't have to explain yourself," she said
sweetly. "Eat your dinner. Leona's waiting for us."

"Us?"

"You might get to be a guinea pig, too."

"The hell I will—" She vanished again, and the door
swung back and forth gently.

"Don't fight it," Dulcy counseled. "Sybil can be very
determined."

He barely heard her. She had moved quickly, without
Dulcy's grace, without the languid sensuality of most
women of his acquaintance. As she darted away from him
with a delicious grin on her dark face, he was conscious of

a sudden uprush of desire more intense than he'd felt in years.

"So can I," he said softly, more to Sybil's vanished figure than to Dulcy's shell-like ears. "So can I."

Chapter Three

He didn't like Leona Coleman, not one iota. For all her dizzy charm, he had the odd feeling that it was an act. The other Seekers of Truth or Enlightenment, or whatever, at least seemed sincere enough. Leona struck him as patently manipulative. And he especially didn't like it that she was manipulating Sybil.

Particularly now that he was feeling decidedly mellow toward her. He'd eaten just enough of the highly spiced, unrecognizable food she'd handed him to still his hunger, and then he'd followed her back into the crowded confines of the Spook Group. He had met Deke and Margaret Appleton, a surprisingly mundane couple in their early seventies. He'd corresponded with Deke, one of the best water dowsers in the country, and he matched his expectations: a short, rosy-faced little man with dreamy blue eyes. His wife was a matriarch who topped him by almost a foot and had clearly turned her social tendencies to the material at hand. She was the perfect, overwhelming hostess in her self-consciously British tweeds and overloud voice, and Nicholas wished he had stayed in a motel for his first night instead of accepting Margaret Appleton's heavy-handed hospitality.

He had been standing there, bemused, listening to her holding forth on energy lines beneath the main altar at Chartres Cathedral when Sybil had reappeared out of the crowd. She put a hot earthenware mug into his hand and slipped away before he could break Margaret's stranglehold. He stood there, a polite prisoner, and took a sip.

Bless the woman. It was coffee—strong, hot, black, just the way he liked it. And there was enough whiskey in it to float a battleship. He took another long, appreciative sip and began to consider Sybil's undeniable merits.

But his temporarily sanguine mood had now faded. He was sitting on one of the chintz sofas, sandwiched between a dairy farmer from Walden and a librarian from Greensboro. The dairy farmer hadn't changed his boots since he'd done the evening chores, and the faint scent of manure mingled with and drowned out the smell of whiskey from his coffee. The librarian favored musky perfume and coy glances. If there'd been a spare inch in the now candlelit room, he would have moved to it. But every space was packed, a hush had fallen over the expectant group, and Sybil sat cross-legged on the floor, her hands resting comfortably on her knees, her thin shoulders relaxed, as Leona began her damned mumbo jumbo. Nicholas felt his tension increase.

It was a simple enough technique, he thought objectively, listening to Leona's voice drone on and on. She was hypnotizing Sybil, or aiding Sybil in hypnotizing herself, and the suggestive voice was creating a dreamy mood throughout the room. It would have been easy enough to succumb, after the long day and the generous shot of whiskey, but that was the last thing he had in mind. He was intent on watching Leona, catching her little tricks. Not that he planned to say or do anything about it. He merely wanted to observe.

He'd gone through just what Sybil was about to go through, had been guided by one of the best. Past-life regression involved self-hypnosis, being guided back through time until a likely period was picked, and listening to the fantasies come forth. His own had been quite colorful, involving the French Revolution and his sexual adventures with a Countess Félicité. He'd imagined himself to be some sort of revolutionary, and according to Swami Benana he'd come to a bad end, but it was entertaining while it lasted. He'd listened with real amusement to the tape the Swami, whose real name was Harry Johnson, had made.

But Harry, while he was absurdly gullible, had at least believed in what he was doing, and had done it in the spirit of fun. Leona was intoning in a singsong chant that was making his blood run cold. Sybil sat there, at her mercy, her eyes closed, waiting for God knows what.

"Where are you now, Sybil?" Leona asked gently. "Can you tell us what's happening to you?"

Sybil opened her eyes. They were dazed, with none of their earlier clever mischievousness. Nicholas quickly drained his coffee and tried to keep himself from putting a stop to this farce.

"It's long, long ago," she said, her voice dreamy. "I'm in a cold place. I'm wearing skins around my body."

"Tell me more," Leona urged.

"There are horses. I've been training horses," she murmured, and an appreciative gasp arose from the enthralled company.

Nicholas shook his head silently. She must have been reading Jean Auel. They were going to have to sit through half-baked retellings of the *Clan of the Cave Bear*. It might take all night.

But Leona wasn't interested in a secondhand Ayla. "Come ahead a bit, dear. Into the warmth and light. What are you wearing now?"

There was a long, eerie silence, and then suddenly Sybil giggled. It was an enchanting sound, sexy and delicious, and once more in the darkness Nicholas felt that astounding reaction.

"Not much at all. An emerald necklace," she said. "And diamonds around my ankle."

A sudden sense of horrified disbelief swept over him. He sat forward, intent, staring at the two women in the center of the darkened room.

"What day is it, my dear? What is your name?" Leona cooed.

Sybil grinned, an impish upturning of her suddenly sexy mouth. "It's July 13, 1789. And I am Félicité, Countess de Lavallière."

He must have groaned. There were sudden, hushing noises, glares in his direction. With an extreme effort he bit down on the protest he was about to make.

"I must have complete silence," Leona addressed the hushed crowd like a cross schoolteacher. She returned to her subject, her voice low and crooning once more. "And what are you doing, Countess? Why aren't you wearing anything?"

"Because I'm waiting for my lover, of course."

The librarian beside him sighed gustily, and the musk wafted around him.

"Who is your lover, Countess?"

"Oh, I'm not allowed to tell. It is very bad of me, very naughty, but I don't care."

Leona had clearly had enough of that low, sexy chuckle. "Very well, let's move ahead."

"I don't want to," Sybil piped up. "I want to talk about Alex."

"We will move ahead—"

"He is so handsome," she said with a lusty sigh. "He has the most wonderful eyes, *au diable, et . . .*" Her musings had dropped into very idiomatic and graphic French. Her accent was perfect, and Nicholas understood every word she said. He wondered if he was blushing.

"We will move ahead," Leona said again, her tone brooking no disobedience. "It is winter now, and—"

Sybil's face had crumpled in despair. He watched in suspended amazement as her huge brown eyes filled with tears, her mouth trembled, her body seemed to cave in around her. "No," she screamed, and the sound was loud and shocking in the packed living room. "No, he can't be dead!" And she collapsed, weeping, on the baby-blue carpeting.

Nicholas had had enough. "Take her out of it," he ordered, his voice cutting across the excited murmur of voices.

"Really, I can't be interfered with," Leona protested stubbornly. "It's never worked this well."

Nicholas rose to his full height, knowing he made an impressive sight in the flickering candlelight, knowing and using it to his advantage in this group of gullible souls. "Take her out of it, damn you. Now!"

He was careful not to overplay. He kept his voice low, a silky menace, knowing that half of this scene was carefully staged theatrics and knowing his performance had to fit. But half of it was a woman weeping for her dead lover, lost in time, and he wanted her brought out of it with a desperation that amazed him.

"All right," Leona acquiesced with poor grace. "Though we're missing a wonderful chance. . . ."

"Get her out of it," Deke piped up. "We don't want to see poor Sybil so miserable."

Nicholas knew he should sit down and keep silent. But Leona was shaking Sybil, her voice sharp, and still she lay there weeping, murmuring the name of her lover over and over again. Without further hesitation he stepped over the people sitting on the floor in front of him and reached Sybil's side, brushing away Leona's rough hands and substituting his own gentle ones.

At the different touch she opened her eyes, which were swimming with tears. "Alex," she whispered in disbelief. "I thought you were dead." She spoke in French, and without thinking he responded in the same language.

"I'm right here, my love." And she sank into his arms.

He held her as Leona intoned her mumbo jumbo words, held her gently as she slowly returned from her self-induced fantasy. "You're back now, Sybil," Leona said, still sounding disgruntled. "You're here in Danbury, and Professor Fitzsimmons is holding you."

He felt her stiffen. Slowly he released her, preparing himself but still startled to see the expression on her face. It was a combination of surprise and irritation, as if he'd been too forward and she couldn't quite figure out why. The only thing at odds were the tears still swimming in her eyes.

"Copping a cheap feel, Nicholas?" she murmured under her breath. "I thought you took care of these things yourself."

"You ought to have your mouth washed out with soap," he muttered back, rising to his full height.

"Try it," she taunted, loud enough for Leona to hear.

"I must ask you to resume your seat, Nicholas," she said sternly. "We've lost valuable ground."

"You're not doing it again," he said flatly. "Not to Sybil."

"I most certainly am. She's been the most receptive subject we've had so far and—"

"No," he said. "Practice on someone else."

"I don't believe you have any say in the matter." Leona, too, could be silky-voiced. The two of them, along with everyone else in the room, turned to Sybil.

He could see her hesitate, and he knew damned well she'd like to spite him. But she wasn't a fool; she knew her limits.

"Not tonight, I think," she said gently. "That was pretty rough. Let's do it later."

"It may not work as well later."

She gave Leona a reassuring little pat. "If it's meant to work, it will. Haven't you always told me that?"

Score one for Sybil, Nicholas thought sourly. Leona had no argument left.

"Turn on the lights," the old woman announced. "I think we've all had enough. And I, for once, need sustenance. I feel quite depleted."

"What about you?" Nicholas hadn't moved from Sybil's side. The people around them had begun talking, filling the room with an irritating buzz, but for the moment he had the odd, pleasant feeling that they were alone there, surrounded by white noise.

"Drained would be a better word," she said, taking his hand and rising to her feet.

"It's amazing what tricks our minds can play on us," he said.

"Is that what you think it was? A trick?"

"Do you remember what you dreamed?"

"Dreamed," Sybil echoed. "Not much. Part of it was very erotic, I do remember that. But most of it was so horrible I don't even want to think about it." She shivered in the overheated room.

He hesitated for a moment, then on impulse quoted an old saying. "He who sits down to eat with the devil sups with a long fork." But he said it in French.

She looked up at him in complete confusion. "What?"

He began to repeat it, but she shook her head. "In English, please. My French is third-grade level and completely lousy."

He just stared at her. Her French had been superb, a precise, Parisian French. And he looked up, past her shoulder, to stare directly into Leona's triumphant little eyes.

THE DRIVE HOME from Deke Appleton's seemed longer than seven miles. The roads were icy, but the Subaru could handle them. The heater finally decided to work, and at least the snow had stopped. Sybil shivered slightly, wrapped her scarf around her aching head, and drove onward, her eyes watering from concentration.

So Dulcy and Nicholas hadn't hit it off. The thought should have depressed and disturbed her. There was no reason why she should find it such a source of secret delight. Doubtless he liked short, buxom brunettes instead of tall, willowy blondes. There was no way he could prefer plain ordinary women of indeterminate everything. She was still safe, if she wanted to be.

Of course she wanted to be. Right now she didn't need her life complicated by someone like Nicholas Fitzsimmons. To be sure, he was a very handsome man; one couldn't help but respond to such good looks. When he wasn't wearing that bad-tempered pout he was even more irresistible. She'd brought him the whiskey-laced coffee as a peace offering, and the quick, grateful look he'd cast her way had almost taken her breath away. Not to mention the expression in those disturbing eyes of his when she'd awakened from Leona's induced nightmare to find him holding her with all the tenderness of a lover.

But then, there'd been that startled, disbelieving expression on his face when he'd babbled in French at her. She could understand a couple of words, but her grasp of the language had been rudimentary, to say the least. Languages were never her forte; she did better in English and art, less well in practical matters involving tenses and genders and declensions.

She hadn't even said good-night to him. She'd ducked out like the coward she was, before half of the Spook Group was ready to leave. She'd see him soon enough; Deke and Margaret were going to drop him back at his car tomorrow on their way to the airport. And she'd have to see him settled into the Black Farm. She'd hoped to foist that particular duty off on Leona, but the antagonism between the two of them made her own relationship with Nicholas seem like love at first sight. No, she'd have to do the dirty work. Maybe in the bright light of day he wouldn't have that odd effect on her.

Except that in December in northern Vermont there was unlikely to be any bright light during the day. Most likely more snow, maybe more sleet, certainly more gloom. Maybe she'd take the day off and go Christmas shopping—that would cheer her. Or maybe she'd just sleep in, play with the dogs and let Nicholas find the farm by himself.

No, she couldn't be that much of a coward. She'd get a good night's sleep, and tomorrow she'd be in much better shape to deal with a bad-tempered, dangerously handsome, surprisingly charming thorn in her side. After all, he probably hadn't spared an extra thought to her all evening. She'd get him settled, and they could forget about each other.

And maybe hell would freeze over.

THE BED WAS TOO SOFT, too narrow and too short. Nicholas was used to sleeping in a queen-size loft bed, and the narrow little cot to which Margaret Appleton had shown him resembled a torture chamber. He knew without asking that the Appletons were one of those couples who didn't own anything larger than a twin bed. With a grunt of frustration he punched the limp pillow and accomplished the impressive feat of turning over without falling off the narrow mattress.

Not that he would have slept well anywhere. For all the discomfort of his body, the discomfort in his mind far outweighed it. So far he couldn't find a way to reconcile himself with what he had seen and heard and, most particularly, what he felt.

He didn't believe in past-life regressions. It was that simple. He didn't believe in reincarnation, either, or at least, he was still highly skeptical. Most past-life regressions were the result of a combination of self-hypnosis, fantasy and half-formed memories from bad historical romances the subjects had read in their youth. They had nothing to do with real life and hard facts.

But...

Sybil's French had been perfect. And the look of blank incomprehension on her face, when he'd spoken to her later, hadn't been feigned. Of course, there were explanations for that. People knew a lot more in their subconscious than their conscious let them realize. She'd quite probably assimilated a great deal of French from foreign movies and years of French class that her mind had resisted.

But...

She'd looked different when she was under hypnosis. That sensual grin, that sexy chuckle were nothing like the face she'd presented to the world at large yesterday. Perhaps yesterday was a bad day, perhaps she was usually like that gamine and the transformation had surprised only him.

But...

She'd known about Countess Félicité and the onset of the French Revolution. And she'd had a lover with his middle name, Alexandre, a lover who'd met a bad end. But Félicité was a common enough French name, and, of course, any fantasy countess would have a lover. They probably both got the name Alexandre from Dumas *père ou fils*. There was no way either Leona or Sybil could have known about his own fantasies, but coincidences do happen, and they must have happened last night.

But...

It still didn't explain his reaction. His eerie, half-submerged recognition when she chuckled. His body and his reluctant mind had been flirting with an unwanted attraction to her all night. When she'd wept in his arms, he'd given up the fight. For some reason he wanted her, more than he'd wanted anyone in a long time. The musky librarian left him cold, the glorious Dulcy had no effect on him whatsoever. For some inexplicable reason he wanted Sybil, and he couldn't get that wanting out of his mind.

He was going to have to watch Leona. He didn't trust her, and he didn't like her effect on Sybil. Then again, he didn't like Sybil's effect on him. Hell, right now he didn't like anything much.

Tomorrow it would begin to make sense. In the bright light of day, Sybil would lose whatever arcane attraction she held for him. He'd get settled into the Black Farm and begin his research, and avoid the Seekers of Enlightenment or Truth from now on. Superstition and mumbo jumbo had always been contagious, how could he have forgotten? He had to keep his mind clear and his options open.

And if one of his options included Sybil Richardson, he was open-minded enough to consider it. Though he knew damned well she was going to bring him nothing but trouble.

He punched the pillow once more, imagining Leona's round face beneath his fist. He'd never run from trouble before, and he wasn't about to start now. Sybil might prove a very delightful sort of trouble indeed. If he were one of her flaky friends, he'd run his hands along the side of the bed to dowse it. Instead of courting splinters, he turned over and finally went to sleep, only to be plagued with erotic dreams of a Countess Félicité who looked exactly like Sybil Richardson.

Chapter Four

Sybil Richardson had a headache, a nervous stomach, a scratchy throat and the worst case of nerves she'd had since she faced her assembled family last Fourth of July. She sat at her desk in the office of the SOWWs, thankful to be alone, and tried to talk herself out of her ill-feeling.

Sure she had a headache. When she had braided her hair this morning she'd been in too much of a hurry, not to mention in a bad mood, and doubtless had braided too tightly, then stuck hairpins into her scalp. Her stomach was nervous because all that she had managed to swallow all morning was black coffee. She had overdosed on that because for once Leona wasn't there to disapprove or to make her weak peppermint tea with too much honey in it, and Sybil had gotten carried away.

The scratchy throat wasn't unexpected on such a raw, blustery day, and the nerves were probably because she hadn't slept very well last night. And that must have been because of that disturbing nightmare, half terrifying, half erotic, all about the French Revolution.

She was lying to herself, she admitted with a sigh, taking another sip of the cooling coffee and slipping a few of the more lethal hairpins from her coiled braids. There was one reason for her current state of physical and spiritual dis-ease, and one reason alone. And that reason was a man who had just been dropped off in the snowy driveway and who was now peering at his precious car like an anxious father.

She considered throwing on her coat and rushing out to forestall his invasion of her territory. The sooner she got him settled into the Black Farm the sooner she'd be rid of him. Or would she? Deke had already made it clear that Nicholas should have free rein over his office and the adjacent library on the second floor of the old building. With Sybil's luck he would be there every day, haunting her, driving her even crazier than Leona did.

Well, she could take it. She could deal with the reactionary old men who made up the board of trustees, she could deal with her family in small and even large doses, and she could certainly deal with one rather large, distinguished-looking gentleman afflicted with antiquated ideas and a bad temper. Sure she could.

She heard the silver bells on the front door ring, she heard the stamping of snow-covered feet in the hallway, but she made no move. Better to make him come to her, rather than to seek him out. She could sit there, cool, remote, a distant, amused smile playing around her mouth, while he blustered. . . .

The footsteps moved away, back toward the bookstore, and Sybil swore, the amused smile vanishing. "I'm in here," she called out, disgruntled.

"I know." His voice drifted back, and if anyone was amused, he was. "I'm just checking your book supplies."

"Hell and damnation," Sybil muttered, shoving herself back from her desk and starting after him. The last thing she wanted was to have him poking around her shop, sneering at her choices, mocking her passions. "Wait a minute," she yelled. "I'll be right there."

She raced out of the office, not even bothering to put on her shoes, and the snow he'd tracked in sank into her wool socks. She cursed again, slipped on the next patch of melting snow, and barreled directly into a tall, immovable figure.

Hands reached up to catch her arms, strong, surprisingly gentle hands. Her eyes were level with his shoulders, her flesh still smarted from the impact of their bodies, and she waited for her usual feelings of irritated intimidation to wash over her. They didn't come.

She stepped back, yanking herself out of his grasp with only a trace of startled panic. "You tracked snow in," she said belligerently, staring at the unbuttoned top button of his blue wool shirt.

"You aren't wearing any shoes." His voice was warm, low and beguiling, with none of last night's bad temper apparent. She looked up, startled, directly into those topaz-colored eyes and for a moment felt very much as she'd felt last night, as if she had drifted into a hypnotic state. But dangers had lurked in that blissful lassitude, and danger lurked in those wonderful eyes of his. She stood there, wiggling her damp feet, reminding herself that he was Trouble.

"I don't wear shoes in the office," she said. "What did you want to see in the bookstore?"

"I wanted to see what percentage of your stock was purely dowsing and what was this new-age crap."

Any accord that might have begun between them vanished as swiftly as the snow had melted on the carpet. "As much as I want," she snapped. "Why?"

"Research, Sybil. I'm interested in how much other things have infiltrated the bastions of pure water divining."

Her reaction was quick. "Give me a break! No one wants to interfere with your prejudices and opinions. Leave us ours."

"I don't want to interfere, I just want to document them. My book isn't just on water dowsing, it's on the division between traditionalists and the new wave."

"And we know which side you're on."

"I have an open mind," he said loftily.

"Sure you do. While you check out the 'new-age crap' in my bookstore," she snapped, finally bringing her condescending smile into play.

He didn't appreciate it. "I never said I was tactful."

"You don't have to be tactful. You're a college professor, you get to cram your ideas down students' throats and no one will dare disagree with you. Well, I'm not your student, Professor Fitzsimmons. And I think you're full of—"

"Sybil!" Leona's soft voice cut her off in midsentence. She had just a moment to register Nicholas's look of irritation before that bland, superior expression swept over his handsome face as he turned to greet the newcomer.

"Hi, Leona," Sybil said sheepishly. "Nicholas and I were just having a discussion."

"I heard it," she said. "Do you realize the negative energy that is flowing through this place right now? Your aura is very tight and small, Sybil. Very tight and small."

"What about mine?" There was just the suggestion of a sarcastic drawl in Nicholas's voice.

"Bright red, Mr. Fitzsimmons. Red and small and tight and angry. This is not the kind of energy we need here in the office," she said. "I think the two of you should keep away from each other."

"I'm sure you do," he said softly.

Sybil cast him a brief, curious glance before rushing to placate her friend. "Don't worry about it, Leona. I'm just in a bad mood today—I'd fight with Mother Theresa herself. And we'll get our negative energy out of here. I'm going to see Nicholas settled into the Black Farm while you watch the office. I should be back in less than an hour."

"Perhaps I should go instead," Leona offered. "You could stay here and clear the office."

"Clear the office?" Nicholas echoed. "Isn't that a little extreme?"

Leona gave him a reproving look. "Professor Fitzsimmons, you know enough about all forms of dowsing to know I meant psychic clearing, not a physical overhaul. Sybil can sit and meditate, sending waves of healing energy through this place to clear out the angry vibrations."

"Does she do this on company time?"

Sybil couldn't help it. She giggled, earning Leona's further displeasure. "Never mind, Leona. I'd probably do a lousy job of it. Why don't you take care of it while I'm gone, and I'll come back in a much more peaceful mood."

"And how will you manage that, cooped up with the professor?"

"I'm sure I can come up with something," Nicholas purred, and the sexual innuendo was so clear that for a moment Sybil was startled into silence. "And please, don't call me professor. It makes me sound ancient and stuffy. Call me Nick."

Leona didn't blink her dark little eyes, and there was no answering smile to Nick's sudden use of charm. She turned to Sybil. "And I can smell the coffee," she added accusingly.

"It smells wonderful, doesn't it?" Nick said.

"It smells like death," Leona intoned.

"Oh, yuck, Leona," Sybil protested. "That's going too far."

"It kills the brain cells and destroys psychic receptivity," Leona stated.

"Yes, but it tastes so good," said Sybil.

"Get your coat on and take the professor over to the Black Farm. I'll pour out that nasty stuff and brew us a nice pot of peppermint tea. It'll be waiting for you when you get back."

Sybil considered saying "yuck" once more, then dismissed the notion. Leona was clearly distressed, and Sybil hated to distress anyone. Unless it was the tall man beside her. "That would be lovely, Leona," she said gently. "I promise you it won't take me long."

THE HELL IT WOULDN'T, Nick there and then resolved. He had every intention of keeping Sybil Richardson at the Black Farm as long as he possibly could. Apart from the fact that he hated to give her over to Leona's tender mercies, he wanted to see if he could make her laugh again. That soft, unexpected giggle had the same effect on him that her transformation as the Countess Félicité had. And while he would like nothing better than to toss her down on the nearest bed Black Farm had to offer, he'd settle for just one more giggle, one more imperceptible lowering of that guarded distrust she kept wrapped around her.

Maybe he'd have to learn tact. It had never been a commodity he'd dealt in; he preferred brutal honesty cutting through all the social lies that wasted time and intellect. But clearly Sybil, for all her obvious intelligence, had a soft spot for some of the crackpot beliefs held dear by the fringe elements of the water witching community, such as it was. If he didn't want to spend all his time dodging her glares, he'd better learn to put a guard on his tongue.

Given time, she'd see reason and learn that her auras and past lives and dashboard dowsing were nothing more than parlor games.

Given time. The phrase echoed oddly in his head. He was only planning to be in Danbury for less than six weeks—just through the Christmas season and into the first weeks of the new year—and then he was off for England. What made him think he'd have time to show Sybil Richardson the error of her ways? And what made him want to?

Hell, he must be getting soft in his old age. It had been more than a year since Adelle had moved out, and while he hadn't been lonely or celibate since then, maybe he was fool enough to want to fall in love again. But Sybil Richardson would be a hell of a lousy choice, worse than Adelle, and it hadn't worked with Adelle.

Of course, it had worked for a while. For three very nice, comfortable, fun years. But Adelle wanted to get married, Adelle wanted babies, and Adelle had wanted them immediately. While he thought for a while that he could provide those things for her, when push came to shove they both realized he couldn't. Somehow, sometime, when they weren't looking, they'd fallen out of love and into friendship. And that friendship couldn't withstand the strain of marriage and an incipient family.

They'd broken their engagement, canceled the wedding, sent back the presents, and Adelle had moved out. Now she was married to an advertising executive in Dedham and her first baby was due in two months. She was supremely happy, he was happy for her, and not for a moment did he have doubts. Regrets, maybe, but not doubts.

So for the past year he'd been enjoying his freedom. He was only thirty-four, he had enough money and an enjoyable amount of limited fame, and he was considered attractive by attractive members of the opposite sex. Surely he could hold out until he found some nice, leggy British lady untainted by crackpot ideas.

Sybil returned from her office wrapped in a lavender down coat that was leaking feathers, a handwoven shawl around her narrow shoulders, her heavy braids sagging ominously around her small, narrow face and a wary expression in her brown eyes. Nicholas, knowing he was crazy, decided that maybe leggy British ladies weren't all they were cracked up to be. And maybe he'd learn tact after all.

She waited patiently enough as he brushed the snow off his car. This time her Subaru started without complaint, and she took off with a little more reckless abandon than he could have wished as he pulled out onto the snow-packed road to follow her. For a moment he wondered if she was driving too fast in hopes that he might go off the road trying to keep up with her, and then she could once more sneer at his beloved car. The moment the thought entered his brain he dismissed it. For one thing, she'd driven just as recklessly the night before. For another, he didn't think she was that petty.

No, what it all boiled down to, he thought as they sped in tandem over the narrow back roads, was that she was a lousy driver, and with his newfound determination to be tactful, he would say absolutely nothing about it.

"You know, you're a hell of a lousy driver," he said when he climbed out of his car. They had slid down a long, winding driveway, ending up in front of a good-sized red clapboard house. The barn beside it was in as good shape as the house, far better kept up than many of the farms he'd passed. Apparently the Black family hadn't been hit by the economic crunch most farmers were going through.

Sybil was staring up at the old house, an abstract expression on her face, and he waited for her spirited defense. "I know," she said absently. "That's why I have four-wheel drive, so I can get out of all the drifts I slide into." She reached into the pocket of her coat, pulling out a clanking set of keys, and a billow of feathers wafted into the air around her.

"Since I'm not a lousy driver, I expect my Jaguar will do just fine, then," he said, slightly distracted by the way the feathers were settling back onto her coat.

"Maybe."

"What have you got against my car? Most people consider it to be very nice."

"My ex-husband had one just like it," she said in a disgruntled tone of voice.

"Aha."

"Don't aha me," she snapped. "Colin's Jaguar was an essential part of his nature. Jaguars tend to be that important, and I'm assuming it's an essential part of you. And while they're very nice cars indeed, I don't like the kind of people who own them."

Ex-husband, he thought. *That's part of it.* "What if I told you that I'm not really a Jaguar person?" he said suddenly. "What if I told you that I bought it on an impulse, to cheer myself up?"

"Then it would depend on what kind of car you used to have," she said, giving him her full attention for the first time.

"A 1963 Plymouth Valiant."

Her mouth dropped open. It was a very nice mouth, with small, white teeth, and he wondered if he should take advantage of its vulnerability. Before he could move she snapped it shut again.

"I don't believe you."

"It had 367,000 miles on it when it died," he said solemnly.

She grinned then, a wide, warm smile that brought the frozen Vermont temperature up at least ten degrees, and Nick felt the strands wrap tighter and tighter around him. "Then you deserve the Jaguar," she said. "What color was your Valiant?"

"Gold."

"Mine was pale blue," she said with a reminiscent sigh. "It didn't quite make it to three hundred thousand."

"I'm surprised it made it to one hundred, given your driving."

She stuck her tongue out at him, her brown eyes bright with mischief. "Come in and see where you'll be staying for the next six weeks."

He moved up behind her as she was fiddling with the keys. "I didn't think people locked anything around here."

"Oh, we lock houses when no one lives in them. There are plenty of lowlifes who rip off summer houses and sell the good stuff down in the big city."

"Big city?"

"Boston or New York. Though why they bother to lock this place..." She let it trail off as the door swung open into an old-fashioned hallway.

"Why shouldn't they lock this place?" he demanded, suspicious.

It was easy enough to tell when Sybil Richardson was lying. Her pale cheeks flushed pink, her brown eyes looked edgy and her voice grew light and breathless. "No reason," she lied. "Close the door and I'll show you around."

He did as he was told, biding his time. There was no way he was going to let her go back to Leona until he knew exactly why no one would break into the Black Farm. Looking around, he realized that it wasn't for lack of things worth stealing. The house was in perfect condition, renovated within the past twenty years with a lot more taste than Deke and Margaret Appleton had used. There was a large living room with shiny hardwood floors, Indian rugs in perfect condition, comfortable new sofas and beautiful old tables. A large wood stove stood in front of the fireplace, with piles of dry wood beside it.

"It'll be up to you if you want to heat with wood. This place has got electric heat—that's what's on now, but on a really icy day when the wind blows it isn't enough. Besides, it costs a fortune."

"I think I can afford it," he said dryly.

"I expect anyone with a Jaguar can," she said. "There's a full bath off to the left and a bedroom, and the kitchen's on the other side. There are four more bedrooms upstairs, but they're closed off right now. You can open them up if you want, but it'll make the place even harder to heat."

"Okay," he said mildly enough.

"You can put your car in the barn if you want—there's no garage. Or you may just want to leave it out."

"Why would I want to leave it out in this climate?"

She shrugged, her cheeks flushed, her eyes looked edgy and her voice came out light and breathless. "No reason. I'll show you the kitchen."

He followed her with mock docility, waiting his chance. He saw the bedroom with its old-fashioned double bed and pile of pillows, the modern bathroom, the remodeled kitchen and woodshed. The whole place was warm, welcoming, completely charming. He couldn't figure out why it was empty, waiting to be rented, and why Sybil Richardson was lying her head off.

He stared at the bed, with its carved mahogany headboard and the snowy windows beside it. He could imagine long mornings curled up in that bed, with Sybil's small, compact body beside him.

"Where do you live?" he asked suddenly.

She blushed, and he wondered if she was coming up with another lie. "The last house on this road," she said with an odd trace of defiance.

"How far from me?"

"A mile and a half."

"And who's my closest neighbor?"

"Right now I am. We're not far from the lake, and in the summertime there are people in the cottages. They're all closed down now, and it's just you and me."

"Cozy."

"Don't count on it." She whirled away, heading back through the living room. "If you don't have any more questions I'm going back to work."

He caught up with her in the front hallway. She hadn't even bothered to take off her coat, and she'd left a trail of feathers behind during her sudden rush. Her braids were slipping down, and he wondered how she'd look with her hair full and loose around her defiant little face.

He felt her stiffen as he put his hand on her, felt the sudden surge of awareness shoot through her, the same awareness he was feeling. He considered letting her go, then dropped the idea. He kept his hands where they were, on her arms, holding her loosely enough, but holding her nonetheless.

"Just one more question, Sybil," he said. "What makes you so uncomfortable about Black Farm?"

"Maybe it's you," she said, squirming just enough to show her displeasure, but not enough to break the bond.

"That's not it. You manage to put up with me pretty well, all things considered. Do you want to tell me the truth this time, or are you going to lie again?"

"Why should I lie?"

"You tell me."

She wet her lips nervously, but her blush didn't deepen and her eyes were steady. She shrugged, but he didn't release her. "Someone was murdered here."

"Somehow I'm not surprised," he said with a sigh. "In the barn?"

"You're quick," she said. "In the barn. Old John Black was kicked to death by one of his horses. Except that the barn was locked from the outside, and he'd withdrawn ten thousand dollars from the bank earlier that day and no one ever found it."

"Ten thousand dollars isn't very much to kill someone for, Sybil."

"It was in 1936."

"1936?" he echoed. "You mean I'm supposed to worry about a murder that took place fifty years ago? Or are you going to tell me his ghost haunts the place?"

"No one's ever seen a ghost," she said grumpily. "But there's a bad feeling about this place, a very bad feeling. No one stays here for long."

"Neither will I. Just six weeks, and then I'm gone. It's a lucky thing I'm not sensitive, Sybil. You might have me racing into your bedroom in the middle of the night, terrified of John Black's shade."

"Try it," she snapped, yanking herself out of his grip.

"Is that an offer?" He considered reaching for her again, considered and then dropped the idea. She'd probably bite him if he tried to kiss her.

"That's a veiled threat. I have six dogs, and they're trained to attack." She headed for the door. "I'm going back to work. If you need anything, the telephone's in the kitchen. Call somebody else."

"Yes, ma'am," he said meekly. "See you, neighbor."

Sybil snarled, slamming open the front door and exiting in a waft of feathers.

He stood there in the open doorway, watching her go. She did need the four-wheel drive—in her rage she drove off the narrow driveway twice, and the second time she nearly didn't make it back out of the drift. Then she was gone, tearing off down the road at speeds better suited to Indianapolis. He stared after her, a speculative expression in his topaz eyes, and turned back into his haunted house, shutting the door behind him.

Chapter Five

It had been too long a day, Sybil decided as she drove down the progressively narrow lake road to her house. First a sleepless night, followed by too much of Nick Fitz-simmons, followed by a lecture from Leona that was made even worse because it was so kindly meant. Add to that too much coffee followed by too much peppermint tea and her stomach was in an uproar, her nerves were screaming, and all she wanted to do was load the wood furnace, pour her-self a large glass of Courvoisier and crawl into bed. She had a pile of books near at hand that threatened to topple over every time she climbed into her bed, and she had her choice of a range of subjects, from map dowsing to auras to pyramid power to crystal power to runes. Somehow she thought she might dive under the bed for the latest Jackie Collins.

She tried to keep her face averted when she passed the Black Farm, but curiosity overcame her. She could see the elegant tail of the Jaguar at the end of the road and detect a thick white plume of smoke curling upward in the dark-ening sky. He must have settled in well enough without the further help she knew she should have supplied. He'd find the small general store with no trouble, and Hardwick had a Grand Union if he demanded more variety. The state liquor store was only ten miles away, and clearly the man knew how to start a fire in a wood stove. She had absolutely no reason to feel guilty.

Her own driveway was only half a mile down the road, not the mile and a half she'd told Nick, but it never seemed farther away. She stomped on the gas pedal, slid sideways and careened into her well-plowed dooryard, just missing the Honda Accord parked there.

Her house was well lighted, and her own wood fires had already been tended. The front door opened and Dulcy's tall, willowy figure was silhouetted by the warm light behind her. The pack of killer dogs zoomed past her, barking wildly in the gathering dusk.

Sybil jumped out of the Subaru before twenty-four paws could do any more damage to the scratched-up paint job, then squatted down to welcome her vicious attack dogs.

The English springer spaniels swarmed over her, licking her, howling their pleasure at her return, panting and rolling in the snow and generally making a good-natured nuisance of themselves. The four puppies decided Sybil's shawl was a suitable toy, and it was pulled off and in the middle of a tug-of-war before she could retrieve it. She lunged for it, fell in the soft new snow and lay there for a peaceful moment.

"It's a good thing I'm still here," Dulcy drawled from directly above her, "or they'd find you frozen to death like something out of a nineteenth-century ballad."

Sybil rolled over and surveyed Dulcy's feet. "Not with my killer dogs. They'd keep me warm."

"Killer dogs? Your spaniels are so gentle and cowardly they'd probably lick a burglar to death. What's the problem—aren't the allergies enough to keep your family at bay?"

"Yup," Sybil said, climbing to her feet and rescuing her shredded shawl. "But I don't think Nicholas Fitzsimmons has asthma."

"If you're trying to keep Nick away, I'm afraid I blew it." Dulcy started into the house, her silver-white hair flowing behind her. "I told him I was on my way to feed your sweet little dogs and that he ought to come see them."

Sybil followed, shutting the cold and the romping dogs out, shutting her sudden surge of irritation in. "Thanks a lot. When did you see him? I thought he decided you weren't his type."

Dulcy smiled that secret, cat-got-the-canary smile and curled up on the sofa, picking up her cognac in one long-fingered hand. "He has."

"But you thought you'd change his mind?" Sybil kept her voice even as she pulled off her coat, dumped the ruined shawl into the overflowing wastebasket and kicked off her boots.

"No, Sybil. I was simply being a good neighbor. I dropped off some of my herb jam as a welcoming present for him. Even Leona sent over some of that nasty rosemary wine she makes. I'm sure you're planning to do the same."

"Guess again." She poured herself a glass of the cognac Dulcy had left out. Her friend had taken the one Waterford brandy snifter, so the Courvoisier had to settle for one of the Indiana Jones glasses Sybil had bought from Burger King. Neither the cognac nor Indy seemed to mind. "I've already done my part in welcoming him. From now on he can muddle through on his own."

"Then what's that casserole in the fridge?"

"Maybe I'm hungry." She took a defensive gulp of the cognac and then had to force back a choking gasp. Her eyes watered, but she remained calm.

"So why do you have two casseroles?"

"That was before I met the man. I thought he was going to be a crotchety old reactionary with a heart of gold. I figured I could charm him into being pleasant."

"And instead he's a crotchety young reactionary with a handsome face. Maybe your charm could be put to even better use."

"Forget it," Sybil said, throwing herself into one of the overstuffed chairs. "Leona says I'll diffuse my energy if I get involved."

"Leona is . . ." Dulcy began sharply, then took a deep, calming breath. "Leona is full of opinions," she finished evenly. "There's no need for you to agree with all of them."

"I don't. But she makes sense."

"Sometimes. I never thought celibacy was all it was cracked up to be. Some of the great psychics of history have been fairly randy creatures." Dulcy took another decorous sip of her cognac. "And don't bite your lip like that. I know you're dying to ask me what the hell I know about celibacy."

"I wouldn't do that," Sybil protested, a small grin playing around the corners of her mouth.

"Only because you're too nice. But you thought it just the same. Why don't you use some of that niceness and some of that discretion on your new neighbor? He deserves it as much as Leona, maybe more."

The dogs were scratching wildly at the door. Sybil rose, let them in, then wrestled the puppies for the chair while Annie and Kermit, the two parents, took their dignified places on the sofa beside Dulcy. "Why don't you like Leona?" she asked.

Dulcy sighed, draining her cognac. "Who says I don't like her?"

"Everything about you. Your expressions, your polite behavior toward her. The only people you're polite to are people you don't like."

"Maybe you could learn to be as polite to Nick."

"Why don't you like her?" she persisted.

"Maybe I don't trust her."

"Why not? She's sweet, kind, and has the same interests we do. She even spends lots of time with the old ladies in the Davis Apartments, just as you do. I've never heard her say a single mean thing about anyone."

"Maybe that's why I don't trust her. Anyone without noticeable malice has to have a lot hidden away."

"Well, at least we don't need to worry about Nick having hidden malice. His is there for everyone to see."

"I don't think he's malicious, Sybil. Just a little... contentious, perhaps. I think with the proper handling he could be quite... lamblike."

Once more Sybil stifled the surge of irritation. "Well, go for it."

"Not me, kiddo. He didn't come to Danbury for me."

"He didn't come to Danbury for anyone. He came to do research on water witching."

"So he thinks," Dulcy said with her serene smile. "In the meantime, the poor man is going to open a can of corned beef hash for dinner. Do you think that's fair for a newcomer to town when you have chicken marengo in the fridge?"

"Life isn't fair," Sybil grumbled.

"It is the way you play it." Dulcy rose to her full, impressive height, pulling on her handwoven lavender cape, which only added to her ethereal effect. "Take him dinner, Sybil. I've loaded your stove, fed the dogs and walked them, so you've got nothing else you have to do. Be your sweet, fair self."

"For someone like Nicholas Fitzsimmons?" she argued, already talked into it.

"Especially for someone like Nicholas Fitzsimmons. Things don't happen without a reason, Sybil. He had a purpose in being here, and someone has a lesson to learn from it."

"And you think I'm that someone?" she said morosely, following Dulcy to the door, with the dogs trailing behind them.

"It seems like a possibility."

"I shouldn't listen to you."

"No, and you shouldn't listen to Leona, either. You should only listen to yourself, to your inner voices."

Sybil tried it one last time. "My inner voices tell me to go to bed and let Nick eat canned meat."

Dulcy smiled her secret, glorious smile, and Sybil wondered how Nick could have resisted it. "Do they really?"

Sybil gave up. "No, and you know they don't. My inner voices say to change my clothes, fix my hair and drive back to the Black Farm."

"Good girl. Listen to your voices." Dulcy started out into the chilly night air, now pitch-black. Her pale hair was a beacon of light in the darkness.

"You still haven't told me why you don't like Leona," Sybil called after her.

Dulcy didn't answer. She merely waved an airy hand behind her before climbing into her Honda.

Sybil went back inside, shutting the door behind her. The dogs had already resumed their spots around the wood stove, ready to settle down for a long winter's nap.

"I don't want to go out," she said plaintively. Annie lifted her black-and-white head and stared at her with gentle, disbelieving eyes. "No, I really don't. I want to stay by the fire and read trashy books and drink cognac and eat all the chicken marengo by myself.''

Annie yawned, dropping her head down onto her paws, and one of her puppies rolled over, paws in the air. "I suppose I could call him. He's probably already eaten. After all, it's after—" she looked at the mantel clock "—quarter to six. Well, still, he probably doesn't want any more visitors. If Leona and Dulcy took goodies to him, then other people probably did, too. He won't need anything." Kermit shifted, his head flopping halfway off the sofa. "Okay, okay, I'll call him."

"The number you have called, 555-7740, is not a working number. Please call your operator for assistance." Sybil dropped the phone down in its cradle with annoyance. She didn't need to call the operator to know that she'd messed up. It had been up to her to have the Black Farm telephone reconnected—she should have called New England Telephone two weeks ago when she first heard Nick was coming. Now there was no question—she'd have to go back there, if for no other reason than to explain the phone situation.

NICK STARED at the phone in his hand in frustration. He should have had enough sense to try it earlier, when he could have driven out to Danbury and called the phone company. Even if he wanted to attempt it in the pitch-darkness, the business office would be closed and chances were the trip would be wasted.

Of course, instead of turning left at the top of his driveway he could always turn right. Somewhere down that road were Sybil Richardson and her killer dogs. He could show up, exert his long-lost charm and ask to use her telephone. If he played his cards right she might even invite him to dinner, and he wouldn't have to make do with the

canned corned beef hash that had looked edible enough in
the dim light of the almost empty cupboard.

He'd have to think of someone to call first—preferably
someone who wouldn't be home, so he'd have to keep
trying. It had been Sybil herself he'd been trying to reach
when he discovered the phone didn't work, and that was
for a lame enough excuse as it was. What it all boiled down
to was that he was restless, bored and lonely. And he was
restless, bored and lonely for Sybil Richardson.

Not that he didn't have visitors. There had been a steady
stream of them, from Dulcy with her herb jam to Leona
and two of her elderly cronies, bringing rosemary wine, of
all the disgusting things, and hard little cookies made entirely of whole wheat. He'd forced himself to nibble on
them, poured the rosemary wine down the sink, and
wished he had thought to go to the store before the early
winter sun set.

He would survive. He had gourmet Gummi Bears in his
glove compartment, instant espresso in his travel kit. At
first sign of daylight he'd hunt for a restaurant that would
feed him. If worse came to worst, he could drive all the
way back to St. Johnsbury and have an Egg McMuffin.

Unless he wanted to go searching for Sybil Richardson.
The more he thought about it, the less he thought of the
idea. He was hungry, he was lonely, but at this point things
would be much better if she made the next move. He didn't
want her to feel she was being stalked. Even if that was
exactly what he was contemplating.

He threw himself down on the comfortable couch,
glowering at the wood stove. Not even a nice fire to watch,
he grumbled to himself. Nothing to drink, nothing even to
read. It looked as if it was going to be a hell of an evening.

Now what would one of the Danbury Seekers of Enlightenment do in a situation like this? Certainly not sit there and sulk. He could always lean back and meditate, send thought waves across the frozen countryside to his neighbor. He slid down on the couch, stretching his long legs out, a cynical grin on his face as he closed his eyes.

"Come to me, Sybil Richardson," he intoned in a spooky voice that was a good match for Leona Coleman at her campiest. "Come to me and bring me food."

The dry wood in the stove crackled cheerfully in response, and Nick slid lower on the couch. "Come to me," he murmured. "Bring me food and drink and leave your killer dogs behind. Come to me, Sybil." His voice was low and eerie in the empty house, and for a moment he remembered John Black's fate fifty years ago, and a faint twinge of nervousness ran across his backbone. He opened his eyes, glanced at the shadows in the dimly lit living room and for a moment considered getting up and turning on every light in the place.

He dismissed the notion, figuring he was getting a little nuts with hunger. Maybe he should just go to bed. Maybe...

There was a loud rap on the front door. He could hear it all the way in the living room, and he sat up, startled. He hadn't heard a car, hadn't heard anyone approach in the stillness of the December night. Maybe it was John Black's ghost. Except that according to Sybil the place wasn't haunted, and she wouldn't have lied to him to spare his sensibilities. As far as she was concerned he didn't have any.

He headed for the hallway, pausing by the thick wooden door. Someone was rattling the lock, someone in a bad mood. He could guess who that someone might be, but it was too coincidental and downright creepy. He couldn't really have summoned her across the miles, could he? The knocking began again, loud and irritable.

"Who is it?"

"Who the hell do you think it is, you paranoid flatlander?" Sybil's irritated voice came from the other side. "Unlock the damned door."

A slow grin creased Nick's face. "How do I know it's really you and not a ghost?"

There was a long, furious pause. "If you don't open this door, I will leave, and I'll take my chicken marengo and my bottle of cognac with me."

Nick flung open the door before the last word was out of her mouth. She stood there, small and defiant, a basket full of wonderful-smelling goodies on her arm. "Red Riding Hood, I presume," he said thankfully, reaching out for her, reaching out for the basket. He tugged them both into the house, shutting the darkness out.

"Your phone doesn't work," she said flatly.

"I know. It's the damnedest thing—"

"No, it isn't," she interrupted. "I forgot to have them turn it on."

He stopped his rummaging in the basket long enough to look down at her. She looked like a resistant little kid, awaiting a deserving punishment. "On purpose?" he questioned softly.

"Of course not. I didn't realize you were so obnoxious. I thought you'd be a sweet little old man."

He laughed, too pleased with the smell of the chicken and wine to snap back. "And instead I'm a sour, big, not so old man."

"You got it." She stood there, making no effort to take off her shedding down coat. "Anything else?"

"You brought coffee," he said reverently. "And cream, and pie and..." A silence fell over the hallway. "Courvoisier," he said, and his voice was hushed with awe. "I could kiss you."

She was getting nervous, he could tell. The hall was a small place, and he was a tall man. She edged toward the door. "I thought you might not have had a chance to get to the store," she said on that breathless note. "Well, I'd better be going." She opened the door, clearly hoping to dash out.

He put a quick stop to that, reaching over her head and slamming the door shut again. "You can't leave me. I'm not only starving, I'm lonely."

"I don't think I'd be the best company...." He set the basket down on the floor and became busy unfastening the buttons on the front of her coat. "Nick, don't..."

"Humor me." He moved closer, pushing the coat off her shoulders, his body almost touching hers. Simple intimidation tactics that were being amazingly effective. He could feel the heat from her small, surprisingly lush little body, could sense the battle going on behind those startled brown eyes.

It was a battle he lost. She reached up, yanked her coat back on and pushed him away. "Forget it. I have to feed my dogs."

He knew when to back off. He shrugged, moving away, but not before he saw a delicious flicker of disappointment in her face. "At least I was higher priority."

"I was on my way home. Otherwise the dogs would come first."

She was lying again. He remembered Dulcy's seemingly artless prattle that had told him a great many things he'd wanted to know.

"Well, thanks for the dinner," he said.

She grabbed the doorknob. "I'd do it for anyone."

"I'm not supposed to jump to any conclusions, then?"

"You got it."

"You want to tell me something, Sybil?" His voice stopped her as she stepped out into the chilly night air.

She hesitated, and he knew she wanted to run back to the Subaru. But she was made of sterner stuff than that. She turned. "Yes?"

"Why are you afraid of me?"

"I'm not afraid of anyone," she said with a weary sigh.

"Then why are you lying to me?"

"I'm not...."

"Dulcy fed your dogs. Your car drove past here to your house an hour and a half ago. I was outside and I saw it. Why won't you stay and have dinner with me? Are you afraid I'm going to attack you? I promise you, I can control my raging lusts."

"I'm sure you can." Her voice was as clipped and cool as the December night.

"Then why?"

She smiled sweetly. "Because I don't like you." And without another word she ran out, got into her car and raced down the driveway.

He watched her breakneck pace with smugness. "And that, Sybil Richardson, is another lie," he said. And he turned back to the house.

THE DOGS GREETED her return with their usual enthusiasm, but even their high spirits failed to help her gloom. She'd given him the last of the cognac, and she wasn't desperate enough to resort to her ever-growing cache of Leona's rosemary wine.

She let the dogs out one last time, loaded the stoves and pulled on her ancient and blissfully comfortable flannel nightgown. Climbing into bed, she pulled her battered copy of the I Ching from the pile beside her, sending the precariously balanced books tumbling onto the floor.

Of all the various bits of arcane tools she'd come across in her search for deeper meaning, her favorite was the I Ching, the ancient Chinese book of changes. By casting coins and reading the appropriate hexagram, she'd gotten herself through more difficult times than she cared to remember. She sat back, closed her eyes and tossed the three coins as she cleared her mind.

For now, her only problem was dealing with Nicholas Fitzsimmons, she thought, casting the coins for a second time. She didn't usually lose her temper like that, she wasn't usually so responsive to jibes and . . . was it flirtation? It had seemed uncomfortably close.

She tossed them the third time. Dulcy was right. There was a lesson to be learned here, and she was fighting it. Maybe the I Ching would show her the way.

She rolled the coins three more times, opened her worn yellow book and turned to the appropriate hexagram. She immediately slammed it shut, sinking down into her bed with a howl of despair that woke the puppies.

"Of all the hexagrams to have gotten," she moaned, "why did I have to come up with Marrying Maiden?" With a groan of surrender, she switched off the light beside her bed and buried her face in the pillow.

Chapter Six

It was a brilliant, sunny morning, the first in days, and Sybil determined she was going to enjoy it. Leona wasn't coming in at all, and with any luck Nick would be so busy settling in and doing the shopping he would have forgotten about yesterday that she wouldn't see him, either.

Her mornings were traditionally allotted for office work: her afternoons were for the bookshop. She would finish the long overdue monthly mailing, then take her knitting into the back room, turn on her new tape and sit there in the sunshine drinking herb tea and feeling righteous. It was going to be a glorious, wonderful day.

Of course, she hadn't taken into account that she couldn't depend on Nick's absence. It took her twice as long as usual to finish up the mailing, since she kept getting up to see if his Jaguar was coming down the road. Every time the phone rang she jumped a mile: every time the wrong voice spoke on the other end she felt a wave of emotion drain through her—an emotion she called relief but that still felt a lot like disappointment.

She didn't finish till quarter past twelve, and by that time it was too late to go out for lunch. Business had been brisk in the pre-Christmas rush. She might have an unending stream of three or four customers in the afternoon, and she couldn't afford to lose a single one. She could afford to miss lunch, however, and if she had any hunger pangs, the tape would take care of it.

She shoved *How to Lose Weight without Trying* into the cassette player, climbed onto her stool by the old-fashioned manual cash register and pulled out her knitting. It was a rich, flame color and shapeless, with a wonderful texture that was mainly the result of dropped stitches. She hadn't improved much in the past two years, but she refused to give up. This latest would be a Christmas present for someone in her family, she still wasn't sure who. It all depended on what it ended up being. It had started out as a vest, turned into a cardigan and was now looking like a lumpy sort of afghan. It would probably end up as the same kind of ill-fitting pullover her other efforts had made. Sighing, she dug her needles in, keeping the tension of the yarn too tight, as the sound of waves washed over her and a mumbling voice whispered, "Food is for nourishment, not for pleasure. Food is for nourishment, not for pleasure."

Sybil remembered her missed dinner the night before, the yogurt that was two weeks past its due date for breakfast, and she sighed. "Food is for pleasure, not for nourishment," she muttered, dropping a stitch. "Food is for pleasure, not for—"

"I'm glad to hear that."

Sybil jabbed the knitting needle into her palm. Apart from that she managed quite well, looking up into Nick Fitzsimmons's golden eyes with only a faint quiver of alarm. "I didn't hear you come in."

"I have been told I have a light footstep," he intoned.

Sybil abandoned her knitting, temper forgotten in sudden interest as she recognized the quotation from *Dracula.* "You don't strike me as the vampire type." Which was a lie. With his black hair, commanding height and mesmerizing eyes, he could very well be a Transylvanian immigrant.

He moved into the room. He had already shed his jacket, if he'd even been wearing one, and his close-fitting navy sweater and faded jeans accentuated his height and leanness. "What type do I strike you as?" he murmured.

She cocked her head to one side, considering. One part Frank Langella, one part William F. Buckley, a dash of Dan Rather, a soupçon of Sting, a side order of Henry Kissinger and a tiny little streak of James Dean. It was a bizarre and potent combination, she recognized ruefully. "Miss Piggy," she said.

He laughed, placing a heavenly smelling paper bag on the counter beside her. There were delicious-looking grease spots leaking through the brown paper, and Sybil recognized the aroma of tomato-mushroom bisque from the restaurant in town. For a moment she felt faint. "How can you say such a thing when I have brought you a peace offering?"

He was toying with her, she knew he was, and there was a satanic gleam in those wonderful golden eyes of his. Only a devil would waft tomato-mushroom bisque under the nose of a starving woman.

"Peace offering?" She tried to make her voice sound cynical, but it came out in a plaintive bleat.

"Pleasure, not nourishment." He nodded toward the bag. "Soup, pastrami sandwiches and even, if I remember the floor of your car properly, Tab."

Sybil slid off her stool, contemplating temptation. According to the ancient legend, Persephone had been kidnapped by Hades and carried off to the Underworld. She would have gotten off free and clear if she just hadn't succumbed to hunger and eaten six pomegranate seeds. Surely there was a lesson to be learned in all that. This dangerous, disturbing man was standing in front of her, bearing gifts of pastrami and NutraSweet. Surely she could resist.

She wavered for an instant. "What do you want in return?"

His answering smile was blissful innocence itself. "Absolutely nothing. I'm returning your favor of last night and going you one better. I'm going to eat it with you."

She eyed him suspiciously. "Pastrami?"

"And Tab."

How could he know her greatest weakness, a weakness she'd been trying hard to conquer. "Well," she said finally, "if you are a vampire, the pastrami should keep you at bay."

"Don't believe everything you read. Vampires probably love garlic."

"Nothing's sacred," she said, leading the way into the old kitchen that was still part of the renovated farmhouse. "I take it you've found everything you need? Food store, restaurant, liquor store?"

"Actually, I made do with the Danbury C and E restaurant. I figured you could tell me where to go later."

"I'd be delighted," she murmured, setting out plates and silver.

"I didn't mean it that way," he said, unruffled. "What does C and E mean, anyway?"

"Come and Eat."

"Oh, no."

"The food's worth it," she pointed out, opening the bright pink can of Tab and breathing a blissful sigh as it hissed a welcome. "So what did you do this morning?"

"Nosy, aren't you?" He dug into his sandwich. "I went visiting."

Dulcy, she thought in sudden misery. No, Dulcy would be working. "I didn't realize you knew anybody in town," she said carefully.

"I met them yesterday. The Muller sisters came calling with your buddy Leona, and they asked me to stop in for morning coffee."

"And you did?"

"Why do you sound so skeptical? They're a couple of fascinating old ladies. They fed me coffee strong enough to keep me going for weeks, sticky buns and all the local gossip. I had a great time."

"I wouldn't think they'd be your style."

"We still haven't come up with what my style is. And I like little old ladies. They were very informative."

She drained the twelve ounces of Tab and started in on the soup. "At least my conscience is relatively clear—they couldn't have told you anything that embarrassing."

"Actually, we didn't talk about you."

She looked up sharply. "Sorry. I tend to become a little self-absorbed in the winter."

"Not because I didn't have every intention of pumping them about you, but we got off on the subject of their recent losses."

For some reason she felt better. "I know, isn't it awful? They lost every penny of their savings in that stupid investment program."

"So they said."

"At least they have enough to live on," Sybil continued. "They'll be comfortable, but that's about it. They won't have anything to leave their nieces and nephews."

"Miss Edla said they weren't the only ones."

Sybil had finished the soup and had gone on to the sandwich. "No, they're not. It seems as if half the old ladies in town have lost their nest eggs."

"Doesn't that strike you as odd?"

She stopped eating long enough to look up into his beautiful eyes. "No, why should it? Our farmers are all in trouble, too. The economy is lousy right now, and has been for a while."

"Not that lousy."

"Listen, people are making bad investments. I can understand how it happens. Half of them are farm widows. When their husbands die they sell off their farms and move into town and invest their capital. They've never had any major financial dealings before in their lives, and it's no wonder they run into trouble. Danbury is full of women with the same sad story."

"Have they lost it all in the same place?"

"Of course not. The Mullers invested in orange juice futures when there was a bad winter. Ally Johnson lost hers in a computer company. Merla Penney and Cleora Lyles invested in a wood stove company after everyone had already bought one. It's just been bad luck."

"If you say so."

Sybil pushed her plate away and stared mournfully at the empty Tab can. "Apparently you don't think so," she said. "What's your explanation?"

"I think they're being swindled."

"If they are being swindled, why didn't the crook take everything? All of them have enough to live on, they just don't have enough to leave their children and grandchildren. Have we got a crook with a conscience?"

"Not if we have one robbing helpless widows, we don't."

"Which I don't think we have," she said firmly. "I think you're imagining things. Cabin fever's already set in and you've only been here two days."

"Maybe it takes an unbiased mind to see what's going on right under your nose," he replied, an edge to his smooth voice.

"Well, if we're looking for an unbiased mind we're going to have to look farther than the great professor."

He opened his mouth to snap at her, then shut it again, and she could see he was making an effort at controlling his temper. She wondered why. "Keep that up," he said, "and I won't give you the other can of Tab I bought."

She nearly disgraced herself and begged. Instead, she drew herself up very tall. "That was kind of you," she said. "But I've already had one."

"You drank it in fifteen seconds flat."

"Nice of you to notice."

"I'm observant."

"I'm trying to quit."

He fished the second pink can out of the bag and set it on the table. "Don't let me tempt you."

She grabbed it before the words were out of his mouth. "You're rotten, you know that?" she said amiably enough. "I just hope you don't discover any of my other weaknesses."

He didn't say a word; he just grinned. It completely transformed his handsome, somewhat austere face. If he'd looked satanic before, now he looked like a fallen angel, and Sybil felt her heart doing a graceful flip.

"Okay, so if there's a crook, who do you think he is?" she asked, humoring him.

"She."

"I beg your pardon?"

"Who do I think *she* is."

Sybil stopped with the can of Tab halfway to her lips. "I don't suppose you mean me?"

"Wishful thinking. You're not evil."

"You think I'd want to be evil?" she demanded, outraged.

"I think you might flirt with the idea."

"So if it's not me, who is it? Dulcy? You're way off base with that one. Dulcy's spent half her time trying to help the old ladies. She's an advocate for the poor and elderly in St. Johnsbury and she does half her legal work for free."

"It could be a cover-up. You have to admit it would be a pretty effective one."

"I don't have to admit anything. You've been here two days and already you're concocting crimes and coming up with suspects. Don't you think you've got a lot of gall?"

Again that wicked smile. "Did you think I didn't? Besides, I didn't say I thought it was Dulcy. I just said I thought it would be a good cover-up. She's not the only one who's been a good friend to all the old ladies."

Sybil took a deep, furious breath, knowing exactly whom he was talking about. "Leona wouldn't hurt a fly," she said fiercely. "She's a little old lady herself; she wouldn't swindle one of her own kind."

"Who would she swindle, then?"

"No one. You make me so angry! You've been in town less than thirty-six hours and already you've been listening to nasty gossip and jumping to foul conclusions. Just because Leona's a newcomer—"

"How new?"

"She's been here two years. As long as I have. I'm surprised you haven't decided I'm her accomplice."

"I haven't decided anything," he said in a maddeningly calm voice. "I just noticed some curious coincidences involving your good buddy. I'm not jumping to any conclusions."

"It sure sounded like it—" She was interrupted by the jarring ring of the office telephone. "I'll get it."

Nick was there ahead of her and his reach was longer. He picked up the kitchen phone. "Society of Water Witches," he said in an unctuous murmur.

"Give me that phone!" Sybil snarled, reaching for it.

She might have been a Pygmy batting at a giraffe. "I beg your pardon, whom did you wish to speak to?" he said, ignoring her futile attempts.

"Nick . . . !"

"Sara Lee?" he echoed.

With a howl of rage she ripped the phone out of his grasp. "Hello, Mother. Yes, it's me."

Nick just stood there, staring, and that fallen-angel grin of his spread across his face once more. Leaning against the doorjamb, he waited, all mischievous patience, as Sybil dealt with her surprisingly loquacious mother.

"Yes, I'll be down before Christmas. No, I can't leave the office for any longer than that. Listen, Mother, I'm very busy. Yes, one can be busy at the Society of Water Witches. No, that wasn't a nice man who answered the phone, it was a very nasty man. Yes, I'll call you back tonight. Goodbye, Mother."

"Nasty man?" Nick echoed as she replaced the receiver with far more gentleness than she'd wanted.

"Very nasty man." She braced herself, waiting.

"Sara Lee? As in pies and cakes and frozen goodies?" The laughter in his voice might at any other time be beguiling. But not when it was at her expense.

"Saralee. One word, named after my maternal grandmother, who never baked a day in her life. All she did was make money."

"Saralee," he murmured, his voice slipping over the syllables in an oddly erotic way. "It suits you. Far better than Sybil ever did."

"If you call me Saralee," she said calmly, "I will personally do everything I can to make your life hell. And I can do a lot."

"You've already been more distracting than I care to admit. Okay, Sybil." His voice mocked the name. "Show me where I can work and I'll keep out of your hair."

She had to admit that Sybil didn't sound half as nice as Saralee did in his rich, sexy voice. Had to admit it to herself, not to him. Maybe she would wangle more vacation time, fly down to Princeton and the bosom of her family and stay there until Nick was ready to leave.

No, she must be out of her mind. Even Nick wasn't as bad as the assembled Richardsons with their tactful concern. Besides, she couldn't close the bookstore during the Christmas season—it was the only time she made any money. And she wouldn't let Nick Fitzsimmons drive her out of her comfortable home in Danbury.

She'd have to warn Leona, of course. She'd had a hard enough time, coming into a tiny, tight-knit community like Danbury without having Nick give her trouble. It was all absurd, of course, but it wouldn't do any good to tell Nick that. He would believe what he wanted to believe.

"Deke's office is at the top of the stairs," she said, her expression giving nothing away. "The library's in the room next door. But careful with the books—some are very old and rare."

"On water witching?"

"On everything. We even had a couple of ancient books of curses and spells someone's ancestor brought over from England. They're practically indecipherable but fascinating enough."

"Don't tell me you believe in spells and witchcraft?"

"No, I don't believe in spells and witchcraft," Sybil snapped. "They're a curiosity, that's all. Go away, Nick. Let me get back to work."

"I take it the truce is over?" He stood there, still blocking the doorway. She wished he were six inches shorter and six times uglier. "My bribe didn't work for any longer than that?"

She reached over, drained the second Tab, and gave him a flashing, gorgeous smile. "Ten minutes of sweetness per Tab," she said.

He looked startled, then straightened up and headed toward her out of the doorway. She ducked underneath his arm, brushing past him as she went. "Thanks for lunch," she called back, heading for the bookshop and her private phone line.

"Give Leona my love," he called after her.

Sybil, trying to remember where she'd be able to reach her friend that day, shivered.

DEKE APPLETON'S OFFICE was small and cramped, with the sloping ceilings proving a decided menace to a man who topped six feet three. The library was a little better, the table provided more work space than Deke's desk, and it had a view out over the small, picturesque little village. All he needed to make it perfect was Sybil Richardson in plain sight.

She was right about the books. There were real treasures there, including books from the nineteenth century on water witching that he'd heard about but had never been lucky enough to see. The books on regular witchcraft were in a locked, glass-door cabinet, cheek by jowl with Aleister Crowley and his ilk. For a moment he was tempted to go back and get the key, then thought better of it. Sybil—no, Saralee—needed some time away from him.

He had to be very careful not to push her too far or too fast.

For that matter, it wouldn't do him any harm to ration his exposure. For some reason, the more he saw her, the more attracted he was to her. And there was no earthly reason for it. He was used to women with a great deal more physical beauty, and certainly more charm of manner. He was used to statuesque blondes who flirted, not sullen little sparrows who every now and then looked up at him out of those melting brown eyes.

So, okay, here he was, finally able to start work on the dowsing book and, instead, he was standing there having erotic fantasies and suffering from the expected physical reaction such fantasies usually provoked. If nothing else, he could at least make a catalog of the books he was planning on using. And if worse came to worst, that glass-door cabinet would be a simple matter to open, even without the key. He could distract himself by reading some ancient witch's prescription for syphilis.

Or he could think about how he was going to trap Leona Coleman without her little champion getting in the way. Because he had no doubt at all that Leona was everything he suspected, and worse. And while her pernicious influence on Sybil was at this point only psychological, he didn't trust it to remain that way. According to the Muller sisters, Sybil had "Money," though she didn't care to use it. If it were up to Leona, she might no longer have that option.

Gingerly he lowered himself into a chair, stretching his long legs out in front of him and contemplating the quiet, musty room. His plans were simple. He had to research his book, trap Leona and break through Sybil's defenses until she was ready to be involved, both physically and emotionally. He still wasn't quite sure why he didn't want to settle for a brief affair, but the longer he was around her, the more he wanted, and he wasn't getting anywhere rationalizing about it.

He had to accomplish all this within six weeks. He was going to have a busy time of it, and the only way to accomplish everything was to get started. First things first, he told himself, and headed straight for the book of spells.

Chapter Seven

Sybil couldn't get through to Leona. She'd gone off to Hanover with Mary Philbert and they weren't due back until dinner. By the time darkness had closed down around the old building, she no longer wanted to. After all, she thought, adding row upon tangled row to her knitting, what would be accomplished by passing on Nick's infamous suspicions? They were patently absurd, no one else would even dare imagine such a thing, and to tell Leona would only hurt her feelings. It would be much better if she kept an eye on Nick, to keep his nosiness under control, rather than worry her elderly friend with pointless gossip.

She just had to hope he wasn't crass enough to start spreading those sorts of malicious tales around. For all his faults, and they were countless, he didn't strike her as the vindictive sort. He probably didn't for one moment believe that about Leona; he probably made it all up just to torment her.

But on the off-chance that he did believe it, on the vague possibility that he would start harassing Leona on some misguided suspicion, she would have to be doubly observant, and very careful. She would have to keep an eye on Nick Fitzsimmons, to make sure he wasn't causing any trouble for her friend. She couldn't just ignore him, as she told herself she longed to; she'd have to keep close tabs on him. The thought was infuriating and depressing, but highly stimulating.

She had her busiest day in the entire year, with a grand total of eight paying customers and almost a hundred dollars' worth of business. She almost forgot the presence in the office upstairs—forgot, until she heard the measured tread, the shifting of a chair, an absentminded cough.

The Mullers came at the end of the day. Miss Edla, the plumper and more talkative of the two, peered at her out of nearsighted, fading blue eyes that were quite mischievous, while Miss Minna devoted her attention to choosing between a lapis lazuli pendulum and a tiger's eye one for her totally uninterested niece.

"We like your young man," Miss Edla said, leaning over the counter confidentially.

Sybil dropped another stitch. "My young man?" she managed to say in an admirably bewildered tone. "I don't know who you're talking about, Miss Edla."

The frail old lady giggled. "Of course you do, Sybil. I haven't lived for eighty-three years without learning something. We had your young man to tea this morning."

"Oh, you mean Professor Fitzsimmons?" she said in a voice that would have fooled half the population of northern Vermont. "He's not my young man, Miss Edla. We don't even get along very well."

Miss Edla wasn't fooled. "He was asking all sorts of questions about you. We didn't tell him much, just enough to whet his interest. And when he left we dowsed it. There's no question about it, Sybil. He's your young man."

Sybil didn't use rude language in front of little old ladies, so she gritted her teeth into a semblance of a smile. "Not if I can help it," she said.

Miss Minna looked up from her perusal of the pendulums. "I don't know if you can, dearie," she murmured. "We've got a very good track record in predicting these things. We haven't been wrong yet."

No, they hadn't, Sybil remembered gloomily. "There's a first time for everything," she said.

"Of course. But this isn't it. Here..." Miss Minna removed the knitting from Sybil's slack fingers, pausing long enough to cluck in dismay over the tangled mess, and replaced it with a jade pendulum. "Try it yourself."

"Miss Minna, you know I can't dowse—"

"Everyone can dowse," Miss Edla said sternly. "Go ahead, try it."

With a long-suffering sigh, Sybil held the pendulum over her left knee. "Clockwise for yes, counterclockwise for no," she ordered in a bored voice. As usual the pendulum responded. "Are my eyes brown?" Yes. "Am I thirty years old?" Yes. "Do I love my family?" A less enthusiastic yes. "Are the Muller sisters with me?" Yes.

"Try something a little harder, dear," Miss Minna ordered, her blue eyes bright in the afternoon.

"Will there be peace in our time?" she asked, and the pendulum swung back in a depressing no.

"Not that hard, Sybil. You know what to ask."

She did indeed, and she didn't want to. Her results had been far better than usual—for once she was trusting the answers the pendulum was giving her. She didn't want an answer that could turn her world upside down.

But the Muller sisters were watching her, their matching blue eyes curious and trusting. And not for anything, not even Nicholas Fitzsimmons, would she let herself be a coward.

She hedged her bets just a trifle. "Will Nick and I ever get along?"

The pendulum wasn't sure about that one. It swung clockwise for a bit, then looped around to counterclockwise, then swung aimlessly.

"You see," she said to the sisters. "I told you we can't get along."

"That's not the question, Sybil." Miss Edla used to be a schoolteacher, and she hadn't lost the iron touch. "Stop avoiding the issue."

Sybil sighed, staring at the tiny piece of jade that was ordaining her future. "You tell me what the question is, Miss Edla."

"Will you and Nick fall in love?"

"No!" she said violently.

"I didn't ask you, Sybil. That's for the pendulum to answer."

"I'm not asking that question."

"Then phrase it your own way."

Sybil stared at the pendulum, then took a deep breath. So intent was she on the question she was formulating that she didn't hear the footsteps, the admittedly light footsteps, on the hall stairs.

"You asked for it," Sybil muttered, "you got it. Will Nick and I be lovers?"

The pendulum stopped its aimless twirling and began a slow, clockwise motion. It grew in intensity, moving faster and faster, so that it was spinning around in her hand, parallel to the ground in the enthusiasm of its positive response. "Damn," she muttered. And looking up, she stared directly into Nick's golden eyes. Those eyes were bright with malicious amusement.

"Parlor games?" he questioned, walking into the tiny bookshop, which was suddenly crowded to overflowing with his large presence.

Sybil stared up at him. She could always hope that he hadn't heard her question, but fate wasn't usually that kind. Besides, he wouldn't have that grin on his face if he thought she'd been asking about the weather or water veins under the building.

She closed the pendulum in her fist and shoved it into the pocket of her jeans. "Parlor games," she agreed.

"I'm heading home now. I'm taking a couple of books with me. Do you have any problem with that?" He was carrying a couple of the oldest leatherbound volumes, and Sybil knew she should put up a token protest.

"Not in the slightest. I think you'll be more comfortable working from home."

"Oh, I have no intention of doing that. There's no suitable place in the Black Farm to spread out. The library upstairs suits me just fine. As long as I'm not distracting you." It was said so innocently. Sybil wanted to stamp on his foot.

"You're not distracting me," she said through gritted teeth.

"I'm glad to hear it," he said, his eyes still bright with mischief. "Where's the best place for me to get herbs around here? And I don't mean the supermarket kind, I mean homegrown."

"Dulcy." She came up with the answer quickly, knowing if she hesitated she wouldn't want to send him there at all. One more inconsistency in her bewildering behavior.

"Oh, my yes. Dulcy has the finest collection of herbs in New England. She grows them, dries them and even manages a small mail-order business," Miss Edla volunteered. Sybil was doubly glad she hadn't hesitated. Nick already thought he knew too much about her and her reactions to him.

"Why don't you sell them in your shop? You have everything else under the sun."

Sybil smiled. "There are a few areas of disagreement between Dulcy and myself. One of those areas is her herbs and the uses she puts them to."

"Dulcy's a white witch," Miss Minna offered. "She grows her herbs for spells."

"And healing," Sybil added fairly. "But it's an area I tend to keep away from. I think it's dangerous to mess around in things I can't understand."

"That's what I've been trying to tell you," Nick said mildly.

"Only when it comes to witchcraft. It's an area where there's been active work toward causing harm. Even white witchcraft makes me uneasy, so I keep away from it."

"Very wise. I'll give Dulcy a call this evening."

"Do that," Sybil said evenly, ignoring the irrational stab of jealousy that had come over her once again. "Why do you want herbs?"

Nick only smiled, and his clutch on the ancient leather books tightened. "Parlor games, Sybil. Parlor games."

The Muller sisters left with him, thank heavens. The last thing she wanted to do was answer any more questions, deny any more suppositions, defend her skepticism or her honor. She watched them leave. A light snow was falling, illuminated by the street lamp that was one of seven in the entire town of Danbury. Standing motionless in the front window of the old house, she watched them go, and she reached into her pocket for the pendulum.

She pulled it out, watching it swing aimlessly. She wouldn't be proved a coward in front of the Mullers, and she was damned if she'd be a coward with only herself watching.

"Will Nick and I fall in love?"

Yes, said the pendulum, swinging clockwise, and Sybil bit her lip. Might as well go the whole way.

"Will we live happily ever after?"

Again that aimless swinging, that irritating refusal to answer. She was about to pocket the piece of jade once more, when an irresistible question came into her mind.

"Is Leona harmless?"

Once more the pendulum began to spin, but it turned in a negative, counterclockwise circle. Sybil stared at it, opened her mouth to ask another more specific, damning question; then she shut it again and shoved the jade back into her pocket. After all, if the pendulum was clearly wrong about her and Nick, it couldn't be trusted about Leona, either. She would have to rely on her own instincts, and her instincts told her...

Damn, she didn't even trust her instincts anymore. Her instincts told her to trust the pendulum. It was only her brain that knew better. And maybe it was time to listen to her brain. It could hardly get her into the kind of trouble her instincts and the pendulum seemed intent on leading her.

Parlor games, she thought, locking the bookshop and heading for her coat and boots. It was her own fault for not treating the pendulum with proper respect. No wonder it lied to her. Hadn't it?

NICK TOOK A DEEP, meditative sip of his cognac and surveyed the various oddments laid out on the kitchen table in front of him. The ancient book of spells and curses lay propped up behind them, open to a page entitled "Love Philtres for Reluctant Partners." The herbs lay in front of him, encased prosaically enough in Ziploc bags, and the wooden salad bowl, still slightly redolent of rubbed garlic, waited nearby.

Dulcy had proved more than helpful. Not only did she have everything he requested, from something as mundane as lemon thyme to something as arcane as wormwood, she had been willing to drop them off on her way to a meeting that night. It had been too late when he realized he had forgotten to ask for the orrisroot, and when he called her back she had already left. He'd kept the book carefully hidden when she arrived. He had politely offered her a drink and politely offered her recompense for the herbs, both of which she refused.

"Part of my housewarming present," she said, tossing that silvery mane over her shoulder. "Just make sure you follow the instructions."

"What instructions?" he'd asked, looking properly innocent.

She had only smiled, that wise, knowing smile. He didn't like deliberately mysterious women, and he didn't like ethereal smiles. And he certainly didn't like self-styled white witches. But he had been polite enough, waiting with barely concealed impatience for her to leave, and then had taken his basket of goodies into the kitchen to dump them onto the scrubbed pine table.

Everything was there. He stared down at the neatly marked packages, a cynical smile on his face—one that faded when he picked up a package marked orrisroot.

Coincidence, he firmly told himself, taking another warming sip of the cognac. To prove he didn't put any stock in Dulcy's claims, he mixed the potion with a deliberately casual hand, stirring the fragrant herbs and muttering the various incantations required. The vodka was the final ingredient. It would have to suffice—heaven only knew where he'd get honey mead in this century. He poured generously, the liquor releasing even more of the rich aroma. It was supposed to sit for an hour. Then, somehow or other, he was supposed to administer it to his intended victim.

That might prove easier said than done. For one thing, after today she was highly unlikely to show up at his house again. For another, even if she did, the concoction didn't smell all that appetizing.

He drained his cognac, moving back into the living room and the wood stove that was a poor substitute for the glow of a fire. Sooner or later he'd find a way. The idea had fascinated him since he'd run across the recipe for the potion, tucked between remedies for the French disease and a potion efficacious for those of dangerously costive disposition. It was a combination of boredom, lust and too much Courvoisier that made him determined to finish what he had started. He was never a man to admit defeat, particularly in something as minor as an ancient love spell.

Maybe he would discover a real aphrodisiac. Think of the chaos he could unleash upon the world—the idea boggled the mind. Think of the money he could make for such a discovery. But no, he didn't particularly need or want a lot of money. He could patent it, and then only sell it through Sybil's pathetic little store. Then she'd become rich and famous, and in her gratitude she'd turn to him....

But if the love potion happened to work, she would have already turned to him. It was an unquestionably appealing thought. Now if there were only some way he could get her over here, if worse came to worst he could hold her down and pour the nasty stuff down her throat.

No, subtlety was the ticket. The phone company had outdone itself and fixed the phone late that afternoon. He could call her up, invite her over on some irresistible trumped-up excuse, and then ply her with that concoction. Or maybe he could just ply her with the cognac—it had proved quite effective over the centuries in seducing reluctant maidens, and he had no gentlemanly qualms about taking advantage of her. He wanted her any way he could get her. Maybe the simplest plans were the best. Though he would still like to see how she reacted to the orrisroot punch.

First things first. What in all creation would get her to enter the lion's den at quarter past eight on a Friday evening? Leaning back on the couch, he took another sip of his cognac and put his inventive brain to work.

SYBIL STOOD OUTSIDE the doorway, huddled in her down coat, telling herself she was crazy. Nine o'clock at night was no time to be visiting Nicholas Fitzsimmons. As far as she was concerned, there was no time to be visiting him at all. She had the weekend ahead of her, two days of uninterrupted peace. So why had she driven back out on this snowy night, looking for trouble?

She could admit her first reason. She wanted to see if Dulcy's blue Honda was still parked in front of the Black Farm. She only intended to look, then to turn around and go back and congratulate herself on her matchmaking abilities.

But Dulcy wasn't there, and that same incomprehensible relief swept over her. All she'd meant to do was turn around in the end of his driveway and head back home, but somehow she found herself driving down toward the farm.

Well, she had excuses enough. She was still worried about Leona. Having the damned pendulum confirm Nick's suspicions was distressing, and sitting home worrying about it didn't help matters. She needed to prove that smart-aleck pendulum wrong, and she could do that either by proving that she wasn't going to fall in love with Nick

Fitzsimmons or by convincing Nick his suspicions were unfounded.

Either way, she couldn't just let the situation with Leona fester in the back of her mind like an untended wound. She was someone who faced up to things, unless they were connected with her family. And facing up to Nick, nerve-racking as it threatened to be, was better than sitting home worrying about it. Right?

Right, her cynical brain replied. *Stop looking for excuses and knock on the damned door.* And raising her gloved hand, she did just that.

It took him a moment to get there. She'd practiced all the things she planned on saying, rehearsed all the pithy little comments she planned to make. When he opened the door, tall and dark with the light behind him, his topaz eyes gleaming down at her, all conscious thought left her brain. She stood there, silent, staring, unable to shake the sudden, uneasy suspicion that she confronted a creature of the night.

The creature of the night broke the silence. That fallen-angel grin lit his face, and he reached out and pulled her into the warmth and light. "Welcome to Carfax Abbey."

"You still don't make it as Dracula," she said, hiding the sudden shiver that swept over her backbone. She moved out of reach of those long, graceful hands of his. "Is this a bad time?"

"A bad time for what?"

"A bad time for a visit. I wanted to talk to you, and since your phone doesn't work..."

"Actually, it does. They fixed it late this afternoon. And you couldn't have picked a better time for a visit—I just made some of an herb drink I found in an antique recipe book. You can be my first victim."

She gave him a long, suspicious glance before shrugging out of her down coat. "I don't need anything. I won't be staying long."

"You'll be staying long enough to have a drink. Don't be graceless, Saralee. You can certainly manage the amenities for an hour or so." Once more he put his hands on her, warm, strong hands, and he pushed her gently in the direction of the living room. "Go in and have a seat and I'll bring you your drink."

"Is that what you've been having?" she demanded.

He smiled, a curiously mischievous smile, and she wondered, if she looked closely, whether she might discover fangs. "Cognac," he replied. "A little too much, but it won't do me any harm."

"Then I'll have cognac too."

"Sorry, I drank it all." He was lying; she knew it, but there was no way she could prove it. He gave her another gentle push toward the living room, the warmth and light spilling over into the darkened hallway. "Come into my parlor," he murmured, and she could hear the laughter beneath his deep voice.

"Said the spider to the fly," she snapped back. "Stop shoving. I'll go along quietly."

"And you'll drink my herb drink? It's the least you can do when I keep you supplied with Tab."

She stopped inside the doorway, turning to stare up at him, all her suspicions aroused. He just smiled at her, with such sweet innocence that she knew she was in deep trouble. She could always run while he was getting his herb drink.

But no, she wasn't a coward, and she wasn't going to let Nick intimidate her. She'd sit there, drink his damned drink and calmly, rationally, convince him that Leona had nothing to do with the recent raft of bankruptcies among the old ladies of Danbury. Then she'd leave, immune from any sort of attraction, and when she got home she'd give the pendulum to the dogs to eat.

She smiled up at him with equal innocence. "I'll drink your herb drink," she said. "If it's good, we can make up a batch and sell it in the bookstore."

"You know, I thought of that," he murmured, a devilish light in his eyes. "It would be . . . interesting."

She turned away from him, moving into the warmth of the living room. "I'm sure it would."

Chapter Eight

It was amazing, the subtle changes someone's presence wrought in a room. Already the living room of the Black Farm was altered, different, a chair pushed closer to the wood stove, books scattered on the coffee table, a sweater tossed over the back of the sofa. It looked and felt less like an empty house with an unhappy history and more like a home, and it was undeniably welcoming.

She perched gingerly on the edge of the chair nearest to the wood stove. For all the deceptive comfort of the place, she was already regretting her rash visit. Nick was up to no good, that much was clear, and his mysterious herb drink had something to do with it.

Maybe it was just some of Leona's rosemary wine, and he wanted to see whether it had some nefarious hallucinatory powers. Or maybe he had concocted a hallucinatory potion himself. She rose quickly when he entered the room, that seraphic smile on his satanic face, and the brown liquid in the tulip-shaped wineglass looked unpromising indeed.

"Here you go. I promise you, the stuff is completely innocent. It's just a simple mixture of common herbs and a bit of vodka to bind it together."

She eyed it warily. "It's a love potion, isn't it?"

His grin broadened. "My, my, you do have a high opinion of yourself, Saralee. Why should I want to ply you with a love potion?"

She didn't even blush. "Because you've got an odd sense of humor. You took the book of spells and potions home with you, Nick. I've read it from cover to cover, and the only potions of any interest are for love potions. Unless you're trying to cure me of syphilis or help me conceive, I think you are probably fooling around with the aphrodisiac."

"Guilty."

"It doesn't work."

"Let's try it and see." He moved closer, his tall body dwarfing hers.

"I don't have to try it. I made some up a long time ago and tried it then. Nothing happened. Besides, it tastes very nasty. Like liquid cigarettes."

"Humor me."

She shook her head. "I can't imagine why you bothered doing it. You're the great skeptic—compared with you I'm Rebecca of Sunnybrook Farm, and even I don't believe in love potions."

Nick set the glass down on the mantel, reaching around her, and for a moment she felt trapped. And for a moment it felt good. When he moved away she released her pent-up breath, silently, so that he wouldn't hear it. "I was curious. Bored, too. And you accused me of having a closed mind earlier today. I wanted to prove you wrong."

"Messing around with antique spells isn't going to prove me wrong, it's just going to prove a waste of time."

He smiled, a slow, devilish smile. "So if it's harmless, ineffective and a waste of time, you won't mind trying it."

She opened her mouth to protest, then shut it again. "Okay," she said finally. "I'll drink some. Then I want to talk about what I came over here for."

"What's that?"

"Leona and your outrageous suspicions."

"I don't want to talk about Leona," he said flatly. "She bores me."

"Then I can leave right now." She started toward the hall, but he reached out and caught her, his strong hands a deceptively gentle restraint.

"Okay, we'll talk about Leona, and you can tell me how pure and innocent and kindly she is."

"She is!"

"I'm sure," he said. "But we'll talk about it after we try my experiment."

Sybil sighed. "Okay. Hand me the potion."

"Not yet. We have to do this in a scientific manner."

He was standing very close to her. He hadn't yet released her arms, and his topaz eyes had a gleam that made her very nervous. She swallowed once, wishing she could move back, away from him, unwilling to let him know how he affected her—particularly since she wasn't sure herself.

"Okay, we'll do it in a scientific manner."

"We need a basis for comparison."

"How do you plan to do that?"

He smiled. "Simple. I'll kiss you before you drink the potion and we'll see how you respond. Then I'll kiss you after the potion."

"What if the potion works? I may fling you to the floor, rip off your clothes and have my wicked way with you."

"I'm prepared for that eventuality."

"Nick . . ."

"Stop arguing. This is for the sake of pure science." His hands slid up her arms, pulling her closer, so that she was within inches of him. For a moment she panicked, struggling, and his hands were very strong. "What's the matter, Saralee?" he whispered, his breath warm and sweet on her upturned face. "Afraid I'll be irresistible?"

She stopped her useless struggles. "Not likely. Do your worst, then."

"I have every intention of doing my best." His mouth descended, touching hers, briefly, gently, a mere flirtation of a kiss that left her astonishingly aroused and longing for more. She kept her eyes open, and they looked up into his golden ones with more than faint mistrust.

She tried to pull away again, but he still held her firmly. "That was just to get you used to the idea," he murmured, a thread of laughter in his voice. And pulling her into the warmth of his body, he kissed her again.

She tried to keep her mouth closed against his, but it was a losing battle. Slowly, seductively his tongue reached out, breaching her defenses, slipping into her mouth, invading her, possessing her, as his hands molded her suddenly pliant body against his. He tasted of brandy, she thought as her eyelids fluttered closed. He tasted of love. And she moved her hands up to rest against his shoulders, and her fingers clutched at him.

She would have liked to think that she had been the one to pull away, but she doubted it. After all, it had been more than three years since she'd been kissed like that. Hell, maybe she'd never been kissed like that. When she opened her eyes she was standing alone, and despite the roaring fire in the wood stove she was cold.

"Ready for the potion?" he inquired innocently.

She looked at him. He appeared totally unmoved by that kiss, he just stood there, waiting patiently. But when she looked closer she noticed the rapid rise and fall of his chest. It would have been too crass to let her eyes drop lower, but while she had been concentrating on what he was doing to her mouth, the rest of her body still felt the imprint of his. And it hadn't been the imprint of an un-aroused male.

Two could play at that game, she thought. If it took every ounce of her ability, she could appear undisturbed, too. She smiled coolly. "Ready." She stepped toward him, taking the wineglass from his hands and holding it to her lips.

It looked like weak tea with cigarettes crumpled in it. It would probably taste worse. "Here's mud in your eye," she said deliberately, toasting him with the glass. She took a cautious sip.

"You've got to have more than that," he protested when she grimaced in distaste.

"How much more?"

"Half the glass at least."

"Nick . . ."

"For the sake of science."

She looked up at him suspiciously. When it came right down to it, if she didn't drink the nasty stuff he'd have no reason to kiss her again. And she very much wanted an-other kiss—just one, and then she'd stop. Surely one more couldn't hurt her.

She took a deep gulp, drinking most of it, then handed him the glass. "For the sake of science," she said.

"You want to sit down for this one?" he inquired, set-ting the glass on the mantel.

"You think you're going to sweep me off my feet?" she responded. "It hasn't begun to affect me yet, Nick. I'm still wonderfully impervious to your charm."

"Sure you are, Sybil. So why don't you sit down so we can do a proper job of this?"

She managed, just managed, to emit a long-suffering sigh before sinking down on the sofa. She spoke no more than the truth—she wasn't overcome with any sudden upsurge of uncontrollable lust. She'd been suffering from that from the second time he kissed her.

He sat down beside her, very close, a light of humor and something else in those hypnotic eyes. His hands were warm and strong as they reached out and touched her neck, cradling her head, his long fingers stroking her jaw. He must have felt the trembling in her pulses, there was no way he could have missed it.

"What I don't understand," she murmured, putting off the inevitable, "is why you bothered trying this on me. Why not on Dulcy, or someone more amenable?"

"If I tried it with someone more amenable, it wouldn't be much of a test, would it?" His thumbs were tracing the line of her lips, a gentle, erotic caress that Sybil felt in the very center of her being.

"No, I suppose it wouldn't," she agreed, trying to sound prosaic. Her voice came out breathless, her lips moving against his thumbs were a tentative kiss. "But I would have thought you'd at least try it with someone you really wanted."

His eyes were dancing with humor and something more. Something even Sybil had to recognize, whether she wanted to or not. "Oh, Sybil," he said, his voice soft, "what makes you think I don't want you? I don't know if I've ever wanted anyone so much in my life." And before she had a chance to do more than open her mouth in astonishment he pushed her down on the sofa, his mouth claiming hers as his hands held her still for his shattering kiss.

A white hot spasm of longing swept over her, one so intense that she practically cried out. Her hands reached out to pull him closer, her tongue touched his, shyly at first, then with renewed hunger, until all that existed were their mouths, twining, joining, thrusting and retreating, heat and love and desire all tumbled together. Somewhere in the back of her brain Sybil reached for sanity, trying to tell herself that it was simple hormones, it had nothing to do with magic potions, nothing to do with a man she was sure she disliked. He simply knew how to kiss, and she was normal enough to respond. She told herself that as she clung to him, fighting the reaction that was threatening to turn her into a helpless victim of a passion that was nothing but trouble.

Just when the last bit of her control was about to shatter, just as she was about to do what she'd joked about and begin to rip off his clothes, he pulled his mouth away, mere inches, far enough for her to catch her breath, far enough for her to reach for the fast disappearing traces of common sense.

"What do you think?" he whispered, his voice husky. "Did it work?"

She was stretched out on the sofa, and he was lying half beside her, half on top of her. The weight of him was hot and strong, arousing and protecting, and she wanted to pull him all the way over her, into her. She could feel his heart racing against hers, feel the hardness of him pressed against her hips, could see the dazed look of desire he was trying so hard to keep from his eyes. And she knew she must look even more vulnerable.

She took a deep breath. "Nope," she said.

He moved so quickly she was taken by surprise. One moment she was cradled in his arms, in the next she was lying alone on the couch, chilled by the sudden withdrawal of his heat and strength. He was over by the mantel, and his eyes were hooded.

He shrugged. "It was worth a try. Guess we won't market it quite yet."

She sat up, pulling her clothes together with hands that trembled. She supposed he could see that she was shaken; he probably knew perfectly well that she was lying. It didn't matter. He'd chosen to let her be, and his insistence that he really wanted her had been just one more manipulative trick.

"Want some coffee? It'll only take me a moment."

She rose, giving him a regal smile that was only slightly lopsided. "No, thank you. I think I've had quite enough stimulation as it is."

He paused. "You found it stimulating?"

She met his gaze fearlessly. "You do know how to kiss," she said. "I certainly grant you that much. You just aren't much of a potion maker."

He nodded. "Would you like some cognac, then?"

"I thought you said you drank it all."

"I lied."

So did I, she thought with just a trace of mournfulness. "No, thank you."

He grinned then. "Another shot of love potion?"

"Don't push it, Nick," she warned. "I think I'd better just go home."

"I thought we were going to talk about Leona?"

"I don't feel like it now."

"Why not? I thought you were impervious to my charms."

"I'm impervious," she said. "I'm just tired. I'm sure by Monday you'll realize your suspicions were all ridiculous."

"Monday? Is the office closed on the weekend?"

"It is. I'm sure you'll find something to entertain you. Maybe you could try coming up with a cure for constipation out of that book."

"For those of a dangerously costive disposition? I might have a hard time finding a guinea pig."

"If you do with that book what I'd like to suggest you do with it," Sybil said sweetly, "then you can practice on yourself."

It took him just a moment. Then he laughed, a rich, delighted sound that was almost as beguiling as his kisses. "Saralee Richardson," he said when his amusement had died away, "I think maybe that potion backfired on its maker."

"I'm sure you'll be able to come up with an antidote." She moved toward the hallway, and this time he made no effort to stop her. She could feel his eyes following her, their gaze distracted, and for a brief moment she reveled in the tiny sense of accomplishment. If Nick Fitzsimmons had thrown her for a loop, she had at least disturbed his seemingly invincible amour propre.

He'd left her coat hanging over the banister, and she pulled it on without any help from him and headed toward the door without a backward glance. He said something beneath his breath, and for a moment she was tempted to ask him to repeat it. It had sounded like "I'm not sure I want one."

"I'll see you Monday," she called over her shoulder and stepped out into the chilly night air.

"If not before," he replied, still in the living room.

She shut the door behind her and walked to her Subaru. It had a light dusting of snow mantling its battered exterior, making it look almost as elegant as Nick's Jaguar. If one didn't have a good eye for beautiful lines, she thought, climbing in and offering up a silent prayer that her station wagon would start on the first try.

It started on the second try, and Sybil let out her pent-up breath as she let out the clutch, zooming up the driveway at breakneck speed. The sooner she got home, back to the safety of her house and the companionship of her dogs, the happier she'd be. For a few minutes back there she'd felt the solid foundation of her universe shift and slide, like geological plates during an earthquake. Everything she held dear, everything she believed in, had shimmered and dissolved for a brief moment when she was in Nick's arms. And she had to wonder whether the damned potion had worked after all.

"DULCY?"

"It's seven in the morning, Sybil," the tired, cranky voice came back over the telephone wire. "Saturday is my only morning to sleep late."

"I know that, Dulcy. And I wouldn't have called you this early if it weren't desperately important."

Her first response was a long-suffering sigh. "What is it now?"

"How do you know it's not something life-threatening?" Sybil countered, much aggrieved.

"Trust me, I'd know. Don't play games with me, Sybil, it's too early. What's the problem?"

"I need some herbs."

There was a long pause on the other end, and then, to Sybil's amazement, Dulcy laughed. "Do you indeed? Shall I waste my time asking why, or do I just guess?"

Sybil bit her lip. "I don't suppose you'll believe that I want to do some cooking."

"No. I think you must have fallen prey to Nick's little experiment. Don't tell me it actually worked?"

Sybil ignored the unmistakable glee in her friend's voice. "Of course it didn't work!"

"Then you don't want an antidote?"

"You're not making this any easier for me, Dulcy."

"I don't intend to. If you don't want an herbal antidote, what are you calling me for? Do you want to try a love potion for him?"

"God, no!" she said quickly, before she could even consider the enticing idea. "I don't need an antidote, the damned potion didn't work, but I decided it wouldn't do any harm to try one. You and I both know that it's the power of suggestion that makes spells and curses work, not actual magic. And I've simply fallen prey to the power of suggestion."

"Did you sleep with him?"

"Don't be absurd. He doesn't even know I had any reaction to the filthy stuff."

Dulcy laughed. "I wouldn't be too sure of that. Nick struck me as a very observant man."

"Then it was wishful thinking on his part," Sybil snapped. "My main problem is the nightmares."

"Nightmares?"

"Well, perhaps not really nightmares," she admitted, running a hand through her heavy mane of hair, which she hadn't yet confined in braids. "Just disturbing dreams."

"You can tell me about them when I get there and we'll analyze them," Dulcy announced.

"Forget it. You're too young."

"That raunchy, eh?"

"No...yes," Sybil admitted finally. "That raunchy. I probably won't be able to see the man without blushing. I'm sure it was just tension and lack of sleep. But I figured I'd hit all bases."

She could practically hear the smile in Dulcy's voice. "I know just what you need. Make a big pot of coffee and I'll be there in half an hour."

"Bless you," Sybil said with real relief. "I knew I could count on you."

Dulcy's delicious chuckle, the one Sybil had learned to distrust, came over the line. "You surely can, my friend. I have just the thing."

Slowly Sybil replaced the receiver, telling herself her sudden qualms were no more than part and parcel of a sleepless night. She would have been better off if it had been sleepless—her dreams had been so erotic and so real that she was still quivering from an advanced state of sexual tension that nothing seemed to diminish, not a cold shower, not Saturday morning cartoons on the TV, not meditating on the sins of Nicholas Fitzsimmons.

But Dulcy was coming; Dulcy with her common sense and her bag of herbs would take care of things, put her back on the straight and narrow. Wouldn't she?

But somehow, Sybil couldn't rid herself of the suspicion that she'd gone from the frying pan to the fire. With that gloomy thought breakfast came to mind, and she headed into the kitchen, the dogs trailing behind her. Maybe food would drown her sorrows. Or at least blunt her unmanageable cravings. Sighing, she opened the refrigerator.

"Damn you, Nick," she muttered to the link sausages. "You and your love potions." Slamming the door shut, she sat down at the butcher-block table to await her deus ex machina in the unlikely form of a white witch cum lawyer named Dulcy Badenham.

Chapter Nine

Dulcy wasn't long in coming. The coffee had just finished running through the drip machine, Sybil had thrown on a loose pair of jeans and a tiger-striped sweatshirt, and the dogs had had their morning romp. The wood stove was cranking out enough heat for two houses, and the dreams of the night before seemed a distant aberration. Until she remembered them, and felt herself growing hot all over again.

Dulcy was dressed in lavender, wispy clothes and wonderful handwoven woolens that played up her otherworldly air, an air that was instantly dispelled as she strode into the house and dumped her huge multicolored tote bag on Sybil's table.

"Pour me some coffee," she ordered, stripping off her cape and diving into the bag. "And I'll get things started. You can also tell me all the details about last night."

Sybil was already pouring. "There are no details. Did you know what Nick had in mind when he asked you for the herbs?"

Dulcy smiled, pulling out a pile of Ziploc bags. "Any fool could guess. Didn't you know what he was plying you with?"

"Thanks a lot. I don't happen to be a fool, either; I knew exactly what he was giving me."

"Why didn't you refuse?" She took the wooden salad bowl Sybil handed her and began sprinkling herbs into it.

"Because I knew it wouldn't work."

"So why am I here at quarter to eight on a Saturday morning, mixing up herbs?"

Sybil sank down in the chair, staring morosely at the rapidly growing pile of herbs. "Because I'm gullible. You know it and I know it. My common sense will tell me it's all ridiculous, but my subconscious won't listen."

"The subconscious is a powerful thing," said Dulcy, taking a sip of her coffee and pouring a generous slosh into the salad bowl.

"You don't have to tell me that. That's what killed people during the Middle Ages; it's what kills people in the Caribbean who've been cursed. All they have to do is believe they're going to die and sure enough, they do."

"You're not going to die, Sybil," she said in a prosaic tone of voice. "Got any vodka?"

"Not at this hour in the morning."

"For your antidote."

Sybil lifted her gaze from the disgusting concoction. "Are you sure you know what you're doing?"

"Why did you ask me to come if you don't trust me?"

"Oh, I trust you," Sybil assured her. "I'm just tired and cranky."

"And if you don't believe Nick's potion really worked, it won't matter what I give you as an antidote, as long as your subconscious is convinced it will do the trick. Right?"

"Er...yes," she said doubtfully. "But you might as well give me the right one while you're at it. It wouldn't hurt to touch all bases."

"All I need is vodka and it'll be ready to drink."

"Yuck."

Dulcy's antidote didn't taste any better than Nick's vile brew, she thought as she dutifully downed a glassful, picking out the herbs from between her teeth. Mind you, it didn't taste any worse. As a matter of fact, it tasted exactly the same. She looked up at her friend. Dulcy was sitting back in one of the kitchen chairs, her long, slender fingers wrapped around a mug of coffee, a smug expression on her otherworldly face. "You're certain this is the right antidote?"

"Of course I'm certain. The proper antidote to the love potion in the Hungarian curse book is simply to administer a different love potion. I just whipped you up the one from the old English book of charms and curses. I realize it tastes much nastier than that nice lemony potion Nick gave you, but nasty medicine works better."

Sybil sat listening to this artful chatter with a growing sense of horror. "He didn't give me any nice lemony brew, Dulcy."

Her friend set the coffee cup down very carefully, her pale blue eyes meeting Sybil's with just the right amount of concern. "What do you mean?"

"He fed me something that tasted exactly like your antidote."

Dulcy sat back in her chair, chagrin washing over her face. And if Sybil could see a light of amusement in the back of those fine eyes, it wasn't strong enough for her to call Dulcy on it. "Oops," she said.

"What do you mean, oops?"

"I gave you the wrong antidote."

"I knew it," Sybil howled. "Things couldn't be this easy! Couldn't you tell from the ingredients Nick asked for last night that it was this potion?"

Dulcy shrugged. "I didn't pay any attention. I felt sure he would have taken the Hungarian book home with him. It's so much more interesting than the English one."

"It was the English one, Dulcy." Sybil resorted to another cup of coffee, her third, both to wash the taste of the love brew out of her mouth and to give herself courage to face this latest trauma. "Do you have what you need for the Hungarian potion?"

"Why should I need stuff for that?"

"For the antidote," Sybil said patiently. "If the English potion wipes out the Hungarian, surely...surely..."

Dulcy was shaking her head. "Sorry."

"Well, you must know something?"

"I hate to tell you this, kid, but there's nothing I can do. One dose of love philtre I can combat: two, and you're a sitting duck."

"Great," Sybil grumbled.

"Look at it this way—you don't really believe the stuff works. Just exert a little mind over matter. A glassful of nasty-tasting herbs isn't going to make you fall at Nick's feet. Not if you don't want to."

"I don't want to!"

"Of course you don't," Dulcy soothed her. "And you could meditate, mentally surround yourself with a healing blue light. No, on second thought, that might not be a good idea."

"Why not? It sounds like an excellent idea."

"Because if you surround yourself with a healing blue light you might get more than you bargained for. Who's to say that lusting after Nick Fitzsimmons isn't the healthiest thing you could do right now?"

"I do," she snapped, immediately resolving not to meditate.

"Cheer up, Sybil. You and I both know it doesn't really work. And look on the bright side of things. At least you're better off than Mary Philbert."

All thought of love potions vanished from Sybil's mind as she felt a sudden dread. "What happened to Mary Philbert?"

"The same thing that's happened to too many people. She lost all her savings."

"How?" Her voice came out raw and raspy.

"Some bad investment or something. I don't know all the details, but it sounds as if she's another victim."

"Victim?" Sybil echoed.

"Of the bad economy. Or were you thinking she was a victim of something else?" Dulcy was nothing if not shrewd. "Or someone else?"

"Of course not."

"It's been awfully coincidental."

"Dulcy, it's happening all over the country."

"It's happening too much here. I'm planning to go visit her later this morning, to see if there's any way I can help. Maybe it wasn't just bad luck, maybe I might be able to trace some sort of fraud."

Sybil set her mug down, banishing the last of her self-absorption. "I'll come with you. I didn't have anything planned anyway, and Mary's always been one of my favorite people."

"She's an old sweetie. At least the other ladies are rallying round. A lot of them have been through the same thing, so they'll be as helpful as anyone can be at a time like this. It's a shame Leona isn't around."

"She isn't?"

"She and Mary were in New Hampshire yesterday, and apparently something came up. She drove Mary back and then went on to Burlington. Something to do with her investments. Let's just hope she's not the next victim."

"Yes, let's hope so," Sybil mumbled, not entirely sure she meant it. While losing one's life savings was a devastating blow, if Leona were similarly hit it would at least clear her of any suspicion.

Not that anyone was suspicious, just that slimy Nick. Even Dulcy, who had strong reservations about Leona, didn't seem to suspect anything.

Probably Nick didn't, either, she thought, as she watched Dulcy drive away. He probably just came up with that theory to worry her. He had a definite talent for it, a definite talent for upsetting and exciting and arousing...

"Hell and damnation!" she said out loud, slamming her hand down on the windowsill. "I am going to stop thinking about him."

The dogs looked up at her out of soulful spaniel eyes, and Annie's openmouthed pant looked just a tiny bit like derisive laughter. "Yeah, I know," she muttered, pouring out the last of the coffee. "Fat chance."

"IT CERTAINLY SOUNDS suspicious, Nick, but I don't know how you think I can help." Ray's thick Boston accent came over the other end of the line. "After all, I'm just a vice cop in Boston—I wouldn't have any jurisdiction up in Vermont."

"I'm not asking for jurisdiction, Ray. I'm asking for information. You've got access to the most advanced information system in the world. All you've got to do is punch a few buttons and find out anything."

"You academic types." He sighed. "How many times do I have to tell you, it just ain't that simple."

"Are you telling me you can't help?"

"I'm telling you it isn't as easy as you think. I'll do my best for you, buddy, but I can't promise anything. And these things take time."

"I hate to hear that. You're shattering all my illusions about the wonders of the computer age."

"Ain't it a crime," Ray said with sarcastic sympathy. "Just like telling you there isn't really a Santa Claus. Tell me this old bird's name one more time."

"Leona Coleman. She's around seventy, no taller than five feet, heavyset, dark eyes, white hair. She's lived in Danbury for two years, and I haven't yet been able to find out where she lived before that. I think she gets close to the old ladies and gets them to invest in fraudulent schemes, either by simple friendliness or through her phony psychic stuff. I wouldn't put séances and all that hogwash past her, though if she goes that far it's pretty much of a secret around here. She's trusted and well liked, God knows why, and she's able to cover her tracks. No one's lost her money in the same way, and no one's made any connection between the sudden financial reverses and the sweet little friend."

"But you have?"

Nick leaned back in his chair, propping his feet on the kitchen table that was serving as his desk. "I have. I think it's a question of people being too close to the situation to notice. It takes an outsider to realize something's wrong."

"Have you mentioned your suspicions to anyone?"

Nick grimaced, glancing over at the dregs of his foul-smelling potion. "Just one. She had a minor fit, accused me of harassing the poor old dear. She's not going to listen to reason until I come up with some proof apart from my dastardly suspicions."

"And you want her to listen to reason? I take it this isn't one of the little old ladies."

"You take it right. And I don't want her to listen to reason, just to a few indecent suggestions."

"Lucky Nick. You always manage to fall on your feet," Ray said with a wistful sigh. "Heard anything from Adelle recently?"

"Just that she's happy and big as a house."

"No regrets?"

Nick thought about it for a moment, probing at the thought as one might prod a sore tooth to make sure it still hurt. Nothing, not even a twinge. "No regrets, Ray."

"I'll do what I can for you. Chances are she's using a phony name, and we don't tend to cross-reference people by height. It'll probably take me a while but I'll get back in touch."

"I appreciate it. There's a bottle of Jameson's in it for you."

"Don't go bribing a policeman, my boy, or I'll have to report you to my superior. And he'll make me share the bottle."

"Now that would be a crime. Take care, Ray. Give my love to Connie."

Good old Ray, Nick thought, sweeping away the remnants of last night's psychic punch, draining his second cup of coffee and setting the dishes in the iron sink. It was handy to have a friend in the Boston Vice Squad, even if Ray, with his paunch, his balding pate, and his thick Irish face looked a far cry from the glamour of Crockett and Tubbs. He'd gone to school with Ray's elegant wife, Constance, and the mismatch of the century, Ray's broad South Boston sturdiness and Constance's Brookline breeding, had proved the marriage of the century. They had three great kids, and he was godfather to all of them. It was only when he was at their overcrowded ranch ho in Newton that he thought about Adelle and the baby with any nostalgia.

Hell, he would have married her. Would have fathered her baby. And it would have lasted maybe till the kid was out of diapers, maybe not that long. Whatever they'd had, and it had been strong and intense, had died, leaving him alone, restless, a little empty, and leaving her with a yuppie husband, a home in the suburbs and a baby on the way.

One final, fading twinge, he thought, rinsing the dishes and setting them in the rack to dry. Even in their earliest stages they hadn't talked much. Adelle had, of necessity, devoted all her time and energy to her career. Advertising was a demanding calling, leaving little time for home and hearth. When they did find the occasional time together, out of bed, they would find they had nothing to say to each other. It had been depressing, but they'd been busy enough so that those moments hadn't come very often. And when they had, the relationship faded and died.

He looked out the kitchen window at the forest behind the house. Just another cloudy day in paradise, he thought with a grimace. Flurries again, sifting through the gray sky and settling on everything in sight. Sure, it was beautiful, the crisp clean air, the tall, dark pines, the blue-gray haze of the mountains in the distance. But it would be a hell of a lot prettier with the sun shining.

So here it was, ten-thirty on a Saturday morning, and he was bored, lonely and restless. Not to mention frustrated as hell. That little romp on the couch with Saralee Richardson had taken its toll on his sangfroid. Even in his sleep he hadn't been able to get her out of his mind. "Obsession" was an ugly word, but it came close to describing his feelings about his unwilling neighbor.

He wandered back into the living room, crammed another piece of wood into the stove, then roamed over to the front window. It wasn't as if he didn't have plenty to do; along with the book of English spells, he'd brought home two of the oldest manuals on dowsing. He could sit down and start taking notes; in no time at all he'd get caught up in the subject.

It was getting started that was the problem. All right, if he didn't want to spend the day at the kitchen table poring over dusty old tomes, he could do some of the fieldwork. Three of the finest water dowsers lived within twenty miles of Danbury, and he'd already laid the groundwork with letters. They were expecting him anytime he cared to show up.

He knew where they lived—all three had given him careful instructions. Or at least he thought he knew. Maybe, just to be sure, he should check with Sybil. After all, he didn't want to end up hopelessly lost on the spider's web of back roads around here.

He could call her. She might even be willing to come along, if he swore it was purely business. Even better, he could take that long-delayed right turn at the top of his driveway and find her place for himself, come face-to-face with her killer dogs and see if he couldn't wheedle a little hospitality from her. It was clear she wasn't usually as hostile as she was with him. Something about him rubbed her the wrong way. But he knew as well as he knew his own name that beneath that hostility was a sensual awareness she was doing her damnedest to ignore. And he had every intention of making that downright impossible.

He was humming under his breath as he gathered notebook and pens together, all his lethargy and melancholy vanished. He'd even promise not to mention Leona. After all, he'd done all he could with that for now. He'd wait until Ray came up with something before broaching the subject once more.

Until then, he'd do his absolute best to be charming. It would take a lot of effort, but in Sybil's case it just might possibly be worth it. Because no matter how much he tried to dismiss the notion, he had the funny suspicion that they might have a hell of a lot to talk about, in bed and out. And he had no intention of giving up on her until he found out.

SYBIL SAT IN HER KITCHEN watching the snow fall. There hadn't been much she could say or do for Mary Philbert, nothing more than add to the litany of woe the other ladies of the Davis Apartments were reciting.

As for Mary, she was a tough old bird. She'd spent the first eighty years of her life on a farm, the last two in town in an apartment smaller than her old kitchen. She still had enough to stay in that apartment, she had enough to eat, and the government was supposed to take care of the medical bills for people her age. God willing, she wouldn't have any, she said, but could just go quickly when her time came.

The Greek chorus of mourning old ladies each took her turn, telling of her own financial downfall. For the first time Sybil listened intently for details. But they had nothing, absolutely nothing in common. Once again she told herself Nick had to be half crazy or a victim of city paranoia. Maybe he just watched too many cop shows on TV.

If that were the case, he wouldn't be having much fun at the Black Farm. It was down in a hollow, getting maybe two channels if he was lucky. Even Sybil, with an outside antenna, a rotor and a signal booster, had to make do with four, and one of them was in French. Watching reruns of *Dynasty* in another language lost its novelty before long, and she hadn't yet succumbed to the temptation of buying a VCR. After all, she'd left Scarsdale and moved to

Vermont to simplify her life, get back to basics, not to clutter it up with technology. Even if she grew wistful at the thought of all the movies she never got to see.

But she was bored, lonely and restless. It would be nice to curl up in front of some nice old movie instead of *Wide World of Sports*. This time of year all they ever had was boxing anyway, and even the educational station showed European soccer matches all afternoon. It was enough to depress even the cheeriest of spirits.

What she needed was some distraction. What she needed was for Nick to come and take her away from all this, to needle her and argue with her and maybe kiss her just once more. Just to see if the potion was still having its insidious effect. What she needed was Nick.

She didn't hear a sound. Some instinct alerted her and she looked up, out the kitchen window to her dooryard. Just in time to see a dark green Jaguar pull silently into place. There were too many coincidences for her peace of mind, she thought, staring out at the elegant vehicle, the elegant driver climbing out of the driver's seat and heading for her front door. With a shiver of apprehension that wasn't all unpleasant, Sybil headed for the hallway, the dogs romping around her feet, barking cheerfully in anticipation of a treat.

Chapter Ten

He heard the dogs barking long before the door opened. They sounded like a pack of braying hounds, like something out of Arthur Conan Doyle, hounds of hell ready to rip his throat out. For a brief moment he considered the final indignity of racing back to seek shelter in his car, then resolutely stood his ground. For all that Sybil called them killer dogs, Dulcy had assured him they were harmless. While he didn't think he could trust what either of them said, at least Dulcy was more likely to be straightforward in the matter.

The door opened, and for a moment his eyes rested on Sybil's small, slim figure. Then that vision was obscured by a blur of black-and-white and liver-and-white fur, as a dozen furious dogs leaped at him.

"Kill," Sybil ordered cheerfully.

He wasn't knocked flat on his back, but it was a near thing. Dogs were leaping and prancing over his feet, licking his hands, sitting back and howling a melodious welcome. It took him a moment to sort out two grown dogs and four puppies, none of them with an ounce of dignity.

"Hey, guys," he said in a low, crooning voice, squatting down to their level. Their joy increased as they wiggled and danced around him, uttering little yelps of glee.

"Calm down," he murmured, and slowly they obeyed, now and then butting a silken head beneath his hand for a caress.

He rose to his full height, meeting Sybil's dazed eyes. "Killer dogs, eh?"

She didn't even blush, just held the door open for him. He was nearly knocked over once again by the wave of dogs rampaging through around him, but he held his ground. "You're good with them," she said grudgingly.

"Dogs know who's trustworthy and who's not."

She snorted. "Tell me another one. These critters love everybody under the sun. They'd welcome Jack the Ripper with open arms."

"Yes, but could he calm them so quickly?"

"Oh, I admit you have a certain hypnotic effect on dumb creatures," she said.

"Including you?"

"Don't push your luck, Fitzsimmons," she warned. "What are you here for?"

They were still standing in her slate-floored hallway, snow melting around their feet. Charm, he reminded himself. "I was bored and lonely and I decided I ought to visit my dearest friend in Vermont."

"So why didn't you?"

"I'm here, aren't I?"

That threw her. "Nick, with friends like me, you don't need enemies."

"Come on, Sybil," he coaxed. "Invite me in, give me some coffee and listen to a proposition I have to offer."

"You're propositioning me?"

"Not that way. Though we can, of course, discuss that, too."

"Never mind," she said. "Go into the living room and I'll bring you some coffee. How do you like it?"

"Why don't you dowse it and see?"

"Why don't you…" It took a great deal of effort for her to bite back her no-doubt colorful suggestion, but she did so, reminding him that if she could do it so could he.

"Cream and sugar," he said quickly, repenting.

She looked at him for one long, suspicious moment. "Cream and sugar," she repeated. "I'll be right with you."

He liked her living room. It was small, cluttered and bright, with lots of windows, an old sofa with a beautiful quilt tossed over it pulled in front of the wood stove, colorful and artistically hideous paintings on the white walls and books everywhere. Tucked in corners of the couch, piled under tables, balanced on windowsills, there looked like enough books to stock a small library. He sat down on the comfortable couch, jumped up and pulled a small tome from underneath him, then sank back down with it in his hand. Past-Life Regression, it said in tiny gold letters. Leaning back, he opened it, searching for some logical explanation of his and Sybil's twin fantasies.

The book was snatched out of his hand. "Do you mind?" she said in her most frigid voice. The coffee she placed in his hand was almost as cold, and she moved to the chair opposite him, perching on it as if she were ready to jump up and escape at any moment. "What did you have in mind?"

He paused for a moment, looking at her sitting there, small and defiant. Her dark blond hair hung in one thick braid down her back, and wisps were escaping, curling around her narrow face. Her brown eyes were staring at him stonily, but that pale mouth of hers looked curiously vulnerable. And infinitely kissable.

But that wasn't what he was supposed to be thinking of, he reminded himself, or he'd be trying to get her on this comfortable sofa with him. Taking a drink of the cool coffee, he controlled a shudder of distaste. "I thought I'd do some fieldwork," he said. "And I wondered if you wanted to go with me."

He'd managed to surprise her. Whatever she'd been expecting, it wasn't something as innocent. "What kind of fieldwork?"

"You have three of the best water dowsers in the country within twenty miles of Danbury. I'd planned to visit them, find out how they operate, and today seemed as good a day as any."

"Perley Johnson, Lester MacIntire and Julius Collier?"

It was his turn to be surprised. "How did you know?"

"Don't be naive. It's not latent psychic power; I happen to be the secretary of the Water Witches. I know every dowser around here."

"Of course." He'd only been rattled for a moment. A moment, however, that she'd noticed and been highly amused by. "That makes even more sense, then. I've written to the three of them, and they told me they'd be glad to see me, but I might be more welcome if I brought you along."

"I'd be more than happy to go with you," she said, "but there are problems. Three of them, to be exact. Perley Johnson's already gone to Florida for the winter and won't be back till after mud season, Lester MacIntire's hunting mad and he's gone to Maine to try to push the season a bit, and Julius Collier's over in Burlington at Mary Fletcher recovering from surgery. None of them is around."

"What's wrong with Julius?"

"Hemorrhoids," she said succinctly.

"Clearly he didn't try the potion for those of a dangerously costive disposition."

She tried to keep from grinning, then lost the battle. "Guess not," she said finally.

"Any other dowsers of their abilities around?" he ventured.

"Not really. Not right now. I'm afraid you're out of luck."

He did his best to look pathetic. "Does that mean you're going to send me back to that cold, lonely house?"

"It's not cold if you know how to work the wood stove," she said. "Or you can turn up the electric heat. And maybe John Black's ghost can keep you company."

"La Belle Dame sans Merci," he said. He remembered her fluent French followed by her schoolgirl incompetence. "I suppose you don't know what that means, either."

"Sure I do." She smiled that wicked, beatific smile that was three times more powerful than any ancient love philtre. "The beautiful lady who never says thank you."

"No, it's—"

"Spare me, Nick. You don't have to know French to know it's the beautiful woman without mercy. However, you're wrong. I'm neither beautiful nor without mercy. If you can't stand your own company anymore, and I can't say I blame you for that, you can come shopping with me."

"Shopping," he echoed faintly.

"Shopping. Food shopping, Christmas shopping. I'll even go all the way and treat you to lunch at McDonald's."

He eyed her warily. "I should have known you'd like junk food," he said with a sigh.

"You should have known," she agreed. "Are we on?"

He was going to have a hard time making another pass at her if they were driving around from store to store. Then again, he'd have plenty of time to try it later, and in the meantime he could pump her for information about her good buddy Leona. He hadn't given Ray much to go on, and the more stuff he came up with the better chance he stood of getting results. "We're on," he said. "My car?"

"My car. And I drive." She dared him to object.

He shuddered delicately, setting down the half-drunk cup of coffee on the pile of books in front of him. *"Morituri te salutamus,"* he murmured.

"We who are about to die salute you," she translated blithely. "My Latin's better than my French. Don't worry, Nick. I always consider my passengers when I drive."

"That's what I'm afraid of," he said faintly.

IF THERE WAS A PRIZE given for stupid ideas, Sybil thought, this one had to take the cake. Here she had the entire weekend stretching out in front of her, a weekend free of Nick Fitzsimmons's disturbing presence, and she'd been fool enough to invite him along. It wasn't as if she even wanted company. There was nothing worse than trying to Christmas shop with someone tagging along. They always wanted to linger around auto parts, browse through videotapes or price washing machines.

When Sybil shopped for Christmas she was organized, fast and efficient. No peeking at the nightgown she'd always wanted, which was now miraculously on sale, no looking at novels or pricing new cars. And she certainly had no time for anyone else's more haphazard style of buying presents.

But Nick had been a pleasant surprise. He'd gone where she'd gone, been ready to leave when she left, and had even come up with one or two excellent suggestions concerning her brothers-in-law. He'd been patient as she'd fiddled through her coupons at the grocery store, enthusiastic

when they stopped at the state liquor store, and tolerant at
McDonald's, despite the presence of two birthday parties
and a busload of Girl Scouts jamming the seats. She noticed he hadn't hesitated when he placed his order, hadn't
wasted time looking overhead at the menu, all of which
bespoke a certain familiarity with the fast-food restaurants he disdained. But with their newfound, temporary
accord she refrained from teasing him about it. She realized as they were heading back on Route 2 that she'd actually enjoyed herself, despite her doubts. For a moment
she was sorry she couldn't think of an excuse to extend the
day.

Her only delay was a dangerous one. She ought to drive
him back to her house, get rid of him and finish her last
errand. But it was two and a half miles out to her house,
another five if she were to go back and forth again, and the
early dusk of mid-December had settled down around the
icy road. The fitful snow seemed to be coming down in
earnest. Bold as Sybil was, she really didn't feel like
traipsing around any more than necessary.

"Does it snow every day in Vermont?" Nick asked lazily. He'd even been tolerant of her driving, moaning only
once when she nearly hit a pickup truck. All in all, he'd
been a charming companion, and her suspicions were fully
aroused.

"Only in months with an 'r' in them," she said. She
hesitated, then made her decision. She wasn't going to
spend the evening driving all over creation. She'd simply
have to trust Nick, even if it seemed tantamount to trusting a snake. "I have one more stop to make."

"Fine. I'm in no hurry."

"I have to feed someone's cat."

She could feel his golden eyes watching her in the gathering darkness of the car interior. For once she kept her

attention on the road, trying to ignore the heat of his gaze. "Whose cat?"

They'd managed to avoid the subject all day, but she should have known her luck wouldn't hold. "Leona's," she said.

"Leona's out of town?"

"She had to go over to Burlington for a few days. She asked Mary Philbert to ask me to feed her cat. I usually do when she goes away."

"Does she go away often?"

She wasn't fooled by his casual tone of voice. "Just when she needs to deposit the money she stole from her friends," she replied coolly.

"Whose money does she have this time?"

"Why don't you lay off her? She's a harmless old lady, as innocent as the rest of them. Why have you picked her to harass?"

Nick shrugged. "Maybe because I don't like her influence over you."

"She doesn't have any influence over me!" she cried in exasperation. "We're friends."

"Okay, I'll buy that. I still think her behavior is suspicious."

The Subaru skidded to an angry stop outside the converted farmhouse that now served the tiny town of Danbury as apartments for the elderly. The Davis Apartments were a model of warmth and efficiency and easy access for the less than nimble, and their waiting list was a mile long. It had only been through an extreme stroke of fortune that Leona had managed to get a spot when she first arrived in town. Helen Sinclair had had a bad fall, sending her to the hospital for a month, and when they finally released her it had been to the nursing home. And she sublet her apartment to her new friend, Leona, who had been visiting at the time of the accident.

No one had ever figured out how that skateboard had ended up at the top of the back stairs outside Helen's apartment. There wasn't a single inhabitant under the age of sixty-five, and they weren't in the habit of riding skateboards. But no one could come up with an explanation other than the carelessness of a visiting grandchild, and no one had come forward and confessed. And Leona had moved into Helen's apartment and stayed.

"Stay in the car," she ordered, not giving him any choice. "It'll only take me a minute."

He was out before she was. "The hell I will," he said pleasantly. "It's cold and dark out here. You can watch and make sure I don't steal anything from Saint Leona."

She stood there for a moment, wondering whether she ought simply to get back in the car and drive away rather than risk having Nick invade Leona's privacy. Snow was falling more rapidly now, clinging to her eyelashes, dusting Nick's shoulders.

"You touch anything and you're dog meat," she growled, turning on her heel and stalking toward Leona's front door.

"For your killer hounds? I think I'm safe. What's that in your hand?"

She was fiddling with the front lock. "What do you think it is? It's a key. Leona gave me one for times like these."

"I thought no one locked her house around here. I thought it was so safe and bucolic that people didn't worry about burglars and their ilk."

"Leona does. It's not her fault; she comes from Buffalo, where there's been a lot of crime." The moment the words were out of her mouth she could have bitten her tongue. The last thing she wanted to do was give Nick anything he could use against Leona. If he wanted to delve into her past he could do it without her help.

But he didn't seem to notice her slip. "Then it's understandable," he said smoothly, following her into the compact little apartment.

As always, it was spotlessly neat. Sybil used to tease Leona that she lived more like a monk than a little old lady. Every other inhabitant of the Davis Apartments had knickknacks, oddments, owl collections and spoon collections and Avon bottle collections and even Danish porcelain collections. Leona had a narrow bed with white sheets and a plain white bedspread, a desk, two hard chairs and a black-and-white TV. She didn't even have any books.

"Cozy little place, isn't it?" Nick murmured behind her.

"Leona lives an uncluttered life. You only have to look at her apartment to see what little use she has for the things money can buy."

"Uh-hum," he said, peering around the place. "Doesn't she have any family?"

"Why do you ask?"

"No pictures. Not even a snapshot. Was she ever married?"

There was no reason not to answer him—the questions were innocuous enough and the answers were common knowledge. "She was married. Her husband died ten years ago, and they were both only children with no kids of their own. The only kin Leona has is Gladys."

"Gladys?" he echoed.

"The cat," Sybil said. "And she doesn't look pleased to see you." That was an understatement. Gladys had never been the most even-tempered of cats, but the low, scratching sound in her throat was ominously close to a growl. She had just stepped out of the kitchen, her fat, marmalade-colored form delicate as always, when she caught sight of Nick and began that threatening rumble of sound.

"I usually get along with cats," he said.

"Maybe Gladys is more perceptive than most."

"Is she?"

"Actually, she's nastier than most. She's the sort that if you pet her she turns around and bites you," Sybil admitted with a sigh. "I don't know why Leona puts up with her."

"Maybe they're kindred spirits."

"Nick . . ."

"Sorry. Why don't you go feed that ravaging beast before she decides I'd be a tasty morsel?"

"I don't trust you."

"So what else is new? I'm not going into the kitchen with that damned cat, not even for you, Saralee. Go and feed the little monster and we'll get out of here."

"You won't touch anything?"

"What is there to touch?" he countered, skirting the issue.

Besides being a royal pain, Gladys was a picky eater. She turned up her nose at the open can of kitty tuna in the almost empty refrigerator, ignored with a look of disdain the can of salmon surprise Sybil offered, and finally, grudgingly accepted the can of Bumble Bee albacore that Leona kept for feline emergencies. Gladys cast her one evil look, as if to say, "Don't you dare pat me," and then settled down to pick at her feast.

Sybil didn't make a sound as she walked out into the main room. Nick was standing there in front of Leona's now open desk, staring at the contents.

"Don't you have any conscience?" she demanded.

"Not a trace," he replied instantly. "Come here and see this."

"I don't want to. You may have no qualms about invading someone's privacy, but I do." Her feet were edging toward the desk anyway.

"I'm forcing myself," Nick said.

Curiosity finally got the better of her. "What did you find?"

"That's what's so interesting. There's nothing here."

"Well, that's good."

"No, that's bad. Any normal person would leave canceled checks, letters, bills lying around, if for nothing else than for taxes. This desk is completely empty."

"Maybe she knew you were coming," Sybil snapped.

He shrugged. "Maybe she doesn't trust you."

"That's a lousy thing to say!"

"Then why are you peering into her desk yourself?"

Sybil jumped back. "You tempted me."

"The devil made me do it? I don't know if that would hold up in court."

"Damn it, Nick . . ." she began, beside herself in fury, guilt and that continuing, niggling doubt.

"Who's James Longerman?"

"What?"

"The only thing I found was a scrap of paper that must have missed her eagle eye. It was stuck in the back of the drawer and it says James Longerman, 32650. Any ideas?"

"Not the slightest. Close the damned drawer and let's get out of here. I'm feeling rotten enough as it is."

"Anything in the kitchen?"

"Nick!"

"Well, we've already gone this far," he said reasonably. "May as well be hanged for sheep as well as lambs.

Besides, wouldn't you like to know your suspicions are unfounded?''

"My suspicions?'' Her voice was high-pitched with rage. "You're the one with suspicions, not me.''

"Wouldn't you like to prove me wrong?''

"I don't think an affidavit from the pope himself would convince you,'' she shot back. "And there's nothing in the kitchen.''

"Nothing?''

"Just food,'' she said. "And not much of that. Leona leads an austere life.''

"Leona leads a mysterious life.''

"We're leaving,'' she announced.

Gladys chose that moment to reappear in the main room of the apartment. When she caught sight of Nick, her fat back began to arch, her elegant tail to thicken and that low, evil growling began once more.

He was eyeing the cat. "We may as well. There's nothing more to discover here.''

"That's because there's nothing to discover!''

"Maybe,'' he said, his voice showing strong doubt. And he followed her out into the night air with only a single backward glance.

Chapter Eleven

Sybil stared down at her tangled knitting. She'd been working on it since October, and while it was steadily getting bigger, it wasn't getting any better. Of course, there'd been that three-week period when she couldn't remember how to decrease, and it was only Leona's providential return from a trip to Buffalo that had saved the sweater from growing to gargantuan size. As it was, it would fit Emmie's husband, the six-foot-one beanpole. It would fit someone who was six feet three and had broad shoulders even better. And the color matched his eyes.

She was not going to give Nick a Christmas present, she reminded herself sternly. If there were only some way she could juggle her schedule, she'd be happy if she never saw him at all. But duty and finances insisted she stay at the Society of Water Witches all morning and work in her tiny bookshop all afternoon. And all that time Nick worked overhead, his measured footsteps vibrating through the old house, vibrating through her sensitive body.

He'd been in Danbury for ten days, and things weren't getting any easier. To be sure, he'd been remarkably, frustratingly polite during office hours. So polite, in fact, that she'd been tempted to slash the brand-new studded snow tires on his beloved Jaguar just to see his reaction. She'd controlled the temptation, just as she controlled the almost hourly urge to head up the narrow staircase and ask him some trumped-up question. If he could be immune to her, she could return the favor.

It would be nice if her dreams would stop. Every morning she dutifully wrote them down, then did her best to analyze them over morning coffee. Most of them were erotic and embarrassingly detailed. Fortunately, dreams seldom meant what they at first appeared to mean. Just because she had explicitly sexual dreams about Nicholas Fitzsimmons and woke with her heart pounding and her body covered with sweat didn't mean she actually wanted him. No, it had to mean something else, but she was damned if she could figure it out. And despite Dulcy's prying, there was no way she was going to share the intimate details with her nosy friend, even if it meant discovering that fantasies of making love with Nick in the library of the SOWW building meant she didn't trust her father.

No, that was Freudian, not psychic, she reminded herself. But Nick was becoming tantamount to an obsession. Thank God she was flying down to Princeton that very afternoon.

It was the first time she'd looked forward to visiting her family in years. Usually their glorious perfection did nothing but intimidate her, but not this time. This time she was going to revel in her mediocrity, blend into the woodwork and not even think of Nick Fitzsimmons, much less dream about him. She'd be so busy fending off her family's well-meaning suggestions that she wouldn't even remember his existence.

According to the ladies at the Davis Apartments, Leona would be back sometime tomorrow. She wasn't usually gone for such long periods at a time, and Gladys had gotten progressively nastier as Sybil tried to tempt her with shrimp salad from the Come and Eat, frozen haddock fillets and even herring in sour cream. What she usually got for her trouble was a disdainful sniff and occasionally a hostile swipe from Gladys's cookie-size paw.

But Mary Philbert would take care of her tonight, and tomorrow Leona would return. Dulcy had already taken the dogs back to her house. For the time being Sybil's only duty and concern was for her family, and that was more than enough to keep her busy. If she could just weather the five days down there, then she'd be free to concentrate her energies on resisting Nick's seemingly irresistible attraction. And if she couldn't resist . . .

Sybil set the knitting down, cursing. Somewhere along the way she'd dropped another stitch, and if she didn't notice when she did it there was never any way she could get it back. It would serve Nick right if she gave the sweater to him. Not even her worst enemy deserved such a mess.

Not that Nick was her worst enemy. He was simply a distraction, an irritation and a royal pain. It was bad enough when he was hanging around, flirting with her. It was worse having him ignore her.

Maybe it would help if she had Christmas more in hand. For some reason she was reluctant to throw herself into the spirit this year. She'd made herself decorate the offices and the bookshop, she'd even earmarked the perfect Colorado blue spruce growing in the field behind her house. It would make a lovely Christmas tree, and thank heavens she didn't have to deal with some damned man.

They were the orneriest creatures when it came to Christmas trees, she knew to her sorrow. Send them out to buy one, and they came back with the scraggliest, scrawniest, most pitiful reject ever to make it to a Christmas tree lot. But send the dear man out to chop one himself, or even worse, go with him, and you were in for an all-day marathon, a twenty-mile hike and a case of the sullens when he finally had to compromise his high standards and settle for less than perfect symmetry.

Her father had been like that, her brothers-in-law, her ex-husband. She had no doubt whatsoever that Nick would fit the pattern. She was lucky indeed that she didn't have to deal with anyone's standards but her own.

Well, it was time to get into the proper holiday spirit. When she got back she'd drag the decorations out of the attic, she'd start wrapping the presents she'd accumulated, she'd bake sugar cookies and ginger cookies and *kringler* and *julekage* and stollen and eat anything she wanted. And she wouldn't even think about Nick Fitzsimmons.

Of course, it didn't help that every time she looked at her tangled knitting she thought of his mesmerizing topaz eyes. And it didn't help that all the cozy sentiment of Christmas made her long for someone to curl up with on a snowy winter's evening. Maybe that was why she was avoiding it.

There was no pleasing her, she thought in disgust. It would be the best possible thing for her to get out of town. It would be worth putting up with her family, worth everything just to be in another state away from Nick Fitzsimmons. With all his nose-to-the-grindstone hard work he'd probably be finished with his research way ahead of time, maybe even have moved back to Cambridge by the time she returned.

No, that was impossible. She was only going to be gone a week. Nick would still be here, still burying that aristocratic nose in those ancient books upstairs, still having tea with the ladies at the Davis Apartments, still roaming the countryside, without her, talking to farmers and such about water witching. No, he'd still be here when she returned. Thank God.

NICK STRETCHED his long legs out under the library table, turned to stare out into the winter afternoon and shivered. The upstairs rooms at the Society of Water Witches weren't the warmest places on earth, and if he didn't think Sybil above such petty actions he'd suspect she had turned the heat down on purpose. He could see the wind whipping the snow past the frosted window, however, and knew his suspicions were unfounded. When the wind blew, there was no way this drafty old building could stay warm.

He sat back, listening to the wind howl around the eaves, to the creaking of freezing wood settling, to the sound of Sybil singing to herself one floor below him. She didn't realize how every sound, every sigh, every breath carried up to him. She didn't realize he could sit there and hear every word of her conversations with her various customers, conversations that would, more often than not, involve the interesting newcomer to Danbury.

To his surprise Sybil was always charitable. Much as she tried to detest him on a one-to-one basis, she was unfailingly generous when answering the Muller sisters' curious questions. She even put up with their sly matchmaking attempts with admirable calm, a calm that never failed to amuse him.

She didn't like the distance he'd been putting between them. A brief grin lit his face as he put his fingers together and contemplated that distance. It was almost harder on him than it was on her. Of course, he had the advantage of knowing he was in control, that he was playing the game most suited to driving her crazy and into his arms. That still didn't mean he wasn't frustrated as hell, knowing she was one floor below, knowing if he pushed it he could have her.

But he also knew he wouldn't have her for long. Not if he got to her on anything less than optimum conditions. No, she needed to come to him; she needed to accept that she wanted him. And the only way for her to realize that was for him to be devious, manipulative and downright sneaky.

It was almost time now. He'd been distant, as charming as he knew how to be and out of reach for more than a week. When they were in the same room he'd move just close enough to invade her space, to make her physically aware of him, and then he'd retreat before she could complain. But he could see from the confused, frustrated expression in those wonderful brown eyes of hers that it was working.

The weekend was coming up and it was time to make his move. He'd have to be subtle. He didn't want to blow all his hard work and deprivation. Maybe he could deliberately slide off the road just past her driveway. What it lacked in inventiveness it made up for in believability.

Or he could get the Muller sisters to invite them both to tea. They needed no encouragement to matchmake and they'd taken a fancy to him. There was nothing they'd like better than to cook something up between him and Sybil.

Or maybe, just maybe, he could stop by with some of his notes, ask her for clarification on Perley Johnson's history, for instance, or Lester MacIntire's success ratio. Then he could casually ask her out to dinner, woo her with diffident charm and have his wicked way with her when she asked him in for a nightcap.

He liked that last option the best, probably because it involved a more immediate outcome. He could even set it up ahead of time, mention that he might stop by so she wouldn't get too suspicious when he showed up at her doorstep. Maybe he wouldn't even wait till Saturday.

He heard with disbelief the unmistakable sounds of Sybil locking up. He checked the thin Rolex on his wrist, just to make sure it really was only three o'clock. Sybil never closed up before five, no matter how bad the weather, and while it was a gray, windy day, for once no snow was falling. Maybe she was sick. He hadn't heard any sniffling or sneezing or rushing to the bathroom at frequent intervals, but you never could tell. Maybe she needed a ride home and someone to tuck a quilt around her and feed her savage dogs and ply her with chicken soup.

He slammed shut the book, choked on the cloud of dust that wafted into his face and forced himself to head downstairs at a leisurely pace. He'd pretend he hadn't heard her locking up, pretend he was just coming down for coffee.

"There you are." Sybil was standing in the hallway, and he noticed what he hadn't noticed before. She wasn't wearing her usual corduroys and denims and shapeless sweaters. She was wearing a dress, probably silk, of a pale rose color that did wonders for her coloring and wonders for the body he knew existed beneath the bulky clothes. She had breasts—not too big, not too small—round, luscious hips and a small enough waist to set off both those attributes. She'd even fixed her hair into a loose sort of bun and it framed her small, solemn face. He controlled himself with a strong effort.

He looked down at her feet, shod in neat little leather pumps, at the suitcase beside her, at the cloth coat over her arm and then back up to her face. "You're going somewhere?"

She sighed, and for once something else was overshadowing her reaction toward him. "I'm visiting my parents in New Jersey. I can't make it at Christmastime so we're celebrating early.''

"Why can't you make it at Christmastime?" Stupid question, he chided himself. Until he saw the flush that warmed her pale brown skin.

"Because I don't want to. Besides, Dulcy usually goes up to Canada to visit an aunt and I can't count on her to watch the dogs. So my family gets me now or not at all.''

"You don't like your family?''

"Of course I do!" she snapped.

"Well, then, why don't you sound happier about going?''

She took a deep breath. "Because my family, much as I love them, are overbearing, interfering and more than I can handle. Just like you.''

He grinned. "Does that mean you love me?''

"That means I wish there were someplace I could go where I didn't have to deal with any of you," she said wearily. "I'll be back next Wednesday. There's a key on my desk, so you can come and go as you please. Leona's going to fill in for me—try not to harass her, okay?''

"Leona's back?''

"She will be tomorrow. I hope you've gotten over your absurd suspicions.''

Nick smiled his most angelic smile. "What do you think?''

"I think Leona's a match for you," she said. She was pulling on her coat, covering that lovely little body of hers. "Try to behave yourself, Nick," she added.

He couldn't resist, even if it meant blowing all his hard work. He slid one long arm around her waist, under her coat, and pulled her against him. He caught her chin with his other hand, turning her startled face up to his. "I just want to see if the potion's still working," he murmured, and set his mouth on hers.

Her response was gratifyingly instantaneous. Her hands clutched his shoulders, her head tilted back and her mouth opened beneath his with only the slightest pressure. Suddenly he felt slightly desperate. He pushed his tongue past her teeth, into the warm dark hollow of her mouth, and her own tongue met his, sliding against him, flirting with him, and her breasts seemed to swell and press against his chest, as her fingers clutched more tightly, and he heard a tiny little moan deep in the back of her throat. A moan of wanting, a moan of surrender. He wondered for one brief moment whether he could carry her up those stairs to the uncomfortable couch in the library. Maybe the table would be a better surface.

Then she began to withdraw and he knew better than to hold her against her will. Even as his mind howled a protest, his mouth left her and his arms released her, and they were standing inches apart, breathless, staring into each other's eyes.

Her mouth was slightly swollen, he noticed. And her nipples were hard beneath the silk dress, hard despite the warmth of the hallway. Her eyes were dazed and hostile.

"It didn't work then," she said, "and it doesn't work now."

For a moment he couldn't remember what she was talking about, and then he realized. A slow, seductive grin lit his face. "What doesn't work? The love potion or the kiss?"

"Neither."

"Liar."

She took a deep, calming breath. He noticed her thick, silky hair was falling out of that bun she wore. And for the hundredth time he wondered how that hair would look spread out on a pillow beneath him.

"Goodbye, Nick," she said evenly, picking up her suitcase and moving past him toward the door.

He watched her go, forcing himself to remain motionless, even as her silk dress brushed against his thigh and the faint whisper of her flowery scent danced in his nostrils. "Hurry back," he said.

"It'll be a cold day in hell." She slammed the door behind her, the last of her calm deserting her.

He leaned against the panes of glass that surrounded the door, staring out into the gathering shadows of the December afternoon. He watched the Subaru peel out into the road, watched her drive away. A gust of wind blasted between the cracks in the old wooden door.

Nick shivered. "Honey," he said out loud, "it already is."

Chapter Twelve

Sybil had had worse visits in her family's house on Hodge Road. Growing up there had been sheer torment, always overshadowed by her three sisters and her parents, always feeling like a changeling. If it weren't for the fact that she looked exactly like her father's mother, she might have thought venerable old Princeton Medical Center had made a mistake and switched babies. Maybe the real Saralee Richardson was Brooke Shields or Jane Pauley or the president of NOW. A real Richardson wouldn't be happily buried in the north woods, running a tiny little occult bookstore and working as a part-time secretary for a bunch of kooks.

No one said anything, of course. Their questions, their expressions of kindly interest were so well done that anyone outside the family would have been fooled into thinking they really cared, that they really respected the way she had chosen to live her life. But she knew them too well. She intercepted the meaningful glances that passed between her parents and her sisters, heard the vague explanations of her life-style to family friends, and she wasn't fooled for a moment.

It would have been so much easier, she thought, sitting alone in the bedroom that had been left just as she had always kept it, if she didn't love them and they didn't love her. But she did and they did. She was loved just as much as her more glorious sisters. She just wasn't one of them.

She stared around her room, at the looming posts of her canopy bed. Her parents had bought it for her one Christmas when she was twelve. She'd longed for it, begged for it, and when Christmas morning rolled around she'd received a photograph of it with the promise of delivery in one week. While a photograph wasn't as exciting as the real thing, she'd been overjoyed. Until she watched her sisters opening their big presents.

Hattie was eighteen, already fascinated by medicine. Her parents gave her a skeleton with all the bones named and numbered, and Hattie was entranced. Emmie got a set of law books, and was ecstatic. And baby Allison, two years younger than Sybil, got the oak file cabinet and electric typewriter she'd been begging for.

Sybil had hated that bed from then on. She'd never said a word, she'd slept in it for six years until she left for college, she slept in it every time she came back. She stayed amid the pink chintzes her mother had chosen, chintzes that made her look like a brown elf, and she looked at the dolls lining the shelves, dolls her sisters had discarded by the time they reached third grade, and she never said a word. If she couldn't be glorious, at least she could be pleasant.

She was just as glad she wouldn't have to be there when they opened their presents. Despite their cries of appreciation, she always had the suspicion that they were being just a little too happy about the Vermont maple syrup, the handwoven blankets, the wooden sap buckets and the homemade blackberry jam.

As usual, her parents tried to give her a new car, and as usual she refused. Another excuse for not visiting more often was the age of her Subaru, and while its replacement with an all-wheel-drive Audi was tempting, she resisted. If she really wanted one, she could afford to buy one herself—her trust fund just sat and increased. But she valued her excuses more than a new car, and she resisted the latest offering with only a small twinge.

She had flown down on Wednesday, it was now Saturday evening, and she only had four more days to go, she thought, counting them off on her fingers. She'd make it—nothing horrendous had happened so far. The only bad thing about the visit was Nick. Her dreams had only gotten worse. It was no wonder, considering that kiss he'd planted on her just before she left. She'd driven the two hours to the airport, alternately fuming and dreaming. Maybe she was overreacting. Maybe, despite Nick's many irritating qualities and beliefs, there was nothing wrong in getting involved with the most appealing man she'd met in a long time.

After all, sex hadn't even interested her for years. Part of it was Colin's fault—his lovemaking was polite, energetic and boring. And part of it was the lack of men around Danbury—the closest she got to a possibility was Dulcy's younger brother and, at age fourteen, he was just a tiny bit too young for her. No matter what his other drawbacks, Nick Fitzsimmons was a devastatingly attractive, dangerously sexy man. And she should be pleased that she was healthy and broad-minded enough to notice.

Except that she was doing more than notice, she was being sorely tempted. Ever since she'd had that double dose of love philtre, it had simply gotten worse and worse. Even his distance during the past ten days hadn't helped. Even being four hundred miles away in the bosom of her distinctly uncomfortable family didn't help. Nothing helped; the attraction grew whether he was there to feed it or not. She had the uneasy suspicion that the next time he kissed her she was going to kiss him back.

Except that she already had. And the next time she was going to do more than kiss him back. Maybe giving in to temptation would get him off her mind.

Maybe she really was as big an idiot as she always suspected, even to consider such an outlandish idea. She rose from the oversize chair, built more for tall men and women than for someone of her delicate stature, and flicked on the light. The closer she got to Nick Fitzsimmons the worse it got. He certainly wasn't the type she wanted to spend the rest of her life with, even if he happened to be insane enough to want it. He was too much like the rest of her family—too tall, too handsome, too talented, too bright. What he lacked in Richardson charm he made up for in wit. And she was going to find a short, stocky hunk, wasn't she?

She could hear the noise from downstairs, hear the clink of ice and glasses, the sound of laughter and bright conversation. Her mother had told her it was a small pre-Christmas cocktail party, only about fifty guests. Every one of those fifty would make her feel inadequate, despite the turquoise silk dress that Hattie, with her excellent eye for clothing, had chosen for her. At least Allison was planning an announcement. She'd been very secretive about it, but they all knew she'd been seeing someone in Washington. Someone important, it was whispered. And one more Richardson would make a wonderful marriage.

Of course, Sybil thought as she wandered down the hallway, her own marriage had been a Richardson one. Colin had started his own law firm at thirty-two, been named to governor's commissions, been quoted in *Newsweek* and had letters published in *The New York Times*. Her wedding day, with the four hundred and seventy-five invited guests, was one of the only times she had felt like a real Richardson. She had also felt absolutely miserable.

Well, she'd done her duty, stayed in the marriage far longer than it or Colin had deserved and now was free. It was up to Allison to do it right this time.

"Chin up, Sybil," she ordered herself softly as she descended the stairs. "It can't be as bad as you're expecting."

"Saralee!" Allison stood poised at the bottom of the stairs, and a tall, handsome, strangely familiar man stood directly behind her, one strong hand clasping her shoulder in a possessive gesture. "Come meet your future brother-in-law."

Sybil reached the bottom of the stairs, plastered a suitable smile on her face and looked up. Directly into Geoffrey Van der Sling's beautiful blue eyes. Eyes that didn't, for even one moment, recognize her.

"I THINK YOU'RE CRAZY to fly back into a storm," Emmie said, casting her sister a worried glance as they sped along the New Jersey Turnpike toward Newark Airport. "You don't even know if you'll be able to get on a plane, much less know if any are flying out."

"The weather is fine," Sybil said, huddled in the passenger seat of Emmie's Mercedes. "Just a little cloudy and overcast. We should have no trouble taking off."

"But there's a blizzard in Vermont!"

"No, there's not. Just some heavy snowfall. And the plane I'll probably get on has to stop at Logan on the way up. By the time we get to Burlington, the snow will have stopped and the roads will be clear. If not, I can always spend the night in a motel and drive to Danbury tomorrow."

"Why don't we turn around and go back to Princeton and you can fly out tomorrow? Better yet, stay till Wednesday when you planned to leave anyway. Why do you have to go back so early? It's only Sunday; surely your dogs will be fine."

"I told you, Annie just gave birth to seven puppies," she lied blithely. "I can't leave them with Dulcy."

"I don't believe you," Emmie said.

Sybil looked over at her sister, at the pregnant belly pushing against the leather-covered steering wheel, the mane of gorgeous, naturally blond hair, the concerned blue eyes. Emmie had always been the one she could talk to, the one who understood what it felt like to be a changeling.

Sybil opened her mouth to lie again, then shut it. "You're right."

"You want to tell me what the problem is? It was something that happened last night, I know that much."

Sybil stared down at her gloved fingers. "It was Geoff," she said.

"Geoff?" Emmie echoed. "Allison's Geoff? The senator?"

"The youngest senator in the history of New Jersey, the bright star of the Republicans, the charming, handsome, brilliant Geoffrey Van der Sling. Yup."

Sudden comprehension washed over Emmie's face. "I remember. You went to school with him, didn't you?"

"Yup," she said again, her voice morose.

"And you hate him?" Emmie ventured. "I can't see why. I mean he's a tiny bit pompous and certainly more conservative than you are, but then, everyone's more conservative than you are. What do you have against him?"

"Nothing."

The word hung in the heated interior of the Mercedes. "Oh," said Emmie, finally comprehending. "Now I remember."

"Yup," Sybil said a third time. "I had the biggest, most passionate, most desperate crush on Geoffrey Van der Sling that any adolescent has ever suffered through. I used to write his name all over my journal, I used to plan our wedding, I used to pick names for our children."

"Sybil," Emmie said patiently, and once more Sybil blessed the fact that of all her family, it was only Emmie who no longer called her Saralee, "you can't still want him."

"Of course not. As you said, he's pompous, conservative and to someone like me, boring."

"Then what's the problem?"

Sybil took a deep, shaky breath. "He didn't remember me."

"Should he have?"

"Of course not," she said bitterly. "No one ever looked twice at me, then or now. Not with my sisters around. I worked with him on the school newspaper, I acted with him in the school play, I even joined the Young Republicans and managed his campaign for student council."

"You joined the Young Republicans?" Emmie echoed, fascinated. "True love indeed."

"I spent hours hanging on his every word, running his errands, doing his bidding. And he didn't even remember me," said Sybil.

"Okay, I'll grant you, that stinks. But I don't see why you're running away because Geoff Van der Sling has a lousy memory. Unless you still want him, deep down inside."

"I don't want him," she said firmly. "I wouldn't take him on a silver platter. And I think that's part of my problem. I don't care about him, I don't want him, and I still feel absolutely lousy. It's irrational, but all I want to do is get back to Vermont and hide.''

"Okay. And I don't think it's that irrational,'' Emmie added. "It's just one more thing to give you that absurd illusion of inadequacy.''

Sybil managed to conjure up a grin. "I love the way you put things.''

"That's why you let me drive you to the airport,'' she said, calmly making a turn in the midst of dense traffic that would have had Sybil tearing her hair. "I'm going to tell you something I promised Henry I wouldn't.''

"What would your husband want you to keep from me? I'm hardly any danger.''

"We've had amnio on this baby, since I'm thirty-five. We're finally getting a girl after two boys. And we've agreed. This one is Sybil.''

She stared at her in amazement, swallowing the sudden rush of tears that threatened to choke her. "But what about the others? Or shouldn't you name her after Mother?''

"Not Rebecca,'' Emmie said firmly. "Not Hattie, not Allison and not even Saralee. She's Sybil, and she's your godchild in another month. So cheer up. That's better than marrying a senator any day.''

"You're right,'' she said, her voice husky with emotion that Emmie understood without her having to say anything. "And with Allison's luck she might end up in the White House.''

"Poor thing,'' Emmie agreed, commiserating. "Let's count our blessings and see if they have any restaurants in the terminal. As usual, I'm starving, and your plane isn't due to leave for another hour.''

"Sounds good," Sybil said. Reaching over, she patted Emmie's huge belly. "You better keep my niece well fed."

"Don't worry," Emmie said with a groan. "At forty pounds and counting, I'm keeping her roly-poly."

THE PLANE was due to leave at three o'clock Sunday afternoon. Emmie finally headed back down to Princeton at five, they let the passengers board the plane at six, ordered them off at seven, put them on another at nine, and took off at eleven-fifteen.

Logan Airport was a madhouse. Planes were still flying in and out, skidding on the snow-slick runways, darting through the fog and swirling sleet, landing safely with all the passengers gripping their armrests and gritting their teeth. Sybil filed off with the others, thankful to be out of the claustrophobic plane for at least a few minutes till her connection to Burlington was ready to board. The airport was jammed with people, waiting for delayed and canceled flights, college students starting their Christmas vacations, skiers trying to get back to jobs. The loudspeaker was playing Christmas carols, with the same high-pitched, nerve-racking arrangements usually reserved for department stores, the kind that made people nervous enough to spend too much money just to get out of the place.

But no one was going anywhere from Logan. They were keeping the runways open, the snow was heading north and planes would be flying. Even if it meant a delay.

Sybil had always had strong doubts about using Ransome Airways, simply because of their name. Ransome reminded her of kidnapping, kidnapping reminded her of hijacking, hijacking reminded her of terrorists, and she never flew without feeling paranoid and uneasy. And their planes were much too small.

At least they weren't crowded, either. They were merely a connector for one of the larger airlines, and tonight most passengers didn't feel like making that connection. As she walked down the increasingly deserted corridors toward Gate 67A, she wondered if they'd make the flight for one passenger, or make her wait till they had more to fill up their tiny little plane.

The waiting area was dimly lit, a single clerk was standing behind the counter, waiting to check her in, and one lone figure was sitting over by the windows, staring out into the snowy night sky. They'd make the flight for two passengers, she thought in relief, proffering her ticket.

"Flight's two hours late," the clerk announced in a bored voice.

"Will we be getting out tonight?"

He stamped her ticket and handed her the boarding pass that read Number Two. "Who knows? Snow's supposed to be letting up, but things are bad up in Burlington. Even if you can take off here, they may not let you land."

"But . . ."

"Take it or leave it, lady. You want your boarding pass or you wanna arrange for a flight tomorrow?"

She surveyed the almost empty passenger area, the dim lights, the swirling snow beyond the plate glass. In her rush to get out of Princeton she'd left with only twenty dollars in cash, and she didn't believe in credit cards. Even if she wanted a motel, even if they weren't booked solid around the airport, there was no way she could pay for it.

Besides, she desperately wanted to get home. It would be worth sleeping in the airport, driving through a blizzard, just to get back.

"I'll take it," she said evenly. "Two hours, did you say?"

"At this point" was his discouraging reply.

"Thanks." She walked into the waiting area, casting about for a suitable seat. The dark figure of the man had the prime spot, looking out over the landing strip, but she didn't feel like making friends on such a dismal night. Even though she wondered where in the world he'd found that delicious-smelling coffee.

Sighing, she sank down in the row behind him, rummaging in her purse for the glitzy novel she'd been reading. The man in front of her moved, but she kept her head down, not wanting to catch his glance, not wanting to encourage a no doubt lonely businessman looking for some distraction.

It didn't do any good. She could feel his presence, see his shadow move around the seats, pause at the end of her row and then steadily advance toward her. She ducked her head lower, determined to ignore him. Really, she had no need to be nervous. The clerk was still standing there, still patently bored, and even if the man pounced there were plenty of security guards roaming the place. Even if no one was in sight, there were plenty of stranded passengers within screaming distance.

Besides, she wouldn't have to resort to outside help. All she had to do was look up, fix the importunate giant with her most quelling Richardson glare, and he'd subside like a scurrying rat.

He sank down in the seat beside her. Out of the corner of her eye she saw the long legs encased in expensive wool trousers, the handmade leather boots. At least it wasn't a wino accosting her. Slowly she lifted her head, turning to glare at the intruder.

"Want some coffee?" asked Nicholas Fitzsimmons.

Chapter Thirteen

His first impression was that she looked like holy hell. There were shadows under her eyes, her face was pale and her mouth, as it dropped open in stunned amazement, was tremulous. She'd been crying sometime in the last twenty-four hours, crying a lot, or he'd miss his guess. And he wanted to put his arms around her and hold her, just hold her, until she lost that waiflike look and became the termagant he was used to.

Of course, he did no such thing. "Coffee?" he prompted again, holding out the Styrofoam cup. "It's not bad for airport brew."

She ignored it. "How did you know I was here?" It was an accusation, pure and simple.

Nick grinned. "There's that ego again. I had absolutely no idea you'd be here. How could I? You told me you were going to Princeton, not Boston. And you weren't supposed to be back till Wednesday. Why would I expect to find you stranded at Logan Airport at—" he checked his Rolex "—one-thirty in the morning?"

The spark of anger left her eyes, leaving her pale and deflated once more. "You're right," she said.

"Well?"

"Well, what?"

"Do you want some coffee? And are you going to tell me what you're doing here?"

"No."

"No coffee?" Nick echoed, puzzled.

She took the cup from his hand, took a deep swallow and managed a half smile. "No, I'm not going to tell you."

Half a smile was better than none. "Don't you want to know what I'm doing here?"

"I imagine you came home for a visit," she said diffidently, clearly not caring.

Well, if that's what she thought, it was fine with him. He'd flown back to Boston this weekend for the sole purpose of pushing Ray into finding something more about Leona Coleman. So far, everything he'd tried had turned up blank, but he had high hopes for James Longerman, 32650.

Ray couldn't make any promises. Boston had a slasher loose, and every minute of computer time and every law enforcement professional were being called into play. As soon as he had a spare moment he'd get on it, and with that Nick had to be satisfied.

He looked at Sybil, thought for about a moment, then pounced. "I expect you went back to Vermont early, found out I'd gone to Boston and you came tearing after me."

"Why in God's name would I do that?"

At least he'd managed to get her interest. She was finishing his coffee, but that was a small price to pay. If she cheered up he might even tell her where the soft-drink machine was. "I can think of several reasons. One, you might be worried that you'd driven me away, so you chased after me to apologize and beg me to come back."

Sybil managed a genteel snort. "Not likely."

"Or you could have chased after me to make sure I stayed away."

"A better possibility, but not worth my time and effort." She set the empty cup down on the chair beside her.

"Or you could have missed me so much that you couldn't stand it, and came after me to announce your undying love and to drag me into bed. I still don't believe that love potion didn't work."

It was exactly the right thing to have said. Her backbone stiffened, her gaze sharpened and every trace of the woebegone elf vanished. "Fat chance."

He shrugged his shoulders. "I admit it doesn't seem likely. You want to tell me why you're here?"

"I don't suppose I have any choice if you're going to keep bombarding me with stupid suppositions," she snapped. "It's very simple—my family is a little... overwhelming, and I decided to come home sooner than I had planned. The only flight I could make had me change at Logan, so that's what I'm doing."

"Your family must be extremely overwhelming for you to take such a roundabout flight during a winter storm."

"They are."

"I don't suppose you've had a chance to look at this from another angle," he murmured, enjoying himself.

"What do you mean?"

"Well, don't you think it's odd that we both ended up in the same place at the same time? Don't you think it's fate, or kismet, or somehow meant to be? I know how gullible you are—don't you think this is a sign?"

"If it's a sign, Nick, it says stop," she warned.

"Maybe I think it says yield," he said gently.

She closed her eyes and let out a long, weary sigh, one that still had the faint catch of distant tears on it. "Get off my case, Nick. It's been a long weekend, a long day, and it's not over yet."

"Why don't you end it, then? There are any number of motels around—you could spend the night and take the first plane out in the morning. The weather will be better and you'll be more rested."

"Can't," she said succinctly. "I don't believe in credit cards and I don't have enough money."

"We could always share—"

"Shut up, Nick," she said. "I've had a lousy, miserable last few days and I've had just about enough."

"What was lousy and miserable about it?"

She glared at him. "You never stop, do you?"

"Not often. What was lousy about it?"

"Nothing, nothing at all. My younger sister is marrying someone I had a schoolgirl crush on, but that's just part and parcel of the whole thing."

That little twinge in his stomach felt uncomfortably like jealousy. Except, of course, that he wasn't the jealous type, never had been, never would be. "And you've still got that crush?"

"Of course not. Geoffrey is perfect, and perfectly boring. I think he's just right for Allison—she'll know how to handle him."

"But you feel rotten anyway?"

"Yes." Her nervous hands were wrinkling the trashy novel she was holding. "It's irrational and stupid, but it just makes me feel more like an outcast."

He reached out one large, strong hand to cover hers, to stop her fidgeting. To his surprise she didn't jerk away. "Cheer up, Saralee," he murmured. "You've got me."

"Some consolation," she grumbled. But her hand rested beneath his.

He stared at her for a long moment. Her profile was slightly averted, and his eyes ran down the line of her face, the short, slightly upturned nose, the warm brown eyes, the soft mouth and high cheekbone and the untidy mass of dark blond hair. He still wanted to put his arms around her, wanted to pull her into his lap and comfort her. It was an odd feeling—he didn't usually feel protective toward women. And someone as prickly as Sybil Richardson didn't need a self-appointed protector.

"All right," he said, "tell me which dowsing device you think works best: pendulums, L-rods, Y-rods or bobbers? Which sell the best, and why?"

He couldn't have picked a better subject. Her swift, suspicious glance told him she knew he was deliberately distracting her, knew and appreciated it. "What sells best doesn't necessarily work the best. It's a judgment call, anyway. They all have their merits. Which do you prefer?"

"I don't dowse."

She stared at him in openmouthed amazement. "You're kidding."

"No. I can write, I can analyze, but I can't dowse."

"Everyone can dowse."

"Not me," he said flatly. "But I'm hell on wheels at mixing up potions."

"The Arkansas bobber," Sybil said firmly, "is an obscure but extremely effective device...."

He sat there, a faint smile on his face, as she proceeded to instruct him about every obscure dowsing device known to man. He noticed she hadn't offered to teach him how to dowse, nor did she offer any of her own amazing success stories that most dowsers trotted out by the dozen. A sudden, delicious suspicion swept over him.

"...while Y-rods have been documented as far back as the tenth century—"

"Can you dowse?" he interrupted her.

She frowned. "I told you, everyone can dowse."

"But can you?"

"Yes," she said flatly.

"How good are you?"

"If you want more research for your book, forget it."

"I have enough interviews. I want to know how good a dowser you are."

She glared at him, and for a moment he was afraid he'd blown all his hard work. Then a slow, rueful smile started in her eyes, moved to her lips and bubbled up into a laugh that was nothing short of enchanting. "Lousy," she said. "Absolutely lousy."

By this time two or three other late night travelers had straggled into the waiting area, which was just as well. His gut-level reaction to Sybil was powerful enough to make him lose whatever sense of propriety he had, and now was neither the place nor time for unbridled passion, he thought, staring out into the night. The swirling snow had lightened to no more than an occasional flurry, and outside their row of windows he could see one of Ransome's small planes being readied.

He opened his mouth to say something, but the bored clerk forestalled him. "We'll be boarding in the next five minutes. Please have your boarding passes ready."

"Do you think it'll be snowing in Vermont?" Sybil asked, eyeing the snowy runway with a worried expression she couldn't quite hide.

"It's always snowing in Vermont," Nick said gloomily. "But I don't think they'd fly out unless they were reasonably sure they could land." He put his hand under her elbow, helping her to her feet. "Come on, Sybil. You can drink your way to Burlington and sleep the rest of the way home."

"How am I going to do that? I have to drive."

"No, you don't. The roads will be bad enough as it is; we both don't need to risk life and limb. I'll drive, you can sleep and we'll pick up your car tomorrow when the storm clears."

"How about I'll drive and you sleep? I'm the one with four-wheel drive, remember?"

"I also remember that you're the one who drives like a bat out of hell. If it makes you feel any better, we can drive home in your car, but I'll do the driving."

She glared up at him, yanking her arm out of his grip. "Just when I think I might like you," she said behind clenched teeth, "you blow it."

"Stop looking for trouble and accept your fate, Sybil," he murmured. "We've been thrown together for a reason; if you'd stop fighting it, maybe we could find out what it is."

"You were put on this earth to plague me," she muttered.

Adelle had been an amazon. He'd always gone for long, leggy women, not little sparrows like the defiant creature standing there under his nose. Before he even realized what he was doing, he leaned down and kissed her, swiftly, briefly on her pale mouth. "I was put on this earth to tempt you," he said. "And sooner or later you'll give up fighting it."

"Sooner or later you'll give up trying."

He grinned. "Don't count on it. I can be very stubborn."

"So can I."

"Yes, but this time we both want the same thing. It's just taking you a little longer to realize it." She opened her mouth to protest again, but he stopped her. "Give the man your boarding pass, Saralee. We want to get home before dawn."

THERE WAS NO REASON why she should feel comfortable with him, Sybil thought as she leaned her head back against the seat in the Subaru. She shouldn't have sat with him in the plane, trading barbs and witticisms that grew steadily more sexual and more heated in nature; she shouldn't even have allowed him in her car, much less let him drive; she shouldn't have spoken to him at the airport. In retrospect, she had had other possibilities. Her cash would have bought her a taxi ride to her old college roommate's home in Milton, and Margie would have put her on a plane the next day when the weather cleared. But she'd been too miserable and too self-absorbed to think of it, and once Nick had appeared, too busy battling him and herself to think of such practicalities.

So here she was, halfway between Burlington and Danbury in the midst of a full-blown winter storm, trapped in the cavelike cocoon of an overheated station wagon with a man she found far too attractive for her own peace of mind.

She didn't need complications like Nick right now. She needed her own bed, the comfort of the dogs and maybe a glass or two of Courvoisier and one of her favorite books. All together they'd make her forget her miseries. But she'd finished the cognac, the dogs were at Dulcy's, her house would be cold with only the inadequate kerosene space heater going, and all her favorite books were lusty romances. Right now lust and romance seemed a very dangerous pastime.

"Aren't you asleep?" His voice was deep and sexy as he kept his concentration on the snowy highway ahead of him.

"Yes," she said, watching him. She had to admit, if she'd tried to describe the perfect man for her, at least in a physical sense, that Nicholas Fitzsimmons would fill the bill. He had an absolutely beautiful body. Too tall, of course, and his legs were too long, but damn, they were nice. His shoulders were just broad enough, not too overwhelming and not too scrawny. His hands were especially erotic, with their narrow, beautiful palms and long, artistic fingers.

Not to mention his face. She couldn't look into those topaz-colored eyes of his without thinking of the devil—not the frightening devil of fundamentalist religions and fire and brimstone, but the mocking seducer who tempted and twisted and stole people's souls. And people went to him willingly, just as Sybil wanted to go.

She liked his thick black hair, the widow's peak, the black eyebrows that only added to his satanic image. But most of all she liked his mouth, that thin, sexy line that could do the most devastating things to hers.

Or maybe he reminded her more of Dracula—not the vicious, blood-sucking monster but the erotic, elegant lover who sipped blood and drained souls. She could picture herself, stretched out on a bed, Nick leaning over her, his teeth on her vulnerable neck, as she reached for him....

Why was she letting herself have these erotic fantasies? She needed to remember what a pain Nick was, how infuriatingly pedantic and small-minded and incredibly devious he was. How could she have admitted she was a terrible dowser? He'd never let her forget it.

With a nervous hand she reached up and unfastened her coat. The car was hot, much too hot, though she could see he only had the heat halfway up. There was something otherworldly about the night, the utter quiet of the snow falling around them, the emptiness of the highway. Even the usually obstreperous engine was being more refined than usual.

"Go to sleep, Saralee," he said. "It's slow going—we won't be home for another hour."

"I used to hate that name," she said quietly.

"Why?"

"It's the name I grew up with," she said. "The name I associate with being a misfit, a changeling, a small brown wren in a family of peacocks. Every time I hear that name I feel small and inadequate."

"I can't really see you as a Sybil."

She sighed. "No, neither can I. It was just wishful thinking on my part. I was hoping I'd grow into it, be the sort of person who conversed with gods, but it hasn't happened. Not yet, at least. I haven't given up hope."

"Have you ever been called by any other name?"

She laughed. "Lots. Skinny, Short Stuff, Tubs..."

"Tubs?"

"I was fat when I was twelve. Also Cupcake, because of Saralee, Sis, and then of course my husband called me dear."

Nick wrinkled his nose. "Sounds pretty tepid."

"Colin was tepid."

"Who called you Cupcake?"

Sybil laughed. "A camp counselor. My family couldn't have a fat child sitting around, so they sent me off to fat girls' camp that summer. Very degrading at first, but I had one of the best times of my life. You see, no one else in my family had ever been fat, so none of them had been there. I was judged on my own merits, not as Hattie Richardson's little sister."

"Somehow I can't see me calling you Cupcake."

"Don't even try it," she warned. "Actually, I hate to admit it, but I don't really mind when you call me Saralee. Somehow it sounds different when you say it. Not so disapproving."

"Saralee it is," he said. "Unless you prefer me to call you dear?"

"Try it and I'll break your nose," she said sleepily.

"Or darling," he continued. "Or sweetheart, or honey, or hot stuff, or angel, or sweetmeat, or..."

"Cut it out, Nick," she murmured. "Two can play at that game."

"Go to sleep, Saralee. You can think of endearments when I get you safely home."

Saralee, she thought. She liked it too. She especially liked it in Nick's rich, sexy voice. She also liked the way he said darling, and sweetheart and honey and even sweetmeat. Did he really think she was hot stuff? He certainly seemed difficult to discourage, and she had offered him Dulcy on a silver platter. Maybe she was being a fool for fighting.

Fool or not, she didn't have any fight left in her. She had just enough energy to sink down lower in the seat and prop her head against the iced-over window. A few moments later she was fast asleep.

When she woke up an hour and a half later she was curiously disoriented, as if she were floating through clouds and space. It took her just a moment to realize that was exactly what they were doing, except that the fluffy white cloud was a snow squall with zero visibility and the floating feeling was all four wheels of the Subaru out of control.

Nick was cursing under his breath, slowly and savagely, as he deftly turned into one skid, then into another, somehow, by sheer force of personality or superhuman driving skills or demonic power keeping the car on the road when he couldn't even see the road. They were sliding down a steep incline, and for all Sybil knew they were heading off a cliff.

She jammed her feet into the floor, instinctively searching for the brakes that didn't exist on the passenger's side, as she clutched the seat with numb hands and began some cursing herself.

"Damn you, Nick, don't you dare kill me," she threatened.

"I'm not going to," he said calmly enough as they slid to the left. "At least, not unless I do it with my bare hands at some later time. We're almost home."

"Can't you stop the damned car?"

"I'm trying to." Beneath the calm there was a note she didn't care to encourage. Gritting her teeth, she hunched down in her seat, fingers clenching the cracked vinyl beneath her.

The car slid to the right, straightened out for a brief, glorious moment as the tires caught a last bit of traction, and then lost it again. This time there was no getting it back. Endless moments later they were tilted sideways in a ditch, the nose of her car crushed against what had to be the hardest maple tree in the state of Vermont.

They sat there for a brief, stunned moment. Nick reached over and turned off the lights that made no dent in the swirling white-out, then the ignition. "Are you all right?"

"Just peachy."

"We were only going about seven miles an hour when we hit the tree," he said in a damnably even voice. "With luck it didn't do much damage."

"Do you have the faintest idea where we are?" she demanded, unable to get too worked up over a car that had failed her in a crisis.

"Halfway down my driveway."

"Thank God," she breathed. "At least we aren't going to freeze to death."

He looked over at her. He'd left the overhead light on, and the dim bulb provided faint illumination in the darkness. "You're wearing a skirt, stockings and high-heeled shoes. The driveway hasn't been plowed, and even if we manage to head in the right direction we'll be slogging through at least a foot of new, wet snow. There are no lights, I don't really know how far we are, and—"

"We'll freeze in the car," she said.

"Right." He tried to open the door, but it was wedged shut against the snowbank. He shoved again, cursing, and then turned to her. "Lead on, Macduff."

Chapter Fourteen

Pulling the handle, Sybil shoved at the passenger door with all her strength. It didn't move. She grunted, shoving at it again, and panic began to creep up her spine.

"It might help if you unlocked the door," Nick said mildly.

"It's not locked. I never lock it."

"I locked it while you were asleep. I didn't want to risk having you tumble out onto the highway."

"Damn you, Nick...."

"Just unlock the door, Sybil. We'll argue about it later."

It was a waste of time to fight him. She pulled her thin gloves on, unlocked the door and shoved.

A moment later she was lying face-first in cold, wet snow. She lifted her head, blinking away the slush that clung to her, but she couldn't see a thing. It was a curious kind of chiaroscuro, the blackness of the predawn sky, the invisible whirl of white snow.

Nick's strong hands pulled her to her feet, and she clung to him, ignoring any remnants of pride, as he made a futile attempt at brushing the snow off her. He was right, the snow was at least a foot deep, and she might as well be barefoot for the protection her high heels and stockings afforded her.

Well, she was the tough Vermonter, he was the flatlander. Or at least she had two years' seniority on him. It was up to her to get them out of this mess. "Come on," she muttered, pulling away from him and heading out into the storm.

She didn't get far. His hands caught her, jerking her back. "You're heading in the wrong direction," he said, his voice muffled by the driving wind. "The house is back this way."

"Of course," she said, shivering, wrapping her thin cloth coat around her and wishing that she had her ratty down one with her. Not to mention boots and pants and long underwear. "Let's go." She took two steps back the way she came, her high heel collapsed beneath her, and she tumbled full-length into the snow again.

For a moment she just lay there and cried, hot tears pouring down her icy face. This time Nick didn't help her up; this time he picked her up, tossed her over his shoulder like a sack of potatoes and started off into the blinding snow.

She started struggling, but a swift, hard smack on her well-padded bottom shut her up. "The sooner we get out of here and into the house the happier I'll be," he shouted through the howling wind. "And we'll get there a lot faster if I carry you."

She subsided, doing her best to lie there passively, not liking it one tiny bit. There was nothing about the situation she liked, not the cold, not the snow, not the wind and not the company. Or at least, not in her present position.

He slipped once, sending both of them sprawling, but before she could scramble to her feet and try to make it on her own he was up again, carrying her with seemingly no effort at all and heading directly into the storm.

She dropped her head down, thankful that he had a better sense of direction than she did. She had absolutely no idea where they were going, it seemed to be taking five times as long as it should have, and for all she knew they were bypassing the Black Farm and heading directly into the woods. Maybe John Black's ghost decided to make an appearance and lead them to their doom, and they'd die locked in each other's arms.

It wasn't that unpleasant an idea. If they made it safely to the house, to the warmth and comfort of the old farm, then maybe she ought to find a suitable way to celebrate their close escape, maybe she ought to give in to those ridiculous potions and—

The breath was knocked from her as Nick walked directly into a solid unyielding object that turned out to be the old farmhouse. Once more they ended in the snow, and this time Nick didn't reach for her again. He was too busy cursing.

Sybil ignored him, pulling herself up on shaky, frozen legs and groping for the door. Of course it was locked, and Sybil's own curses matched Nick's.

"Calm down," he muttered, taking forever to find the lock in the pitch blackness. "We're almost inside."

"Almost isn't good enough," she managed through chattering teeth. "Haven't I told you you don't need to lock your doors around here?"

"Old habits are hard to break." The lock gave, the handle turned and the door opened. The two of them tumbled in, into the dark, warm cavern of safety, and collapsed on the hall floor. Nick kicked the door shut behind them and lay there, half on top of her, his breathing deep and labored.

As for Sybil, she was sheer ice from the hips down and from the waist up, her hair was frozen, her hands were frozen, her teeth were chattering so hard she could barely speak. No doubt Nick would count that a blessing.

"Didn't you turn down the heat when you left?" she grumbled in his ear, trying to shift out from under him. In his present snowy state he was only making her colder.

"No, thank God," he said, his voice infinitely weary.

"Thank God," she echoed. "You...w-w-w-want to get off me? You're like a blanket of snow."

"Always willing to oblige a lady," he muttered, rolling off her and standing. He pulled her up beside him, and her legs buckled. She fell against him, against his cold, snow-covered body, and she quickly pushed away. Standing on her own shaky two feet was preferable to embracing a polar bear.

He flicked on the light. The glare was so strong she shut her eyes against it, swaying slightly in the warmth. "I want you to go in the bedroom and take off all your clothes," he said.

"Forget it."

"And then get into the hottest shower you can stand, and stay there until you've thawed out. I'm not talking about sex, Saralee, I'm talking about survival. When you're warm enough, you can find some clean clothes in my drawers. In the meantime I'll get a fire going and find us something to drink."

"No love potions," she mumbled. "Two doses are more than enough."

"Two doses? Who gave you the second?"

"Never mind." She opened her eyes just a crack against the glaring light. "Point me in the right direction."

He gave her a gentle shove and she stumbled away from him, through the darkened living room into the bedroom. She fumbled with the light, staggered into the bathroom and began peeling off her ice-stiffened clothes. She didn't even bother to close the door. If Nick was so hard up that he had to resort to being a Peeping Tom, then that was his problem. All she wanted to do was melt the three layers of ice that had solidified around her body.

At first the water hurt her frozen flesh. Gradually the numbness faded, blood began to flow and her limbs began to move freely again. She stood there and let the blissfully hot streams of water rush over her, stood there behind the smoked glass door, ignoring the sounds from the bedroom beyond, ignoring Nick's shadow as he scooped up her wet clothes and took them away, ignoring everything but the warmth pouring over her frozen body.

It wasn't until the water began to lose its heat that she aroused herself from her stupor and turned off the tap. With warmth, sanity had returned, and so had at least a trace of her sense of self-preservation. It had to be close to five o'clock in the morning, in another couple of hours it would be light and she'd have no trouble making it home. That is, if her car wasn't totaled by its close encounter with a maple tree.

So she just had to make it through two hours of Nick's admittedly tempting company. Hell, she could do that. All she needed was something hot to drink, maybe something to eat, and she could face anything.

The bathroom was deserted, bereft of human presence and her wet clothes. He'd left a couple of towels for her, thick maroon ones he must have brought with him from Cambridge. No Vermont farmhouse ever boasted such wonderful towels.

She peeked out into the bedroom, but it, too, was empty, the door chastely closed. He'd left a silk dressing gown for her, a shimmering, sensual piece of apparel that was the last thing she intended to appear in. Particularly since the tie would be much too easy to unfasten. The dressing gown was lying across the bed, and the covers were turned down. Never in her life had Sybil seen a more inviting bed. It was an old-fashioned one, high off the ground, with maroon sheets that matched the towels and a patchwork quilt that had been there before John Black's time. She wanted to climb up into that bed, pull the covers over her wet head and fall sound asleep. And she'd like it even better if she could fall asleep wrapped around a long, lean body.

Forget it, she told herself. Instead, she headed for his closet, dismissing the wool and linen suits, settling instead for a huge blue plaid flannel nightshirt that came practically to her bare ankles. Rummaging in his drawers, she completed her outfit with a pair of thick woolly knee socks and a towel wrapped around her sopping mane. She surveyed her reflection in the mirror, grinning. If he'd had any thought of a last-minute seduction, this should put him off.

He was standing by the wood stove, leaning against the mantel, and he had a glass of cognac in his hand. He'd changed his clothes while she'd been showering, and he was dressed in black sweatpants and a sweatshirt, with no socks on his long, narrow feet. He looked warm, sexy and dangerous.

He caught sight of her standing in the doorway, and that thin mouth of his twisted in just the hint of a smile. "You didn't like the bathrobe?"

"Not warm enough," she lied, moving forward. "Got some of that for me?"

His smile broadened. The room was warm, hot even, and the dim lighting added to the sense of coziness and heat. "Some of what?"

"The cognac?"

"We have to share." He held out the snifter, watching with unconcealed amusement as she did her best not to touch him.

She took a deep, warming sip, feeling it burn its slow, languorous way down into her stomach, and immediately she knew it was a big mistake. The room, the warmth, the narrow escape and, yes, the company all combined to put her in a far too receptive mood. She'd have to keep all her wits about her if she didn't want to end up back in that comfortable-looking bed. And of course, part of the problem was that was exactly where she did want to be.

She sat down on the sofa, cross-legged, the thick wool socks showing to advantage. She took the towel from her head and began to rub it briskly through her long, wet hair. "How does the snow look?"

"Impenetrable. Why?"

"It'll be light in a couple of hours. I thought I could make it the rest of the way...."

"I smashed your car against a maple tree."

"But not badly, didn't you say?" She knew her eyes were anxious. She couldn't walk home, not in this kind of storm. And she couldn't stay here with him.

"Bad enough. And it's stuck sideways in a ditch. Even with four-wheel drive we'll need help getting it out."

"I'll need help getting it out," she corrected, shaking the long wet strands around her face.

"We'll need help getting it out." He took the brandy back from her, ignoring her start when his warm flesh touched hers. She was still cold, deep within the core of her, and there was only one way to get warm. "Stop fighting, Saralee. It's a waste of energy."

"I'm a born fighter."

"That you are," he said, his voice deep with approval. "But you don't have to fight me." He moved forward, squatting down beside the sofa, and his hand reached out and brushed the loose neckline of the oversize nightshirt. "Was this supposed to keep me away? I hate to tell you, darling, but this nightshirt is one of the sexiest things I've ever seen on anybody in my entire life."

She jumped a mile at the touch of his burning skin on her cool, trembling flesh. "You must be crazy," she said.

"Maybe. Who gave you the second love potion?"

She didn't even hesitate. "Dulcy. I called her for an antidote."

"Why did you need an antidote? I thought it didn't work."

"Of course it didn't work. But I . . . I had nightmares. I figured the power of suggestion might be working, so I thought I'd do something to combat it. So I called Dulcy, and she mixed up a second potion to combat the first one. It was supposed to be a different one, and the two should have canceled each other out."

"Did they?"

Sybil grimaced. He was so close she could smell the cognac on his breath, and for a moment she wondered what it would taste like on his tongue.

"Dulcy made a mistake."

"Did she?"

"She thought you'd made a different potion. A Hungarian one, with completely different ingredients. Instead, she just gave me a second dose of the one you mixed up, and then she said there was nothing she could do."

"She lied."

She would have liked to insist that Dulcy never lied, but her own innate honesty stopped her. "You mean there was something she could do?"

"I mean she knew exactly what I had whipped up. She was the one who gave me the ingredients for it, how could she have not known which one I mixed?"

"You're right," Sybil said, unaccountably depressed. "I can't even trust my best friend."

He still hadn't moved. He was much too close, and as long as he stayed there she couldn't think quite clearly enough. "Maybe she thought it would be good for you," he suggested softly.

"And maybe she just wanted to cause some trouble. Dulcy likes to stir things up."

"Are you stirred up?"

She looked at him then, her wary brown eyes staring into his slightly hooded, hypnotic ones. She was crazy to get involved with him, he was nothing but trouble, he was everything she'd run away from. She was crazy to resist him, he was the sexiest thing she'd ever seen in her entire life and for some strange reason he seemed to want her.

"Are you?" he prodded, his voice low and mesmerizing, and the fingers that had been lightly toying with the flannel nightshirt slipped inside the loose neckline, to brush gently against her cool flesh. He was hot, so hot, and she'd been cold for such a long time.

"Yes," she said, her voice a mere whisper of sound, of reluctant surrender. "Yes."

He sighed then, a small sound that might have been relief, and his eyes drifted shut for a moment. The hand that was stroking her skin slid around behind her neck, pulling her gently to him as he leaned toward her. And his mouth touched hers, briefly, softly, and his lips tasted of cognac.

It was the last possible moment. He moved just inches away, his eyes fluttered open and stared down into hers. "One last chance, Saralee," he whispered, but he lied. It wasn't a chance at all, not with his long fingers still cupping her neck, not with his mouth so close to hers, not with the drugging sensuality of his golden eyes burning into hers. She didn't have a snowball's chance in hell.

She crossed the inches that separated them, rising onto her knees and sliding her arms around his neck. Never in her entire life had she wanted someone as much as she wanted this very dangerous man hunkered down in front of her. It could be the three years of enforced celibacy, the close brush with death or her own exhausted emotions. It could even be the double dose of non-Hungarian love philtre. It no longer mattered. She was through fighting it. For now.

Slowly, hesitantly she pressed her mouth against his. Her lips were trembling, her hands were shaking and he was holding himself very still, giving her no assistance, almost savoring her suddenly clumsy efforts. His mouth was soft, damp, responsive against hers, and she could feel his accelerated heartbeat as she pressed her breasts against his chest. It was more than enough encouragement. Very shyly she touched the tip of her tongue to his lips. They parted instantly, his own tongue caught hers before she could retreat. And the taste of cognac swirled around them, cognac and passion.

He surged upward, carrying her with him, and for a moment she dangled there in his arms, inches off the ground, as they kissed. He was hard against her, very hard, the soft fleece of his sweatpants leaving nothing to the imagination, and she gave a small moan of panic and anticipation. Slowly he lowered her to the floor, his hands sliding down to cup her rounded hips and hold her against him, forcing her to feel his need. It was a need that matched her own.

She slid her hands under the velour sweatshirt, trembling as she felt the hot, lean flesh of his stomach with its light covering of hair. He was hard all over, his stomach, his arms, his shoulders, everywhere. And she trembled, softness against his hardness, and pushed her hands higher under the shirt, to cup his flat male nipples.

He pulled his mouth away from hers with a groan, burying his mouth in the vulnerable curve of her neck. And the hands that had been cupping her hips were busy pulling the oversize nightshirt up and over her head, breaking them apart long enough to toss it across the room, leaving her in nothing but a pair of knee socks.

She tried to move back against him, half in shyness, half in desire, but his hands on her shoulders held her away, and his eyes as they drifted down her nude, aroused body were as powerful an aphrodisiac as any ancient love potion.

Then he pulled her back, and his hands on her flesh were unbearably arousing. She reached for his sweatshirt again, but he forestalled her, pulling it over his head and tossing it after the nightshirt. And catching her hand, he pulled it down between them, to that pulsing maleness that was turning her dizzy with want and a primitive panic. She wasn't used to this, she wasn't used to him, she wasn't sure. . . .

He took her hand and slid it inside the waistband of the sweatpants. As her fingers curled, willingly and wonderingly, around his flesh, his hand found her, hot and damp and ready for him.

It had been so long, she thought. And it felt so good. No, "good" was too tepid a word. It was splendid, it was glorious, it was unbearably sweet. She was trembling all over, covered with a fine film of sweat, and her legs threatened to buckle beneath her. He was hot and hard and heavy in her hand, he was damp and ready for her, but still he made no move, content to stroke her, driving her past all conscious thought, and she knew if she had to wait a moment longer she wouldn't be able to stand it.

"Please," she whispered, her face crushed against the hot, smooth skin of his shoulder. Her free hand clutched at him, the nails digging into his flesh. "Please, I can't stand it."

"What do you want, Saralee?" he whispered in her ear, his voice soft and low. He couldn't be human, she thought. She had physical proof that he was ready to explode, and he could still taunt her, ignoring his own needs.

"I want you," she said. Stupid words, how could he fail to know that? "I want you inside me. Now."

He took his hand away from her, and she cried out in pain at the loss. He pulled away, out of reach, only for a moment, to strip off the black sweatpants. His eyes were glittering in the darkness, and the last little bit of fear shot through her. Was she a fool to want him?

Wisdom no longer had anything to do with it. Or sanity, or self-preservation, or even ego. Sybil no longer existed, neither did Nick. There was just woman, and man, and something dark and light, elemental and very complex, there, waiting.

His hands were hard and strong as they lifted her, up, up, into his arms and carried her into the bedroom. Then she was falling, they were falling, toward the bed, and he was over her, around her, in her, filling her with a deep thrust that left her breathless, and she was pulling him closer, wrapping herself around him, locking him in her arms, her legs, her body, imprisoning him as she was imprisoned by his invading maleness. Each thrust was a demand, a painfully sweet demand that she answered with the arch of her body, seeking that which retreated, only to advance again.

She was trembling, he was trembling, she was crying, he was crying. Then the tempo shifted, jerked, swung crazily and exploded. *Too soon,* Sybil thought dizzily. *Not yet. Don't let it stop.*

And it didn't. For countless, endless moments it held, beyond reality, time and space. It held, so achingly pleasurable that it flirted with pain, then melted back into pleasure, until they collapsed together in a damp tangle of limbs and hair and heat and love.

She couldn't move, couldn't think, couldn't even open her eyes. Every ounce of strength she had left was spent on making her heart beat, her lungs fill with air.

Nick recovered faster, but then, he must have felt this incredible obliteration before. It was unlike anything Sybil had ever experienced in her life. She lay there, barely breathing, unable and unwilling to face him.

A finger touched her eyelid, and she flinched. Despite her best resolve she looked up to see Nick smiling down at her, those eyes of his bright with laughter, his fingertip wet with her tears.

She knew her expression was dazed, solemn, but there was nothing she could do about it. She watched him, waiting, waiting for heaven knew what.

"You're mine now," he said, his thin, sexy mouth curved in a smile that was oddly tender. "I just won your soul." And leaning down, he bit her lower lip, just hard enough to hurt. "Got that, Saralee?"

She was too weary to fight. Her heart was working, her lungs were working, but her brain was still on automatic pilot. "Got it," she murmured in a rusty voice. And closing her eyes again, she shut him and all the troublesome world out, falling into a sated sleep.

Chapter Fifteen

He looked down at her, lying so sweetly, so peacefully, curled up in his arms. Her long, damp hair was wrapped around both of them, her warm brown eyes were closed in sleep, and one small, defenseless hand was pressed against her shadowed face. The other was resting against his shoulder in an unconscious expression of trust.

Who would have thought it? he brooded, stretching out in the small bed that had become pleasantly smaller with the addition of a much-longed-for companion. Who would have thought he'd fall in love with someone like Sybil-Saralee Richardson?

Adelle had been much more his style—leggy, sophisticated, ambitious, not a trace of fantasy in her elegant, cynical body. The woman lying next to him was, at best, passably pretty. Until she smiled, and his heart turned over. Or frowned, and he wanted to kiss her. Or looked abstracted, and he wanted to tickle her. In fact, no matter what she did, she captivated him. Illogical as it was, he was lost.

And the woman lying next to him believed in the most ridiculous things. What had that character in *Through the Looking-Glass* said? "Sometimes, I've believed as many as six impossible things before breakfast." He had little doubt that Saralee Richardson bettered that record.

She'd left elegant suburbia and a yuppie marriage for the rustic simplicity of wood stoves and blizzards, she wore cottons and corduroys and seemed oddly shy about sex. And the depth of his feeling for her left him shocked past denial.

She murmured something, shifting closer to him, and the hand tightened on his shoulder for a moment. He could see the mark of his teeth on her soft lower lip. That sudden act of possessive savagery startled him in retrospect. He'd always prided himself on his open-mindedness when it came to relationships; he believed that he'd never hold a woman if she wanted to leave.

Well, those noble days were over. If Sybil put up much more of a fight, he'd kidnap her and carry her off to Cambridge....

No, he wouldn't, much as the fantasy appealed to him in his current weary, semiaroused state. He'd be patient, charming, tolerant; he'd win her over by hook or by crook or by surreptitious doses of every love philtre known to man. And if that didn't work, then he'd kidnap her....

It was still snowing, and the rising sun had a hard time making inroads on the storm. He ran a tender, inquisitive hand down her back beneath the heavy quilts. Her skin was warm and responsive, even in sleep, and she murmured something low and definitely erotic. He ducked his head down to capture her lips again, but something about the shadows under her eyes, the faint trace of distant tears, stopped him. She'd only been asleep for less than an hour; he could give her a little time. With a storm like that still raging outside, there was no way she could run away. They'd have time.

SHE HAD NIGHTMARES. In the calm light of day she knew she wasn't being completely honest, to call them that. But they were the same sort of dreams she'd been plagued with ever since Nicholas Fitzsimmons had arrived in Danbury. Erotic, explicit dreams, full of sexual detail that seemed, to Sybil's uninformed mind, to be frankly impossible, combined with the typical imagery, which was even more disturbing. She could interpret the dreams in a hundred different ways, but one thing she couldn't avoid—she was physically obsessed with the man.

Not that it should be a surprise, she thought sleepily, curling up against him, nuzzling her face against the smooth, warm skin of his shoulder. Why else would she be in bed with him?

Her energy had certainly gotten diffused last night. If what Leona maintained was true, she wouldn't be able to dowse right now to save her life. Although dowsing was the last thing she had in mind at that point.

His hand was traveling up her back, slowly, gently, the touch of his lightly callused fingertips exquisitely arousing. She should open her eyes, tell him to take his hands off her and climb out of this bed.

But if she didn't open her eyes, she wouldn't have to face anything, would she? She could just lie back and enjoy it, pretend it was just one more of those deliciously, frighteningly erotic dreams she'd been suffering—"suffering" was hardly the word for it. She could just lie there....

"Open your eyes, Saralee."

How did he know she wasn't a heavy sleeper? She kept her breathing deep and steady, gave a realistic little wiggle and kept her eyes shut.

His hand slid around her hip, over her flat stomach, as his mouth gently brushed her lips. Her own mouth felt bruised, delightfully so, and it was all she could do not to open her mouth for him and kiss him back. But she kept her eyes shut.

"Open your eyes, Saralee." His voice was muffled as he trailed kisses down her neck, pushing her damp tangle of hair out of the way as he went. She wanted to help him, wanted to move closer, she wanted his hands and his mouth on her breasts. She kept her eyes shut.

He pushed the heavy quilts out of the way, and the cool air danced across her flushed skin. One hand stayed beneath the covers, stroking her trembling, fluttering stomach, the other slid under her shoulders, pulling her closer.

"Open your eyes, Saralee," he whispered, as his damp, open mouth captured her breast, his rough tongue swirling around the tightly aroused nipple. Her body arched in immediate reaction, her fingers clenched the sheet beneath her and she could feel the heat and dampness burning between her legs. She kept her eyes shut.

He was holding her as if she were a feast for his delight. His mouth was a bold devourer on her breasts, his hand was trailing across her stomach, sliding lower and lower, slipping between the legs that opened obligingly for him. His long, clever fingers knew just what they were looking for, and her body arched again in helpless response. A small, hungry moan sounded from the back of her throat.

"Open your eyes, Saralee," he whispered, moving his mouth from her aching breasts back to her bruised lips. She opened her mouth for him, for his plunging, invading tongue, and she opened her legs for him, for his clever, clever hand. But she kept her eyes shut.

A thousand tiny wings beat at her brain, a swirling mist of impenetrable snow surrounded her. She wanted him, she needed him, ached for him, so much that she was afraid she would weep with longing. And he knew it; he was too experienced a man not to recognize the signs. He had no qualms about taking advantage of a sleeping woman, and she had no qualms about faking sleep. She lay there, drowsy, passive, as his hands pulled her to the center of the soft bed, arranging her body for his invasion.

She could sense his shadowy presence above her in the dim light behind her eyelids. And then she felt him, hot and hard and ready against her.

He pressed against her, entering her very, very slowly, the pleasure of his measured advance sending shivers through her body. She arched up, wanting all of him, wanting it now, but he wasn't to be rushed. His control was absolute, his breathing labored but steady, as he filled her with unhurried, deliberate care. Then he was there, filling her completely. Her body was covered with a fine film of sweat as she tightened around him, savoring the feel of him, the size and strength and wonder—

And suddenly he was gone, pulling from her.

She arched up, reaching for him, but his hard hands held her down on the bed. "Open your eyes, Saralee," he said, and she knew it was for the last time.

Her eyes flew open, looking up into his intent, glowing ones in mute appeal. He still didn't move, and she could feel him there, waiting, teasing, pressing against her with his heat and power.

"That's better," he said, and the raw note in his voice was the only sign of strain. She saw the knotted muscles in his long arms as he held himself away from her, the sheen of sweat on his brow beneath the widow's peak, the gleam of his topaz-colored eyes. "I want you to know what you're doing. I want a participant, not a victim."

She lay there in the center of the bed. The old mattress dipped in the middle, cradling her, and he loomed over her, so that she felt trapped, imprisoned by the bed and Nick's hot, aroused body.

"I know what I'm doing," she said, and her voice wasn't much more than a whisper.

He looked down at her for a long, troubled moment. "Lord, I hope so," he said. Then he brought them together again, this time in a low, hard thrust that pushed her deeper into the hollow of the bed.

They took their time. The bed was soft and warm, their bodies relaxed and comfortable after their first, fevered coupling. This was the time to learn each other, to find what pleased them, where to stroke, where to kiss, where to nip lightly with sharp teeth. When to be fast, when to be blissfully, agonizingly slow, when to be soft and gentle, when to be just the tiniest bit rough.

The windows were covered with snow, and no one could look in. The telephone was off the hook; everyone thought she was still out of town. No one would look for her, no one would question her. She had nothing to do but learn Nick's body and learn a few surprising things about her own.

At first she'd tried to hurry him, being accustomed to her ex-husband's efficient attitude toward lovemaking. But Nick wouldn't be hurried; he wanted to savor, and savor he did. There wasn't an inch on her body he hadn't kissed, he moved her from position to position with gentle, demanding hands, and each new position carried her to new heights. Each time, when she thought she couldn't possibly feel any more, he'd showed her that she could.

Finally it was up to her. It was time to shatter his control as he had shattered hers, time and time again. She pushed him back on the bed, rolled him over and sat astride him, her long dark blond hair rippling down her narrow back, her brown eyes blazing in delight as this time she set the pace. When his hands reached out to cup her hips she moved them away, pressing them down on the mattress as she rocked, back and forth, teasing him as he had teased her, until he was panting and sweating, his golden eyes glazed, until he lost the last trace of his control and arched up into her downthrust, spilling himself into her with a raw, guttural cry that echoed in Sybil's heart as her body exploded around him one last time.

She sank down on him, her body drained and numb. She could hear his heart racing against her cheek, she could taste the salty tang of his sweat, she could feel the faint tremors that rippled over his body, tremors that matched her own. She realized she was smiling, a stupid, goofy smile against that warm, pounding chest, and for a brief moment she wondered what in the world had gotten into her. An old line came back to her—the devil made me do it. A little shiver ran down her backbone.

It was followed by the lazy stroke of Nick's hand, and that odd trace of nervousness temporarily vanished. "I hate to think what would have happened," he said huskily, "if that love potion actually worked."

It took all her energy, but she lifted her weary head to look down at him. She liked what she saw. He looked sleepy, dazed and completely satisfied. He even looked, just a little bit, like a man in love.

"If that potion had worked," she murmured, "you'd probably be dead."

He managed a tired grin. "I'm not quite sure that I'm not. I think," he said, "I've unleashed a monster."

"I think," she said, "maybe you have."

WHEN SYBIL AWOKE the next time the digital clock next to Nick's bed said twelve-thirty and the storm was over. Bright, glaring sunlight was pouring in the uncurtained window, reflecting off the thick white blanket of snow that covered everything. She closed her eyes against that glare, lying back in the bed, alone and sticky and sore.

The house was empty, she knew that without question. For a moment she had the wishful thought that Nick had seduced her and had run, back to Cambridge. At that moment she would have been very happy never to see him again.

But she knew that was too much to hope for. She straggled out of the bed, pulling the top sheet with her, and wandered into the living room. The wood stove was kicking out heat, and somewhere she could smell coffee. Nick might be part and parcel of that coffee, in which case she could do without it, but she didn't think so. The house had an indefinably empty feel that was unmistakable.

The coffee was sitting in its automatic drip pot, keeping warm just for her. The note was lying beside it.

"Couldn't wake you this time. Steve at the garage towed your Subaru in and is giving me a ride to Burlington to pick up the Jaguar. Be back around five. Be here."

Short, succinct, she thought with a curl of her lip, crumpling the note in one fist. There was writing on the back, and out of curiosity she flattened out the paper. "P.S. There's some extra love philtre in the refrigerator."

She ripped the note into tiny pieces and left them on the floor. She poured herself a cup of his coffee, because without it she would die, and stomped back into the living room.

She had no reason to be mad at him. He hadn't taken unfair advantage of her, it hadn't been rape, it hadn't even been seduction. It had been mutual, and that was what she couldn't accept. She would have been all right if it had just been last night. It would have been all right if she'd fooled him into thinking she was asleep this morning. But no, he had made sure she was wide awake and completely aware of everything he was doing to her more than willing body. And everything she was doing to his.

And the big question was, was there any future in it? In them? Was she a convenient roll in the hay, a challenge, a bed warmer for the cold Vermont nights? Or was it something more than that? And did she want something more than that?

She stretched out on the sofa that had been the beginning of her downfall last night. She pulled the maroon sheet around her body and sipped the strong black coffee. To be perfectly fair, she had to admit that there had been advantages to last night. While Colin's lovemaking had never been unpleasant, and What's-his-name in college had been exciting in an illicit sort of way, nothing had ever been as overwhelming as the last few hours had been. For years she had wondered if she were capable of feeling those kinds of reactions. Now she knew she was, and if Nick could bring them out in her, so could someone else. Couldn't they?

Couldn't she be grateful, enjoy the sex and wave a cheerful goodbye when he left? After all, she had a life she enjoyed up here, away from the pressures of modern life. She didn't want to go back, did she? And he certainly wasn't going to stay. So couldn't she just lie back and enjoy herself?

"No." She jumped before she realized she'd spoken the word out loud. But she said it again, for good measure. "No."

It simply wasn't in her nature, or in the nature of most women, for that matter. She couldn't give a man her body without giving him her heart. It was that simple.

It was also, she realized with a sense of shock, too late. Somewhere along the line, while she was fighting with him, and hiding from him, baiting him and avoiding him, somewhere along the line she'd given in. She'd fallen in love with the man. Before she'd given her body, she'd given her heart and mind and soul, and that was exactly why she'd been fighting so hard. What was the use of giving your heart and mind and soul to someone who didn't want them? It was downright degrading.

She'd already failed at one marriage. She wasn't cut out for connubial bliss, for suburbia and two-point-three children and happy ever after. Colin had been sweet, tolerant and undemanding, and she had suffocated to the point that she would have killed to escape.

How much worse would it be with a narrow-minded, overbearing tyrant like Nick? Someone who mocked everything she believed in, who rode roughshod over her objections and second thoughts. How much worse could it be with someone she loved to the point of obsession?

What had he whispered last night? "You're mine now," he'd said. "I just won your soul." And he'd bitten her.

A stray hand reached up and touched her lip. It stung slightly, and she pulled her hand back, trembling. She'd almost forgotten that odd, possessive interchange. Now that he had her, would he still want her? And for how long?

"Be here," he'd ordered. Well, that was definitely out. If she had to walk through a howling blizzard, she was getting home, away from him for long enough to think this mess through. If she stayed here she'd end up back in that high, soft bed, and heaven knows if she would have the determination to climb out again before he headed back to Cambridge.

"Damn," she muttered, draining the coffee. The sheet slipped off her as she stood, and for a moment she surveyed her body, from the tips of her toes, still clad in knee socks, up the nude length of her. Her winter-pale body had bruises, bites and other signs of her occupation during last night and this morning. At no point had Nick hurt her, but he'd certainly left his mark on her.

She sighed, pulling the sheet back around her. First things first, and the first thing she had to do was get the hell out of there. She headed directly toward the phone, dialing Dulcy's number. No answer.

She only hesitated a moment before hanging it up and dialing again. If this one failed her she'd walk.

Three long, fateful rings, and then a cozy little voice murmured, "Hello?"

"Leona," Sybil said, almost weak with relief. "Thank God you're there. I need your help."

Chapter Sixteen

"Didn't I warn you?" Leona questioned in her most plaintive voice, her tiny dark eyes glued to the snow-packed road ahead of them. She drove very slowly and carefully, so slowly and carefully, in fact, that it took her half an hour to traverse a stretch of road that took Sybil five minutes and a normal driver ten.

But beggars can't be choosers, Sybil thought, huddling down farther in the car seat, shivering in her cloth coat, silk dress and bare legs. She'd been lucky to find that much of her clothing; she'd even considered borrowing something of Nick's, but common sense had warned her against it. For one thing, he was more than a foot taller than she was. For another, it would give him the perfect excuse to come over and get whatever she borrowed.

"Yes, you warned me," Sybil said quietly.

"The man," said Leona, "is trouble."

Sybil sighed. She'd taken the shortest shower on record before Leona arrived, trying to wash the scent and sight of him off her body. She couldn't wash away the feel of his hands on her thighs, his mouth on her breasts, his hips . . .

"And you're not the only one who's suffered at his hands," Leona continued.

The flush that had heated Sybil's cheeks paled as an emotional fist slammed into her stomach. "He's been seeing someone else?"

"I hadn't even realized, dear girl, that he was seeing you. No, Professor Fitzsimmons has other interests. Unfortunately, I seem to be one of them."

Guilt swamped all of Sybil's other tangled emotions. "What do you mean?" she asked innocently. Damn, she should have warned her.

"Your friend seems to think I have something nefarious in my past. He's been making inquiries...."

"How do you know?"

Leona kept her face turned firmly toward the road as they crept along at a snail's pace. "Friends," she said mysteriously. "Friends told me people have been asking questions."

"But there's nothing to find out...."

"I'm afraid there is," Leona corrected her with a sigh. "I haven't lived a blameless life, Sybil. No one can live to my age and make that boast. I've made mistakes, but I've paid for them. They were long in the past, I thought gone forever, but your professor seems determined to rake them up."

"Not my professor," Sybil said firmly. "Er, what sort of mistakes, Leona?"

"Nothing dreadful. I have many gifts, and I haven't always used them wisely. I've been used by other people, evil men out for gain, and not realized it soon enough. When they were caught, I appeared guilty, and in a way I suppose I was. I should have realized what they were doing."

"What were they doing?"

"Cheating people out of their money," she said simply, and for a moment Sybil's heart shrank. "Exactly what your professor thinks I'm doing now."

"Not my professor," Sybil corrected absently. "What happened?"

She sighed. "It was all so long ago. My husband, and I'm afraid he was a major part of it, was convicted and sentenced to an obscenely long sentence. He died of a heart attack before he had served even two years of it. It was so long ago I don't even like to think about it," said Leona, dabbing a plump hand toward her dry eyes.

"Oh, Leona, I'm so sorry," Sybil said, her heart breaking.

Leona shook her head. "Don't be. I don't often think about it, only when something unpleasant comes up and reminds me of it. It was a sad time in my life, but I've put it behind me. Sybil, I wouldn't think of cheating my friends. You know me, I don't have such ruthlessness in me."

She knew very well that Leona had a great deal of ruthlessness when it came to small matters, but she dutifully shook her head. "Of course you don't," she soothed. "Nick must be crazy."

"But will he convince the others? He's a very persuasive man."

"Not that persuasive," said Sybil.

Leona spared an instant's attention from the road to cast a surprisingly knowing look at Sybil's attire. "Isn't he?"

She blushed. "We won't let him do this to you, Leona. We won't let him railroad you."

"I'm afraid it might be too late. If he's started rumors..."

"I don't think he has. And we can fight back."

"I can't imagine how, my dear," Leona murmured with uncharacteristic fatalism. "I'll just have to move away from the first place that's felt like home—"

"You will not," she said firmly. "We'll think of something."

"Of course, we could always distract him," Leona suggested.

"Not the way you're thinking."

"Of course not!" Leona was affronted. "I wouldn't think of trading your purity for my peace of mind."

Sybil was feeling decidedly impure that morning, and not averse to a good enough excuse to continue that particular impure pastime, but she accepted Leona's protests. "Then how do we distract him?"

"Let me put my thinking cap on," she said with her usual coyness. "A wild-goose chase might be just the thing. Keep him so busy with phony clues that he won't have any time to spare for harassing me."

"Or me," said Sybil, only slightly mournfully.

"Especially not you, my dear," Leona said firmly. "We don't want you falling prey to his entrapments any more than me. Between the two of us, my dear, we'll put up a maze that no one could get through." She pulled to a stop in front of Sybil's snowed-in house. Thirty-five minutes that day, Sybil thought. An all-time record.

"Wonderful," Sybil said morosely. "You can count on me."

Leona gave her her kindest smile. "I knew I could, dear. I'll head back to the office, shall I? It wouldn't do to have the place unmanned."

"You do that," she said, setting her high-heeled, stockingless feet in the deep snow and repressing a shiver. "I'll be in tomorrow."

Leona nodded. "We'll plan something then."

There were no dogs to leap about, greeting her with their usual doggy enthusiasm when she opened her unlocked door. The kerosene space heater wasn't adequate for the house—the most it could do was keep the heat above freezing so the pipes wouldn't burst. She had snow halfway up her thighs, her silk dress was soaked, her feet were blocks of ice and all she wanted to do was throw herself on her couch and weep.

But Richardsons, even changelings, were made of sterner stuff than that. She kicked off her shoes, headed straight to the bedroom and changed into warm long johns, baggy jeans and a thick wool sweater. She pulled on leg warmers and her warmest pair of socks, and headed for the living room and the wood stove.

It was an hour before the chill was off the house, an hour Sybil spent huddling in front of the hot cast-iron stove, shivering. She was too cold to call Dulcy again, too cold to read, to cold to do anything but stand there, hopping from one foot to the other, trying to get warm.

Her stocking foot landed on something hard and metal, and she let out a curse that would have done Nick at his most angry proud. It was a small brass pendulum she'd lost months ago. She picked it up, holding it in one freezing hand, watching it with unconcealed fascination as it twirled aimlessly.

Did unbridled lovemaking interfere with one's psychic concentration, as Leona contended? There was nothing to do but conduct a little experiment.

She ran the pendulum through a series of standard questions, and for once it was surprisingly responsive. Eyes brown, water running under the living room, snow falling, all of these things the pendulum agreed with.

"Am I going to live happily ever after?" She asked the question softly, half embarrassed.

The pendulum dangled, refusing to answer. "Will I ever find someone to love?"

It gave her an enthusiastic yes. Encouraged, Sybil pushed onward. "Will he love me?"

Another enthusiastic yes. "Will I meet him this year?"

The pendulum dropped, hanging there, and for one crazy moment Sybil had the odd impression that the pendulum was disgusted with her obtuseness. All right, the time for being coy was over.

"Is it Nick?"

The pendulum once more began its clockwise spin.

She stood there, watching it, biting her abraded lip as it spun, around and around and around, higher and higher. She must have thrown it. It couldn't have spun out of her hand, winging itself across the room. It was simply because she was tired and overwrought that she couldn't remember hurling the damned thing.

It was only because she was miserable that, search as she tried, she couldn't find a trace of it in the corner where she saw it land.

DULCY ARRIVED with the dogs sometime in midafternoon. Sybil hadn't called her again, but with her usual sixth sense Dulcy somehow got the message, not only about Sybil's return, but about her morose state of mind. She brought the dogs, she brought take-out Chinese food from St. Johnsbury, and she brought the largest size bottle of Courvoisier the state liquor stores offered.

Together they ate the food, giving the extra egg rolls to the dogs. Together they made a respectable inroad on the bottle of cognac. Dulcy left promptly at five o'clock, refusing to stay longer or to protect her from Nick's probable return.

Not that Sybil told her what she wanted to avoid. She'd been remarkably discreet, but Dulcy had gathered up her cape and her trailing scarves, had taken one look at Sybil's face and laughed.

"Lost your innocence, have you?"

Sybil's back stiffened. She was sitting on the living room couch, surrounded by dogs, and she had no intention of moving. "I don't know what you're talking about."

"Sure you do. I can read between the lines. You smashed up your Subaru at five in the morning and waited until afternoon for a ride home. You must have been doing something all that time."

"I was sleeping on the couch."

"Sybil," Dulcy protested, shocked. "Don't lie to me. For one thing, it's a complete waste of time. For another, it hurts my feelings. I'd rather you told me to mind my own business."

"Mind your own business."

"Don't throw him away, Sybil." She blithely ignored the order. "He's worth the effort."

Sybil gave up fighting. "I offered him to you first."

Dulcy shrugged. "He didn't want me. He'd already seen you."

"I'm hardly the type to overshadow you, Dulcy."

"You aren't the type, my friend. You were *the one*. Nick wasn't looking for a roll in the hay, a pretty face, a gorgeous body."

"Thanks a lot."

"Not that he didn't get all three," Dulcy said hastily.

"Who says he got them?"

"Your face does."

"Well, he's not going to get them again. Not if I can help it," Sybil said, leaning against the couch.

"Why not?"

"There are a million reasons."

"Name one."

Sybil leaned forward, intent, and one of the puppies slid onto the floor with a startled yip. "I'll give you two excellent ones. For one thing, he's out to get Leona. He's had her investigated, he's harassing her, trying to railroad her—"

"You're breaking my heart," said Dulcy, never a great fan of Leona's. "Don't you think Leona can take care of herself? You're not her mother, for goodness' sake."

"I don't like to see helpless old women victimized," Sybil said stiffly.

"Neither do I. But Leona's never struck me as the victim type. She's the sort who'll always come out on top. If I were you I'd spend my energy worrying about the Muller sisters and Mary Philbert. They're the real victims."

"Damn it, Leona didn't steal their money!"

"Is that what Nick thinks?" Dulcy murmured, fascinated. "I hadn't thought of that."

"It's not true."

Dulcy merely smiled. "Give me your second excellent reason for avoiding Nick."

"He's everything I came here to get away from. I've spent my entire life running from people like him, from perfect lives and brilliant people and complicated, stressful life-styles." The moment the words were out of her mouth she wished she could call them back.

Dulcy smiled, seeing the unhappy recognition in Sybil's warm brown eyes. "Do I even have to say it, Sybil? Isn't it time you stopped running away? Isn't it time you face what frightens you? Maybe then you'll realize that there's nothing there to make you feel inadequate."

"Go away, Dulcy."

Unfortunately, Dulcy left. Sybil looked around her, depressed. It was getting nerve-rackingly close to Christmas; maybe she should start to get in the spirit. She'd been so busy fighting her attraction to Nick that she hadn't even made a wreath. Maybe this year she ought to buy one. Her wreath-making talents were decidedly iffy, with the results looking more like an oval than a nice circle. She always stuffed too many dried herbs and flowers in them, to cover the inadequacies, but she usually got those herbs and flowers from Dulcy, and right now she'd die before she asked her for anything.

Think Christmas, she told herself, dragging out the large box of decorations from the attic. Think peace on earth, goodwill to men . . . to all, she corrected herself absently. To all but Nick Fitzsimmons.

She put a tape of medieval carols on the stereo, poured herself another cognac and set to work, with crocheted snowflakes in the windows, antique wooden toys on any surface not cluttered with books, candles of varying sizes and colors all around.

Each time the phone rang she jumped a mile. Steve at the garage called to say the Subaru was bloody but unbowed, her parents called to make sure she'd made it through the storm safely, Leona called to tell her she'd drive her to work tomorrow morning and they could discuss a plan she had. Even Edla Muller called, to tell her she was glad she was back.

But there was no word from Nick.

Well, of course she didn't want there to be. The problem with men, she thought as she strung delicate golden beads from the rafters, was that the moment you fell in love they disappeared. As long as the sensible female fought it, the man responded to the challenge. As soon as she was fool enough to give in and lose her heart, he lost interest.

Well, she could lose interest, too, she promised herself grimly, ignoring the unfairness of her generalizations and rationalizations. She wasn't so far gone that she couldn't fight it once more. If he kept away, she wouldn't be as obsessed tomorrow, she'd be less so on Wednesday, and by Christmas she'd have forgotten all about it. Christmas, 1999, perhaps.

The dogs were lying all over the living room in various attitudes of doggy complacency. They did no more than raise their sleepy heads when Nick walked, silently and unannounced, into the living room.

Sybil was balanced somewhat precariously on a chair, trying to hook a strand of German crystal beads around the hanging lamp. He was heading toward her with a purposeful expression in those wonderful eyes of his, and for a moment she stood there, motionless.

During the day she'd managed to blot out just how good-looking he really was. His face was captivating, almost haunting in its beauty, from the thick black hair that came forward in a widow's peak, the satanic eyebrows, the narrow, almost austere mouth and mesmerizing eyes. If she looked into those eyes, those hungry, hypnotizing eyes for a moment longer, her resolve would vanish. Then who would protect poor Leona from him? And who would protect poor Sybil?

She jumped down before he could reach her, scampering behind the chair. He stopped his forward stride, his eyes met hers and his mouth curved in a cynical, resigned smile. "I don't suppose you're skittering away from me like a scared rabbit because I was a few hours late."

"Are you?" Her voice was husky and breathless.

"It's eight. I thought I'd be back by five or six at the latest, but the Jaguar had been plowed in at the airport and it took a while to get it out."

"I wasn't expecting you."

His sigh was loud, long-suffering and bordering on irritated. "Is it because I took off this morning? Believe me, I tried to wake you up. You were sleeping like the dead. I left you a note."

"So you did. As I recall, it said, 'Be here.'"

"Is that the problem? I can be dictatorial, I know. You'll have to cure me of it." He smiled at her, and her heart began to melt.

Think about Leona, she warned herself sternly. *Think about the Richardsons.* "That wasn't the problem. I just ignored it."

"Then what is it?" He advanced upon her, pushing the chair she was clinging to out of the way, and then his hands were on her, his long fingers caressing her arms through the heavy sweater, and she could feel her knees tremble.

"Nick, this isn't going to work."

"Sure it is," he murmured, enfolding her in his arms, ignoring the token struggle.

"You're not the kind of man I want."

"Sure I am," he said, and she could feel him against her, the heat and hardness of him, and miserably she had to agree. "And if I'm not, I'll change."

"Nick..."

His mouth caught hers, midprotest, in a slow, lazy kiss that was as thorough as it was arousing. Desperately she clung to the last shreds of her resistance, but it was fading fast, disappearing like wisps of wood smoke on a windy morning. One of his hands had slipped beneath her loose sweater and was already cupping her breast, and she could feel the tight curl of desire deep in the center of her, twisting outward.

He lifted his head for a moment, looking down at her, and his eyes were glittering with desire. "So what else is the problem?"

It was time enough for the last bit of common sense to intrude. If he hadn't stopped, if he'd just kept kissing her, she would have ignored her worries and concentrated on the moment at hand.

"Leona," she said.

He held himself very still, his arms still holding her, but she could sense the withdrawal, the slowly building anger.

"What about Leona?" he said with deceptive mildness, but the fiery depths of his golden eyes had turned flat and opaque.

"I can't have you railroading her."

"Are you telling me you'll sleep with me if I leave Leona alone?" The question was gently worded, but there was no way she could ignore the tight lash of anger beneath his even voice.

"No," she said bravely, ignoring the fluttering nervousness that had replaced, or almost replaced, the wanting. "I'm telling you to leave Leona alone, and that I won't sleep with you anyway."

He was very angry, very angry indeed. He pulled away, slowly, and with the withdrawal of his heat she felt cold, deep in the very heart of her. "I don't think," he said, "that I'll even bother to ask why. You'll just come up with more crap about how I'm not the kind of man you want, and it'll be a waste of time. Anyone who could dismiss what we shared this morning, ignore that rare kind of magic, is a fool. When it comes right down to it, Saralee Richardson, you're not the kind of woman I want."

He whirled and stalked, absolutely stalked, toward the hallway, fury radiating through his tall, gorgeous body, leaving Sybil staring after him, miserable, doubt-ridden, half ready to run after him.

She'd taken one step in his direction when he turned, and he was so angry he didn't notice the misery and doubt on her face. "And as for your friend Leona," he said, "I'm going to mop the floor with her." Without another glance in her direction he slammed out of the house.

Chapter Seventeen

He shouldn't have lost his temper like that. He knew it, regretted it, but right now he was so mad he wanted to pound on the leather-covered steering wheel and scream obscenities into the chilly winter night. How could she be so childish, obtuse, criminally stupid? Didn't she realize how rare last night was? You don't just throw something like that away because you're too damned scared to face life.

And that was it. Sheer, simple cowardice on her part. Sex that good didn't come from physical sources alone. There had to be love, love on both sides, to bring the act of making love from a satisfying physical experience to something approaching heaven. When he'd left her this morning he'd been dazed, shaken and more than a little frightened himself. His feelings for her—physical, emotional, even spiritual—were like nothing he'd ever felt.

Right now his intellectual feelings for her were so intensely furious that they threatened to wipe out all those blissful emotions. He should have turned her over his knee and spanked her. Except even that thought was erotic. Damn her, damn her, damn her!

Well, she could have it her way. He'd leave her strictly alone, back in her safe, celibate world for a while, and see how she liked it. Within two weeks, by New Year's Eve, she'd be climbing the walls. And he'd be waiting for her, and this time it would be on his terms.

In the meantime he was going to do exactly what he said. He wasn't going to rest until he found out exactly what was going on with Leona Coleman. He had little doubt he had her to thank, at least partially, for Sybil's sudden withdrawal. Sybil wasn't going to trust him completely until she found out what a scheming, devious criminal Leona really was.

Of course, there was always the remote possibility that he was wrong about her. So far Ray hadn't been able to come up with a thing, but what with the Boston Slasher the police hadn't had much free time to play around with computers. All his instincts told him that Leona was a crook of the first order, and his instincts seldom lied.

Those same instincts told him that sooner or later Sybil would come to her senses, come to him, where she belonged. He just hoped this wasn't the one time wishful thinking took the place of those infallible instincts.

He was driving too fast down the snow-packed road, but he didn't care. Not that he was in any hurry to get back to the Black Farm. It would be cold, dark and lonely there, and the rumpled bed, so much smaller than the queen-size one he had in his apartment in Cambridge, would seem very large indeed. And would continue that way, for all the nights afterward that he had to sleep alone.

He'd give Ray another call tonight, see if he could prod him into finding something. Sybil Richardson was a very stubborn lady; it would take time or solid evidence that she was wrong to move her. And right now, time was the last thing he wanted to waste.

While he was at it, he might as well make a call to his real estate agent. There was no way six springer spaniels would fit into his current apartment.

"DON'T WORRY," Sybil said wryly as Leona popped her snowy white head around the front door of the Society of Water Witches two days later, "he's not coming in today, either. I think he's gone back to Boston for a few days."

"I knew that," Leona said, straightening to her full five feet and moving forward with dignity. "I dowsed it before I came. I just wanted to make certain."

"Don't you trust your dowsing?" The moment the words were out of her mouth Sybil could have bitten her tongue. It was all Nick's fault, this sudden doubt that was plaguing her. He was shaking the foundations of everything she held dear, from dowsing to Leona to what she wanted in life. Why couldn't he just go away and leave her alone?

Except, of course, that was just what he'd done for the past three days. And she didn't like it one bit.

"Of course I trust my dowsing. But your professor—"

"Not my professor—"

". . . is a changeable man. Unpredictable at best. That's why we have to do something about him." Leona plopped herself down on the straight chair beside the desk, her short plump legs dangling.

"I suppose so," Sybil said warily. "Do you have anything in mind?"

"It's got to be something to send him back to Massachusetts and away from us. Or at least something to keep him too busy to be chasing after me."

"Amen," said Sybil, thinking of her own particular chase.

"And I've come up with the perfect idea. We'll send him to see Everett Kellogg."

Sybil just stared at her with a mixture of doubt and admiration. "No one can get near Everett this time of year. I always wonder whether he'll make it through the winter up there, but every spring he shows up, hale and hearty. He must be past ninety."

"I expect he is. He's also one of the best dowsers around, and certainly the oldest. There are things he knows that no one else would, things that happened back at the turn of the century that would be invaluable to someone like your professor."

"Not my professor. And of course he'd be invaluable. That's exactly why I haven't mentioned him to Nick. There's no way, short of a helicopter, to get through to Everett before the spring thaw. And Nick's the sort of man who wouldn't believe me if I told him it couldn't be done."

"Exactly," said Leona, swinging her legs back and forth. "All you have to do is tell him about Everett and warn him that he can't make it. Your... Professor Fitzsimmons will do the rest."

"He could be killed, Leona," Sybil said quietly.

"Nonsense. He'll try to drive up through Gillam's Notch, wreck his fancy car and have to walk back down. He's supposed to be in England in less than a month; he won't have time to replace his car and finish his research. Even if he does, he'll be far more interested in getting to Everett than prying into my background."

"He's going to England?" Sybil echoed faintly.

"Didn't you know? He's here for research, and then he's going to Oxford for a year on a teaching and studying fellowship."

"Oh," Sybil said in a flat voice, trying to ignore the sense of betrayal that was rapidly building. Why in the world should she care if Nick was leaving the country? She wanted him out of her life, didn't she?

"The plan isn't foolproof," Leona admitted. "But it's better than nothing. With luck he'll get pneumonia. That should put him out of commission!"

"Leona!" Sybil hadn't liked the sound of malicious satisfaction in her friend's voice one bit. "Why can't we just send him a fake telegram or something, tell him he has to go to England sooner?"

"Because he'd check. Professor Fitzsimmons isn't the sort just to pack up on a moment's notice. He'd probably fight a summons like that just to be contentious. It's going to have to be Everett."

Sybil looked across at Leona's round, cherubic face, the dark, shining little eyes, the pursed mouth, the plump little legs swinging back and forth. "No, Leona," she said gently. "It's too dangerous. We want him to leave us alone, but we don't want to risk his life. You haven't thought it through."

"Of course I thought it through. Do you think I would endanger someone's life, no matter how much he deserved it?" She was clearly affronted. "I dowsed it. I read the tarot, I cast the runes and, just to make certain, I even used the Ouija board, antiquated as it is. It will be perfectly safe."

Sybil just looked at her. Everything was on the line; the moment was upon her faster than she'd ever dreaded. She was being called upon to risk Nick's life, and the only guarantee he'd be safe was Leona's powers—things Sybil believed in, worked for, things intrinsic to her very being. But could she risk Nick's life for them?

She would risk her own life, no question about it. If she was afraid of a dangerous situation and a dowser told her it was safe, she'd go into that situation full of trust. But she had no right to risk Nick's life. And when it came right down to it, was she trusting her beliefs, or trusting in Leona? No one was infallible, particularly in matters like these.

"No," she said firmly. "I can't let you do it."

For a brief moment Leona's face went perfectly blank. Then she shrugged her plump shoulders and smiled. "Well, it was a thought. We'll just have to come up with a better notion."

The tension that had been singing through Sybil's body vanished, and she smiled with real relief. "Don't worry, Leona. We'll figure out some way to get him off your case."

Leona smiled sweetly.

EVERY NIGHT when she drove past the Black Farm she searched for signs of habitation. It wasn't until four days before Christmas that she saw the lights down at the end of that long driveway, the thin plume of smoke swirling up into the blackening sky.

For half an hour she considered trumped-up excuses to visit him. For another half hour she berated herself for her weakness. For the third half hour she made plans. Whether she liked it or not, he had a devastating effect on her. The hoped-for lessening in her libido hadn't yet taken effect, and the last thing she wanted was to immure herself in that old building with only Nick around, with his mesmerizing eyes, thin, sexy mouth and absolutely luscious body....

Christmas shopping. Three days to Christmas, and she had a million things left to do. Her tree was standing in the corner farthest away from the drying effects of the wood stove, and the handmade ornaments and tiny white lights were beautiful and curiously depressing. Maybe if she bought some colored lights instead. And she had to get stockings for the dogs, presents for Dulcy and Leona and the Mullers, and some wool for her next project. The flame-colored sweater was finished, and it was her worst job ever. It was too big at the top, too narrow at the bottom, the arms would fit an orangutan and the color turned her sallow. If worse came to worst, she'd give it to Nick; it might give her a malicious thrill to see him forced to wear it.

But not tomorrow. She wanted a day to compose herself, a day just to do what she wanted without having to worry about Nick. He'd been gone for almost six days; no doubt he expected her to fall at his feet. Well, she wasn't about to warm his bed for a couple of weeks before he took off for England. He could damn well be just as celibate as she'd been. Or could go after Dulcy.

The next day wasn't everything Sybil had hoped for. Leona was more than willing to fill in at the office, and as Sybil drove by the Black Farm she saw a tall, familiar figure climbing into the dark green Jaguar. Her reaction was like a fist to the stomach. She stomped on the accelerator as hard as she could, fishtailing up the snow-covered road toward town.

Eschewing the limited pleasures of St. Johnsbury, she headed for Burlington, for yuppie stores with gourmet chocolate and Liz Claiborne and Celtic music and imported cheeses. She didn't get there often, and had every intention of spending a fortune.

She bought half a pound of Godiva chocolates and ate them all on the way home. She bought raspberry liqueur for the Muller sisters and a crystal for Leona. She bought dog stockings for the springers, silk stockings for Dulcy and nothing for herself. By the time she reached Danbury in midafternoon, the sun was already sinking lower in the gray December sky, her stomach was protesting the surfeit of chocolate, and she was very close to tears.

The green Jaguar was parked outside the Davis Apartments. For a moment panic swept through her, and then she remembered that Leona would be at the office. They'd hardly be in the midst of a dangerous confrontation. And he couldn't be in there searching her apartment—Gladys would have ripped his throat out.

She drove past, very slowly. He was parked in front of the Mullers' door. Sybil looked back at the liqueur. She had been planning to stop in on her way out to her house; she shouldn't let Nick's presence stop her. But was she ready to see him? She'd spent an almost wasted day in Burlington, simply to avoid him. Why spoil a perfect record of misery?

She reached the deserted center of town, pulled a skidding U-turn, and headed back to the Mullers, just in time to see the Jaguar pull away, heading out toward the old road to Barton.

Edla and Minna were just finishing up their tiny little glasses of sherry, and nothing would do but they had to share another with Sybil. She could see the third empty glass, the crumbs on the plate of Christmas cookies, but with great effort she waited, eating Miss Minna's freshly baked spritz cookies and sipping the sweet cream sherry.

It didn't take long to get to the subject, and Sybil didn't even have to bring it up. "I am worried about the professor, dear," Miss Edla said.

"Are you?" Sybil picked up a cookie shaped like a Christmas tree and licked the green sprinkles off it.

"Do you think what he's doing is particularly safe?"

She raised her head sharply, her brown eyes meeting Miss Edla's faded blue ones. "What do you mean?"

"Well, if Everett Kellogg wanted visitors, I don't think he'd live up in the Notch. And I think Leona must be wrong—the road must be impassable by now. I don't think the professor should be heading out.... Where are you going?"

"After him." Sybil had crammed the cookie into her mouth and jumped for her coat. "Was he going there this afternoon?"

"Somehow he got the idea that it was the best time to go. I think Leona must be very confused—she told him that the road went all the way through in the winter. Of course, we don't drive, but as I remember the road ends rather abruptly."

"Did you warn him?"

"Well, no, dear. After all, Leona gave him complete instructions, and she does drive. I couldn't very well contradict her, now could I?"

She crammed the hat down on her head. "He's heading for the Notch? He wasn't going anywhere else first?"

"He seemed to think we were due for another big storm, and if he didn't go now, then he wouldn't see Everett at all," Miss Minna said. "Funny, the weatherman didn't say anything about a storm."

"Damn," Sybil said. "Bye, ladies."

She ran from the apartment, slamming the door behind her, and leaped into her car like a stock car racer. The Subaru purred into life, bless its engine, and she tore into the road, narrowly missing a milk truck while skidding sideways toward several parked cars, and finally straightening herself and her four wheels. She took off down the road like a bat out of hell, cursing under her breath.

Leona simply didn't realize how dangerous it was. The temperature was hovering around ten degrees, and there wasn't a cloud in the sky. By the time the sun set and the half-moon had risen, the temperature would plummet, well below zero. And Nick would be out there, stuck in a snowdrift, with his damned city shoes on and his damned city clothes, and if he didn't get frostbite or worse he'd be a lucky man.

She should have known Leona wouldn't be discouraged so easily. She was a very stubborn woman, unfortunately convinced of her own infallibility. If her pendulum told her it was safe, she'd walk on water. And probably manage it, too, Sybil thought with a ghost of a smile. But Leona's self-assurance wasn't enough to keep Nick safe.

It was quarter to four, and the shadows were deepening around her on the deserted road. The old road to Barton was paved for the first three miles, and the coating of ice was treacherous indeed. Since the road went nowhere, only to a couple of farms, and then ended halfway up Gillam's Notch, it wasn't a high priority with the road crew. By the time she reached the gravel part, it hadn't even been plowed since the last storm.

The Jaguar tracks were ahead of her, narrow and elegant even with studded snow tires. But the green car was out of sight, heading for a road that ended in a snowbank or a cliff. He could take his pick.

And if it was dark, and he didn't know about the cliff, he might swerve to avoid that wall of snow left by the plow. There might be enough snow buildup along the side of the road to keep him from plunging over into the gulch, and there might not. Sybil shoved her booted foot down farther on the accelerator, ignoring the needle as it pushed past sixty.

The Subaru didn't like the speed. You weren't supposed to use the optional four-wheel drive at speeds above fifty, but there was no way she was going to careen down this road at any speed less than her maximum, and no way she'd do it in two-wheel drive. If the poor car self-destructed, well, cars can be replaced. Nick Fitzsimmons couldn't.

She left the dim lights of the last farmhouse behind her and started climbing. It was getting very dark now, that twilight time when headlights made no dent in the thickening shadows, and Sybil kept cursing and praying under her breath. She tried to send a mental cloud of healing blue light around Nick, but her anxiety and panic kept interfering with it. All she could do was curse and pray and drive on.

Higher and higher she climbed. In the darkness she couldn't remember where the road usually ended, and out of necessity she slowed her desperate pace. As long as he didn't go over the cliff, she'd get there in time. But despite all the heavy snow of late November and December, snowbanks along the narrow road were less than a foot high. A determined driver with the power of a Jaguar could go right through them.

In the end she almost crashed into him. Rounding a corner, she saw the taillights of the car, jammed into the wall of snow ahead of them, and she slammed on her brakes, skidding sideways, heading directly toward the driver's seat of the Jaguar, directly toward Nick's waiting figure.

It took endless moments as she lifted her panicked foot off the brakes and began to pump them, gently, as she'd always been told to do and had never quite mastered. It would be a hell of a note, she thought, with her mind floating miles away, if she smashed into him and killed him while she was trying to save his life.

The Subaru slowed, slowed, slowed, sliding like a graceful figure skater, crossing the last few feet and coming to a gentle, delicate stop against the door of the Jaguar with no more sound than the gentle whisper of metal on metal.

Nick turned and glared at her as she sat there, dazed. With shaking hands she turned the key, only to find that the car hadn't stalled out after all. The starter shrieked in protest, and she shifted it into reverse, backing away, slowly, carefully, taking green paint with her.

It was a colorful gash down the side of the Jaguar, a rip in its elegant hide, but barely a dent to mar it. Nick climbed out, very tall, very angry in the moonlit darkness of the mountain, and stalked over toward her.

She sat there, unmoving, not even opening the window. He yanked open the door and pulled her out. "What the hell are you doing here?" he demanded.

"Wrecking your car?" she offered, her voice a nervous thread.

"It's not wrecked." He didn't even bother to give it a cursory glance. "Steve can tow it out tomorrow. I want to know how you knew I'd be up here."

"The Muller sisters said you were going to find Everett, and I didn't think it was safe..." she faltered.

"Leona said it would be."

"Leona hasn't been up here in a while. Besides, I told her it would be passable until after Christmas, but then, I thought about it and realized it wouldn't be, and when I heard you were coming up here I figured you might not make it...." She was stammering and stumbling as the lies bubbled forth, and it was all a waste of breath.

"I don't believe you," he said flatly. "I think you found out Leona was trying to set me up and you came after me. I don't know if you did it to save me or to keep Leona from making an even worse mistake."

"Leona didn't realize—"

"Why did you come, Sybil?" The anger was gone. His eyes were dark and glittering in the moonlight, his face silvered and dangerous.

"I didn't want you to freeze to death," she said, shivering a little herself.

He just looked at her. "Then come here and warm me up."

Her feet crossed the short space that separated them, and she went into his arms. She was right, he was wearing city clothes and city shoes, and he was cold, so cold. She opened her down coat to press her own warmth against him, wrapping her arms around him and pulling him closer. It seemed only natural for her mouth to reach up for his, only natural to kiss him, breathe her warm, sweet breath into his mouth, rub her tongue against his, her hips against his, her legs against his.

She found she was shivering, not with cold, but with another basic need that threatened to overpower her. And she wished it were a hot summer's night instead of hovering around zero.

Nick lifted his head, and his breath was frosty in the night air. "I think I'm warm," he said. "As a matter of fact, I think I'm burning up. Let's get out of here."

Sybil took a deep breath, looking around her. "We're going to have to back all the way down the mountain."

"That's all right," he said with the ghost of a smile. "As long as you let me drive."

"I'll let you drive," she said. *I'll let you do anything,* she thought. And moving away, she climbed into the passenger seat and waited.

Chapter Eighteen

It was a long, slow drive back down the mountain. Sybil stayed silent, sitting there beside him as he maneuvered the treacherous twists and turns of the narrow roadway. The heater was on full blast, making a small dent in the rapidly chilling air, and she shivered slightly, pulling her unzipped coat closer around her. She hated to think of what might have happened, of Nick trying to walk the five or so miles down the mountain to the nearest farmhouse.

Once he'd made it to the bottom of the hill he turned the Subaru deftly, heading onto the straightaway with his eyes trained outward. She spared a cautious glance at his profile. It looked cold and severe, grim and unyielding, and she shivered again.

"I know what you're thinking," she said.

He didn't spare her a glance. "Do you? I thought you said your psychic abilities were extremely limited."

"A maple tree has enough psychic ability to guess what you're thinking," she snapped, flustered. "It was a mistake, Nick."

"Humph," he said.

"I'm sure Leona had no idea the road was impassable. She doesn't drive up this way; she wouldn't know that it was already closed."

"Really?" His tone was unpromising.

"I know that's hard to believe when someone is as paranoid as you are, but it was entirely coincidental. Leona isn't the monster you seem to think she is; I'm sure she just wanted to help you out."

"Help me out of this mortal coil, don't you mean?"

"Don't be absurd. You wouldn't have died, anyway. You'd have made it to a farmhouse before you froze to death."

"Unless I went off the cliff."

Sybil shivered again. "She doesn't know the terrain. It's just lucky the Mullers told me where you were heading. Leona will be beside herself when she finds out what happened."

"Beside herself that I didn't go over the cliff."

"You're going to believe what you want to believe," she said wearily. "How can I convince you that she meant no harm?"

Nick turned to look at her, his face illuminated by the bright winter moonlight reflecting off the snow. "I should take everything she told me at face value?" he countered softly.

There was a trap, she knew it, but she was too overwrought to guess what it was. "Absolutely," she said.

"Then if what she told me was true, why did you leave me the message about Everett Kellogg?" he said in a silky voice. "According to Leona, you told her to tell me about him. It was your suggestion I visit him today, before the snows got worse. It was your suggestion that I take the Notch road, and not bother to wait until morning. What happened, Sybil? Did you change your mind, decide maybe it wasn't time for me to meet my doom?"

She was shocked into a profound, utter silence. "You don't believe that," she said finally, her voice rusty.

"Give me an alternative. I'll be interested to see how you do it without implicating your good buddy. Either Leona lied to me and did her best to get me killed or at least incapacitated, or you're feeling a great deal more hostile than I imagined."

"Neither."

He glanced at her, and his thin mouth twisted in a smile that was only half cynical. "Okay. Let's hear your explanation."

She took a deep breath. "It's very simple," she said. "Leona must have misunderstood."

"Sure she did."

"I . . . we talked about Everett this week," she said, thanking heaven that much was true. "And we wondered whether it was too late for you to get up to see him. We were going to check with the people who live out this way, to see if the road was still open, before we told you. You're so headstrong you'd have come up here anyway, even if I told you it was impassable."

"I would have done it in broad daylight, driving slowly, with the proper clothes on in case I got stuck. So you and Leona were going to check and see whether it was safe, were you?"

"Yes," she said, grateful he was swallowing it. Enough of it was true—Leona had to have misunderstood the dangers of the situation. Leona was so certain her dowsing was infallible; she really would be horrified when she found out the danger Nick had been in. Wouldn't she?

"You're lying."

She swiveled around in the seat, staring at him as shock and hurt sliced deep within her. "How could you believe that I'd want to hurt you? I want you to go away and leave me alone, but I want you to go in one piece, of your own accord. How could you think . . . ?"

"I don't think you sent me up there, Sybil," he said as he turned the Subaru down her driveway. "I think you're covering up for Leona, and even worse, I think you're still trying to convince yourself that she wasn't trying to kill me."

"Nick..."

"But right now I don't really care. I'm taking your car, whether you like it or not. I'm going home and take a hot bath, and then I'll call the garage and maybe, just maybe, the police."

"How can I convince you—"

"You can't." He slammed the car to a stop, turned off the ignition and glared at her.

She considered pleading with him, considered and then abandoned the idea. He'd do what he had to do; nothing she said would change his mind. She'd already come up with the best excuses, and none of them worked. Worst of all, she couldn't rid herself of the suspicion that he might be right.

"When will I get my car back? I have to work tomorrow."

"Call Leona," he snapped.

She unhooked her seat belt and slid out of the seat, shivering in the icy night air. She could hear the dogs howling and scrabbling at the front door in their desperation to get out and greet them properly. "Better get out of here fast," she said in a subdued voice, "or the dogs will follow you halfway home."

There was no sound from the aging engine as she headed toward her front door. She could feel Nick's eyes on her, but she didn't look back. The back seat of the car was filled with the Christmas presents she'd bought that day in Burlington, and they could damned well stay there. The sooner he was out of there the better.

The dogs swarmed over her, yipping a joyous greeting, wiggling and twirling in midair in their enthusiasm. They made so much noise she didn't even realize that Nick had come up behind her.

"You're half frozen," he said gruffly over the barking of the dogs. "And so am I." He pushed her, gently enough, through the open door, and the dogs swarmed after them.

At least the house was still relatively warm. The temperature had only just begun to plummet, the banked fire in the wood stove had kept the heat at a bearable level, and it took her no more than a few nudges with the poker and a couple of pieces of dry wood to get a satisfying blaze going. Closing the cast-iron door, she turned to look up at Nick.

He was standing there, towering over her crouching body, tall and dark and menacing. He was dressed in black—black cords, black sweater, a long black topcoat better suited to city streets over everything. He'd unbuttoned the coat and was in the midst of shrugging it off when he caught her quizzical eye.

"I thought you wanted a hot bath," she said.

"I could always take one here."

"No, you can't," she said.

A faint smile creased the stern contours of his dark face. "Are you throwing me out?"

She rose to her full height, her muscles and bones protesting the cold and her own weariness. "I'll give you coffee and cognac to warm you," she said grudgingly. "And then you can leave."

"I can think of better ways to get warm."

"I'm sure you can," she said. "But I'm not in the mood for a little slap and tickle right now." She began unwinding her tattered scarf from around her neck. She'd left the

Christmas tree lights on, and their glow was an unwanted romantic touch in the cluttered, cozy living room. With chilled fingers she began to unzip her down coat, ignoring the cloud of feathers that floated around her.

He moved so quickly she had no time to duck, if she had even wanted to. His hands brushed her numb ones away, unfastening the coat and pushing it off her shoulders. It landed in a feathery pile at their feet, but they both ignored it.

"What are you in the mood for, Saralee?" he murmured, his voice low and seductive.

"To be left alone."

She didn't sound terribly convincing, and he made no move to release her. "What if I said I don't believe you?"

"If I had any sense at all I'd mean it." She pushed against him, a token protest. To her dismay he released her, moving across the room to stand looking at the Christmas tree.

"Do you have any sense?" The question was idly spoken; he seemed more interested in the way the silver tinsel fluttered against the green spruce than in her answer.

"Sometimes I doubt it. And sometimes I wonder if I wouldn't have been far better off if you hadn't started messing with potions, if Dulcy hadn't decided to interfere, if I just weren't so damned gullible," she said, her voice raw with the effort her honesty cost her.

He turned his face from the tree, and she could see the tiny white lights reflected in his golden eyes. "You think magic is to blame for this? You think spells and potions and Dulcy's disputed powers are responsible for the attraction between us?" His voice mocked her. "You are too gullible."

"It certainly wasn't common sense that made me fall in love with you," she shot back, stung, too angry to catch the words before they flew.

He was very still now, watching and waiting in the dimly lighted room. The fire in the wood stove crackled cheerfully; the Christmas lights danced around their motionless figures. "In love with me?" he echoed, startled. As if considering something new, she thought bitterly. "As in get married, have babies and live happily ever after fall in love?" he asked.

Sybil was busy cursing her unruly tongue. "I never said anything about that."

"I did."

She stared at him, astonished. She shook her head, as if to clear away the mist of confusion, and sank down in the corner of the sofa, curling in on herself in an instinctive posture of defensiveness. "Don't play games, Nick," she said. She'd wanted her voice to be cool, sharp. It came out absurdly wistful.

"I'm not playing games." Still he moved no closer. "I'm asking you to define your terms. You just said you're in love with me. What does that mean?"

"It means I'm lonely and depressed and ready to fall for the first good-looking man who comes my way," she said somewhat desperately.

His eyes were alight with cynical amusement. "So at least I qualify as a good-looking man."

"But you're the wrong man for me. We both know it. All my life I've been programmed for someone like you; I even married someone like you when I was too stupid to know what I was doing. But it didn't work, and it wouldn't work this time. I need someone gentle, supportive, undemanding, someone who shares my beliefs and interests, who loves the outdoors and winter and the simple life. I don't need an upscale, cynical professor and a yuppie life-style.''

"I don't remember offering."

"You didn't. I'm just making sure you don't."

He nodded, the grin vanished. "So what you're looking for is a cross between Alan Alda and Frosty the Snowman, maybe with a touch of Saint Francis on the side. And you think that will make you happy?"

"It's what I need."

"Bull." He crossed the room in two long strides, and he was looming over her, staring down at her, all frustration and sexual menace. "I'm what you want, you stupid little fool, but you think you don't need me. I'm what you need, but you tell yourself you don't want me. You sit there and lie to yourself, telling yourself some mythical creature will solve all your problems when I'm right here, waiting for you."

His voice was clipped, furious, as he continued. "Sooner or later you're going to have to grow up. Sooner or later you're going to stop playing these mystical parlor games and accept the fact that what we think is true, what we want to be true, isn't always the answer. You'd walk all over your dream lover, you'd get bored with him in a matter of days. If you ever found him at all. And as long as you keep looking for him, you're safe from the de-mands of real life, you're safe from me."

She didn't move, didn't say a word, just sat there, star-ing up at him, as the words lashed over her. "Well, lady," he said, slowly straightening up, "I'll give you what you think you want. And I'll give you what you think you need. I'll leave you alone."

She managed to pull herself out of her dazed stupor. "Good," she said, her voice a whisper.

His mouth twisted into a dour smile. "I'll be waiting, Saralee. But I won't wait forever." And without another word he slammed out of the house, leaving his topcoat behind.

She sat there, listening to the sound of her Subaru as it sped up the shallow incline of her driveway, listened until it faded into the distance. The room was warm; it was time to damp down the stove. It was now just two days before Christmas, her tree was beautiful, and she had just gotten rid of a nuisance.

His coat was lying at her feet. Reaching down, she pulled it around her, wrapping the warmth and scent of it around her. And leaning her face against the sofa, she shut her eyes and wept.

"WHAT ARE YOU DOING for Christmas Eve?" Dulcy carried a tray of empty punch cups into the kitchen at the Society of Water Witches. She and Sybil were cleaning up after their traditional Christmas Eve open house, and for four hours Sybil had managed to forget the ache in her heart.

Of course, Nick's failure to appear helped matters, she told herself as she tossed the plastic cups into the trash and shoved the forty-seventh sugar cookie into her mouth. She hadn't seen him since he'd stormed from her house two days ago. Steve had brought the Subaru back for her, and all her devious attempts at pumping him got her exactly nowhere.

For that matter, Leona had been pretty scarce. The next day Sybil had tracked her down and read her the riot act about Nick's near miss. Her reaction had been everything Sybil could have hoped for. Shock, dismay, disappointment, all showed quite clearly on Leona's cherubic face. If Sybil wondered whether those emotions reached her tiny, dark eyes, she knew it was only Nick's contagious suspicions that made her doubt her old friend.

Leona hadn't showed up today for fear of running into Nick. And Nick probably hadn't showed up today for fear of running into either of them. For all she knew he might have gone back to Cambridge for the holidays. He probably had family somewhere; he couldn't have just appeared out of nowhere. Somewhere there must be parents, siblings, close friends, all of whom wanted him a great deal more than she did.

"Well?" Dulcy said patiently.

"Well, what?"

"What are you doing tonight? I know you've managed to put off your family again. Do you want to come over to my place, or do you have other plans?"

"You don't celebrate Christmas, Dulcy."

She shrugged her elegant shoulders. "Saturnalia's close enough."

"Somehow I just don't think so," Sybil said. "Pagan festivals and earth religions are all well and good, but when it comes to Christmas I get very traditional and sentimental."

"When it comes right down to it you are a WASP, aren't you, darling? A good little white Anglo-Saxon Protestant, with all those Christian hang-ups?" she mocked lightly.

Sybil refused to rise to the bait. "It doesn't do any good to run away from what you are." No sooner were the damning words out of her mouth than she bit her lip.

Dulcy smiled. "Exactly what I've been trying to tell you, Sybil. Think about it."

"I'm not going to think about anything but a good night's sleep," she said firmly.

"Then you're not going to see Nick?"

"I don't even know if he's in town."

"He's in town, all right. He's going to be all alone at the Black Farm this evening. He has to go back to Massachusetts tomorrow, but for now he's— Why are you looking at me like that?"

Very carefully Sybil set the last tray of cookies down on the counter, very carefully she took a gingerbread girl and bit its head off. "Since you seem to know so much about his plans," she said gently, "why don't you go and keep him company?"

Dulcy threw back her head and laughed, a delightful, full-throated trill of mirth that left Sybil stonily unmoved. "Your jealousy is reassuring, darling. I was afraid you were too far gone. I know all about Nick's plans because I asked him. And I asked him when he called me on some trumped-up excuse to find out what you were doing. I've told you before, Sybil. He doesn't want me, he wants you. You're not usually so obtuse."

Sybil crammed the rest of the cookie into her mouth. In the past two days she hadn't gone a waking hour without eating, she'd probably gained fifty pounds, and all the sugar was making her hyper and sick to her stomach. She reached for another cookie, this time a gingerbread boy, and contemplated where to bite first. "It won't work, Dulcy."

But Dulcy was tired of arguing. "If you say so," she said, whisking the remaining cookies out of Sybil's reach and dumping them back into a decorative tin. "If you change your mind, give me a call. I'll be home casting spells for the New Year."

"Not on me," she begged.

Dulcy only smiled.

Chapter Nineteen

There were distinct advantages to living alone, Sybil told herself later that evening. You could do exactly what you wanted, when you wanted and how you wanted. The trick was, taking advantage of all that freedom.

The Danbury Church of Christ had an early service on Christmas Eve, and Sybil had dutifully attended. When she got home at half past eight she turned out all the lights and lighted every candle in the house; she roasted herself a Cornish game hen stuffed with wild rice; she poured herself a glass of the best Chardonnay to be found in the state of Vermont; and she dressed herself in her favorite Christmas dress, made of red velvet, with a deep, square neckline, leg o' mutton sleeves and a full swirling skirt that reached the floor. She even put on lacy underwear and rhinestone-clocked stockings, and turned the radio to a station with the mushiest, most sentimental Christmas music she could find. With the dogs around her, she settled down to enjoy her Christmas Eve.

Normally her taste in music was somewhat more sophisticated, but for now she abandoned the Montreal-based New Wave station and settled for Mel Torme roasting chestnuts on an open fire, with Nat King Cole nipping at his nose. She sat there in her living room, the spaniels around her, picking at her game hen, sipping her exquisite wine and letting the sentimental images of Christmas pile up around her like a midwinter snowstorm.

It wasn't the first Christmas Eve she'd spent in solitary splendor. She usually enjoyed herself tremendously, far more than if she were dragged from cocktail party to open house in the determinedly festive environs of Princeton. Their family celebration had usually consisted of a massive, formal dinner on Christmas Day, followed by the anticlimactic opening of a few, very expensive presents, followed by more parties. There were times when her family seemed addicted to their hordes of friends; certainly a celebration like Christmas seemed more an excuse for socializing than for family get-togethers.

No, she was much happier up here in her snug little cottage, with a light dusting of snow falling outside, a real blue spruce she'd cut herself and dragged home shining cheerfully in the corner, her dogs around her and nowhere to rush off to.

Sybil wrinkled her nose as the radio played a particularly syrupy Andy Williams song, full of candy canes and holly and easy imagery. She preferred Mel Torme's elegant simplicity, or "White Christmas," no matter how many times she heard it.

She gave up on the game hen. It was delicious, but after two days of nonstop eating she'd suddenly lost her appetite. Even the Chardonnay was dull. She took her dishes out to the kitchen, dumped them in the sink and wandered back into the living room.

The presents beneath the tree were wrapped in brightly colored paper. Maybe she was more like her parents than she expected—she was feeling depressed, restless, lonely. She could change her clothes and take Dulcy her present, even visit the Mullers. But no, the Mullers would be at the party held for residents of the Davis Apartments. And Leona would be there, and right now Leona was the last person Sybil wanted to see.

Dulcy would be home, alone. But when it came right down to it, Dulcy wasn't whom she wanted, either. Sybil sank down on the ancient Persian carpet in front of the wood stove, leaning her back against the foot of the sofa, hugging her red velvet knees. For the first time in years, she didn't want to be alone on Christmas Eve.

"Don't be a fool," she said out loud, and Kermit raised his head and woofed softly. "You're well rid of him." With a sigh, she rested her head on her knees.

Andy Williams faded in a rush of strings. Then it was Judy Garland, younger than Sybil had ever been, singing "Have Yourself a Merry Little Christmas."

It was the last straw. She sat there, her head on her knees, and wept, tears of loneliness, misery and despair, as the snow drifted down outside her windows and the tree twinkled brightly in the cluttered living room. The dogs moved closer in mute sympathy, but nothing helped. She sat there and cried, tears pouring down her face and running into her long mane of freshly washed hair, cried until she started coughing and choking, cried until she began pounding the floor in fury.

The song on the radio had long since switched to something more saccharine when Sybil finally raised her tear-streaked face. "You complete, utter fool," she said softly. "What the hell are you doing, sitting alone on Christmas Eve, crying, when the man you love is less than five minutes away?"

It took her fifteen minutes to get ready. It was already past ten, and she didn't bother to change her clothes, didn't bother to braid her long hair, didn't bother to do anything more than scoop up Nick's present, pull her leaking down coat around her and call Dulcy. And even that was eerily abrupt.

"Dulcy?" she said, slightly breathless. "Are you going to Canada tomorrow?"

A low, friendly laugh answered her. "I'll come and get the dogs."

"But—"

"That's what you wanted, wasn't it?"

"Yes."

"So run off to your nemesis. Give him a kiss for me," Dulcy said cheerfully.

A sudden, peculiar suspicion flitted through Sybil's mind. "You didn't really want him, did you?"

"Truthfully?"

"Truthfully."

Dulcy's laugh was only slightly strained. "Let's just say I would have been willing to try. But he came here for you, not for me, and I learned long ago not to fight what was meant to be. You can have him with my blessing, Sybil. Just don't throw him away without a good reason."

"Dulcy..."

"I'll get the dogs. Merry Christmas, Sybil."

"Merry Christmas, Dulcy."

Her knee-high rubber barn boots were a little strange with the long red dress, and her long hair was covered with snow as she trudged out to the Subaru, the package under her arm. She decided against giving him any warning. Last time she'd seen him he had slammed out of her house. He might need a bit of persuading. Then again, she thought, remembering the burning light in his amber eyes, he might not.

She drove with far more than her usual care down the road to the Black Farm. Tonight of all nights she didn't want to risk sliding off the road; tonight of all nights she wanted to take her time, to make sure she knew what she was doing. The closer she got to the farm, the stronger her self-assurance grew. When it came to being half a mile apart and alone and miserable, or together and happy, there really wasn't much of a contest.

He'd learned his lesson well—the front door was unlocked. The Jaguar was parked by the barn, and Sybil winced as she spied the long, jagged scar along the door. The Subaru had definitely come off the best in this encounter, probably because it had less to lose.

She didn't knock; she just stepped into the hall and shut the door silently behind her. The living room was deserted. She could hear the sound of dishes in the kitchen and the faint sound of someone humming. Clearly he wasn't as bereft as she was, to be humming cheerfully to himself. For a moment she considered leaving, then steeled herself, slipping off the rubber boots and dumping her coat on the floor.

She moved across the chilly floors silently, the package crinkling in her hands. He'd found himself a Christmas tree, slightly lopsided, with multicolored lights and shimmering glass balls. He'd opened up the wood stove to expose the fire, the lights were low, and he was playing the same radio station she was. Had he heard "Have Yourself a Merry Little Christmas" and thought of her? Or had he preferred Andy Williams?

She set the package under the tree. Then, on impulse, she sat beside it, cross-legged, her long hair hanging around her shoulders; sat there and waited.

The scent of freshly brewed coffee mixed with the rich scent of pine above her. It was another five minutes before he appeared in the living room, a steaming mug in his hands, his gaze abstracted. He walked over to the sofa and sank down on it, never once glancing in her direction.

He was wearing the black sweat suit he'd worn the night they were caught in the storm. He looked weary, dangerous and very, very sexy. Sybil just sat there, waiting for him to notice her, waiting for some reaction.

What she got was the fifty-third rendition of "Little Drummer Boy." The fire in front of Nick crackled and popped, illuminating his shadowed face, his distant eyes. Sybil got tired of waiting.

"Ahem," she said.

"Jesus Christ!" Nick swore, almost spilling his coffee. He caught it in time, leaping up from the couch, and he opened his mouth to curse again. Then he saw her.

"It is His birthday," Sybil said demurely, keeping the mischievous grin off her face with a Herculean effort.

Nick stood very still, his anger vanishing as swiftly as it came. "And what are you? A birthday present?"

Sybil shrugged, her thick honey-colored hair bunching around her narrow shoulders. "Birthday present, Christmas present. Whatever you prefer."

"How about a wedding present?"

She could feel the color drain from her face. Once more she tried to drum up excuses. He wasn't what she wanted, he wasn't what she needed, it would only end in disaster, she should run like hell.

"Yes," she said simply. "Yes." And she held up her arms to him.

"YOU'RE MAKING a big mistake," she said. Her voice came out slightly muffled, since her face was pressed against his bare shoulder and her mouth was busy trailing lazy, satisfying kisses on his warm, sweat-damp skin.

"Am I?" he murmured sleepily, pulling her closer into his arms. A trail of clothing led from the bed into the living room, with the red dress a swirl of color under the

Christmas tree. The fire had burned down low, and the multicolored lights from the tree were the only illumination in the bedroom. Sybil could feel his tawny eyes on her, watching her with sleepy satisfaction.

"I'm not the right sort of wife for you," she said, feeling it only fair to warn him. "I'm not cut out to be a faculty wife, I don't want to live in a condo, I don't want you to wear a tweed coat with leather patches and smoke a pipe."

"I hate pipes. And I'm not tweedy. And we'll buy a house in the country, with plenty of room for the dogs."

"But I'm not the kind of woman you want," she wailed, miserable at the halcyon picture she could so easily imagine. It snowed in Massachusetts, just not so damned much, and they could have a barn and a pond for the dogs to swim in and babies. . . .

"No," he said. "You're not the *kind* of woman I want. But since you happen to be *the* woman I want, I guess I'll have to make do."

"I failed once," she muttered against his skin. "I couldn't be what Colin wanted me to be."

"You already are what I want you to be," he said, his hand trailing down her backbone, stroking, strengthening, soothing.

"But what if you change your mind . . . ?"

"What if you change your mind? There aren't any guarantees in this life, Sybil."

"No," she said, doubt and misery thick in her voice.

"The only guarantee," he said, "is love."

She moved her head then, to look up at him. He looked so beautiful he took her breath away. "Do you love me?"

He smiled, a slow, infinitely tender smile that banished the last of her doubts. "Completely," he said, rolling her onto her back and leaning over her.

She looked up at him. "I can fight love potions," she said, "and I can fight Dulcy's interference. I can even fight my own heart. But there's no way I can resist you, too." Sliding her arms around his neck, she pulled him down to meet her hungry lips.

SHE DIDN'T GET OUT OF BED till late morning, and by that time Nick had already left. There was no way he could get out of it; his old friends Ray and Connie were counting on him. He'd drive down, have Christmas dinner with them, invite them to the wedding and be back before midnight. The Jaguar was capable of highly illegal speeds and the interstates down to Boston were kept clear.

She didn't put up any arguments. Indeed, she wasn't in the mood to argue about anything, from wedding dates to guest lists to the uses of dowsing. And he never brought up the subject of Leona.

If she'd had any doubts, the Christmas presents wiped them out. She had finished the flame-colored sweater, despairing of its shape and size. As always the hips were too narrow, the sleeves too long, the shoulders too big to fit anyone, but she'd wrapped it to give to Nick anyway, partly because he'd teased her about it, partly because the color of the wool complemented the fire in his disturbing topaz eyes. He laughed when he opened it, laughed when he pulled it on. It fit perfectly.

"I give up," she said, falling back against the pillows. "Everything I knit comes out looking like that. I must have known you were coming."

"Via your Ouija board?" he mocked gently.

"Tarot," she said lazily. "Where's my present?"

"What makes you think I got you anything? Last I knew we weren't speaking; as far as I knew I wasn't going to see you again."

"You knew," she said amiably enough. "What have you got for me? I can just imagine."

She caught it when he tossed it, a small black velvet bag with something heavy inside. A stone of some sort. She opened it, and a deep blue pendulum tumbled out onto the bed.

"I don't believe it," she whispered. "It's Cleopatra's pendulum."

"A copy, I'm told," he drawled.

"The real one is in a museum in Alexandria. I heard they had made a few copies, but I never hoped to own one," she said, picking it up with reverential fingers. "It's beautiful. It must be lapis lazuli. How did you guess that I desperately wanted one? I wouldn't have thought you even knew they existed."

"I dowsed it."

She grinned up at him. "Sure you did. Did Dulcy tell you?" Carefully she squashed down the tiny spurt of jealousy, cradling the wonderful weight of the pendulum in her hand.

"The Mullers," he said.

"Do I have time to thank you properly?" she murmured in a dulcet voice.

"Do I end up like Marc Antony and Julius Caesar?" he responded, moving closer.

She slid her arms around his waist, up under the soft wool sweater that fit him so well. "Not so long as you behave yourself," she said. "Anyway, I wasn't talking about sex. I thought I could dowse whether or not you'd have a good trip."

"I'd rather have sex."

She grinned. "We could always do both. You'll have to take off the sweater, though—you'll give me a rash."

"I wish I could say the same for the pendulum," he said morosely, stripping the sweater over his head and climbing back on the bed.

SYBIL WAS SINGING her own mangled version of "Have Yourself a Merry Little Christmas" as she brewed herself a cup of strong black coffee. Judy Garland in her prime, she wasn't, and she didn't know all the words, but at least she could carry a tune. And that particular tune had become even more special to her since last night.

The doorbell rang and Sybil jumped, cursing slightly as the boiling coffee slopped over her hand. "Come in," she called out, wiping up the spilled mess. It was only one o'clock, too early for Nick to return. She ran her damp hands down the sides of Nick's nightshirt and headed for the door.

Leona was standing there, small, huddled, her dark eyes shining. "I thought that was your voice I heard," she said.

Sybil immediately steeled herself for the disapproval she knew would be her lot, but for some reason it wasn't forthcoming. "Is the professor here?" she murmured, wandering past her into the living room.

Sybil had picked up the trail of clothing, but if she hoped to fool Leona it was a wasted effort. Not that she had anything to hide, she reminded herself forcefully.

She moved ahead of her diminutive friend, diverting her from the bedroom. "He's gone down to Boston for the day. He'll be back sometime after midnight."

Leona allowed herself to be led toward the couch, her face calm and oddly abstracted. "Just for the day, eh? We'll have to move fast."

"I beg your pardon?"

Leona looked up at her, her cherubic face wreathed in smiles. "I can see you two have cleared up your differences. I'm so glad."

"You are?"

"Of course. I had my doubts about your professor when I first met him. And he certainly has been more than mistaken about me. But I'm sure we'll have everything cleared up in the next few days, and we'll all be great friends. Did he...did he say what he was going to Boston for? To see his family, perhaps?"

"Old friends," Sybil supplied, sitting down in the chair and crossing her legs under her. "I'm glad you're so understanding. Nick's just got this weird fixation about you. I'm sure it'll be a simple enough matter to prove him wrong, if we just all sit down and talk it out."

"I'm sure," Leona murmured. "So here you are on Christmas Day, alone, with nothing to do."

"Oh, I have all sorts of things to keep me busy. I was going to bring the dogs over, and then maybe fix something fancy for dinner."

"None of that will take very long," she said. "Indulge an old lady, Sybil. Give me a couple of hours of your time today as a Christmas present."

"Didn't you like the Herkimer diamond I got you?" Sybil teased. "You can't imagine how much trouble it was, finding that particular crystal."

"Of course I did. And that's what I want you for. If we do another past-life regression, with you holding the crystal, there's no limit to the possibilities. We both know that any meditations, any dreams we have while holding on to a Herkimer diamond are increased tenfold." Leona's eyes were shining with unfeigned excitement. "We never did finish that night—your professor misunderstood. Give me one last chance, Sybil. Who knows when we'll have another one?''

Sybil sat very still. For some reason she didn't want to, she didn't want to give over her trust to Leona; she didn't want to search back for past lives, especially for that poor Frenchwoman with her murdered lover. She wanted to stay here, alone, with maybe her dogs for company, and wait for Nick to return.

But what she wanted and what she was going to do were two different things. She'd be leaving Leona soon enough, it would be their last chance, and she owed it to the old lady. Besides, what harm would it do? She'd never been afraid of anything she might find out before; now wasn't the time to start.

"Okay," she said. "Let's do it."

"Not here."

"What do you mean, not here?" Sybil looked over her shoulder at the comfortable, welcoming room.

"The vibrations are crowded and uncertain. A skeptic has been living here, and a man was brutally murdered here long ago. The auras still linger."

Give me a break, Sybil thought, and then was shocked at her irreverence. "Okay. Where do we go?"

Leona smiled—a smug, pleased little smile—and her raisin eyes were like little lumps of coal. "I know just the place."

Chapter Twenty

"Congratulations!" Ray slapped him on the back, grinning like a fool. Nick knew he was grinning back, equally foolishly, and then Connie flung herself into his arms.

"It's about time!" she said. "Who's the poor girl? Another amazon? Let me guess—a lawyer? Someone who works for PBS? A museum curator?"

"A psychic," Nick said, and watched with real delight as absolute incomprehension swept across their faces.

"A what?" Connie gasped.

"A psychic. Except that she doesn't have much talent. A dowser, but she can't dowse. She runs an occult bookstore but it's always in the red. She knits passably well—" he gestured to the sweater hugging his torso "—and she's the secretary of the SOWWs. Society of Water Witches to you guys."

"But you don't believe in most of those things," Connie said helplessly.

"No. But I believe in Sybil."

"Have you two got anything in common at all, Nick?"

"Sure. She believes in everything until it's proved false, I doubt everything until it's proved true. We'll balance each other out."

"But—"

"Don't worry, Connie. All you have to do is meet her and you'll understand."

"I don't believe it," Ray said softly.

"Don't believe what?"

"The man is finally in love."

"I was in love with Adelle. Not in the same way, but..."

"No, you weren't," Connie said firmly. "Take it from an expert, I know love when I see it, and you and Adelle weren't in it. And Ray's right. You've got a wicked case of it right now, praise God. I couldn't ask for a better Christmas present. I just hope she deserves you."

"I hope I deserve her."

"Humility and everything," Ray said in disgust. "Come on in and have some eggnog. The kids have torn the living room apart, but we should be able to find a small corner of peace and quiet. Then I can tell you about your friends the Longermans."

"The Longermans?" Nick trailed after Ray's portly figure, stepping over the dismantled plastic monsters, the wadded-up wrapping paper, the crushed candy canes.

"Leona and James Longerman. James is in Attica right now, doing ten to fifteen for fraud. Apparently he was making a nice little living, bilking little old ladies out of their life savings. Leona got off with a slap of the wrist, but it was clear she was the brains behind the operation. James is up for parole tomorrow, and it looks as if he's going to get out in time to celebrate New Year's Eve with the little woman. Unless you've got something to keep him in there."

"Damn her," Nick swore. "I knew it, I just knew there was something going on. She's up to her old tricks, ripping off the widows in Danbury. God knows what she's done with the money...."

"I wouldn't be surprised if it was stashed up in Canada. You're not far from the border up there—it would be an easy thing to do. She's probably been building up a nest egg, waiting for James to be released."

"I don't suppose you brought any proof home with you? Sybil's not what I call trusting."

"I thought you said she was gullible."

"Unfortunately, not where I'm concerned," he said. "She's very loyal." He heard the telephone ring in the background, but its beep blended in with all the noise from the electronic toys around them.

"I have computer printouts. Will that be enough to shake her loyalty?"

"It should help." He took the cup of eggnog Ray handed him and sighed. "I just hope I don't have too hard a time convincing her."

"Nick?" Connie appeared in the doorway. "Telephone's for you. A woman."

"Sybil," he said, stepping over recumbent children.

"Nope," said Connie. "Someone named Dulcy. How many women do you have up there anyway?"

Nick ignored the sudden premonition that gripped him. "Just one, Connie. Just one."

"ARE YOU SURE you want to drive up here?" Sybil asked, huddling deeper into the passenger seat. She was wearing her red dress, another pair of Nick's knee socks, a heavy cotton sweater and her down coat. For some reason Leona hadn't wanted to stop at her house, even though they drove right past her driveway before they turned off onto the lake road.

The road wasn't in the best condition. No one lived out there this time of year, and while the road crews made an occasional pass at it with the grader, drifts could pile up for days on end with no one noticing.

"I'm sure," said Leona. "Just lean back and relax and we'll be there in no time. We need a quiet, peaceful place, with no one to bother us, so we can concentrate."

"But we'll be back before it's dark? You did promise, Leona. I have to call my parents and wish them a Merry Christmas, and I really should get my dogs."

"Of course. It's just after two now—it gives us till four-thirty. More than enough time."

"But where are we going?"

Leona smiled sweetly. She was driving faster than usual, her sturdy American car slipping slightly on the snowy roads. "The perfect spot. I've borrowed the Barringtons' house."

"But that's closed up for the winter! And impossible to get to—it's down a long driveway that must have three feet of snow on it."

"It's been plowed. The Barrington grandchildren were up for the skiing—they left this morning. We'll have no trouble, and no one will even know we've been there."

"You mean you didn't ask?"

"I dowsed it," Leona said with dignity. "It's perfectly all right."

"Leona," Sybil said, "when are you going to realize that dowsing isn't the answer to everything? We can't just walk into someone's house without asking permission because a pendulum told you it was okay. A pendulum tends to tell you what you want it to."

"You would never have said such a thing a month ago. The professor has had a very negative effect on you, Sybil. I'm disappointed."

"I'm just trying to be reasonable. Listen, I don't think this is such a good idea. Let's go back to my house. I'll make us some herb tea and we can do it there."

"We're almost there, Sybil."

"I don't feel right about breaking into someone's house," she said, trying to stifle the overwhelming sense of uneasiness that was washing over her. "I want to go home."

Leona pulled up in front of the old frame cottage. The pine trees grew tall and dark around it, shielding it from the lake road, closing them in. "I don't think so," she said very gently. And reaching into her dowdy cloth coat, she pulled out a very small, very shiny, very nasty-looking gun.

"DAMN HER," Nick muttered under his breath, shoving his foot down harder on the accelerator. Damn her for not listening to him. If she'd just paid attention to his suspicions she wouldn't be in this mess.

Of course, what proof did he have that she was in a mess? Just Dulcy Badenham's nebulous doubts, nothing concrete at all. Except those nebulous doubts were enough to send him racing out of Ray and Connie's Newton home and heading back to Vermont at the speed of light, or the Jaguar's equivalent of it.

Sybil and Leona were seen driving down the deserted lake road a little after two. And no one had seen them since. Now, perhaps Dulcy was simply being paranoid, but she thought Nick might want to know.

Nick did indeed want to know. If Dulcy was paranoid, Nick was panicked. The drive from Newton usually took close to five hours—he made it in two and a half. It was lucky the interstates were empty this late Christmas afternoon. He couldn't afford the time it would take to get a ticket, particularly since he was driving close to twice the speed limit.

He roared into Danbury at half-past six, heading straight for Leona's apartment. The door, like all the doors in Danbury, was unlocked, and his worst fears were confirmed when he opened it.

Gladys, the devil cat, was gone. So was every stick of furniture, every piece of paper, every trace of human habitation. Only the shades remained, drawn against the eyes of nosy neighbors. Leona had decamped.

And taken Sybil with her? He slammed out of the apartment, racing down the carefully shoveled walk to the idling car. He tore off down the road to the Black Farm, his hands sweating, his heart pounding, muttering under his breath a savage litany of prayers and curses. *Please God, let her be there.* He'd strangle her if she wasn't. *Please, let her be all right.* He'd kill her if she was hurt. Damn it, and damn her for being a trusting fool. If she was in one piece, he'd beat her for scaring him to death. If she was in one piece, he'd never let her go again.

The darkness of the old Black Farm warned him, but he stormed inside anyway, calling her name, his voice echoing with a ribbon of desperation threaded through it. There was nothing, no word, no sign that she'd even been there. Except for his plaid nightshirt, lying across the neatly made bed, waiting for her return.

Dulcy answered the phone on the first ring. "Where is she?" he barked into the receiver.

"I don't know. Are you back already? You must have come back by broomstick."

"Cut the crap, Dulcy. This isn't the time for jokes. Leona's cleared out her apartment in town; whatever she's planning she's not coming back. Think, for God's sake! Where would they go?"

"Nick, I haven't the faintest—"

"Can't you dowse it? Read the tarot, look into a crystal ball, do something! You're the witch around here, you're the one with a direct line to the infinite."

There was an ominous, insulted silence on the other end. "I don't know where she is, Nick, and I can't find out. I've tried everything feasible."

"What about the dogs? You have them there, don't you? Wouldn't they be able to trace her?"

"Those dogs would chase after the nearest rabbit. They love everything and everybody; they'd just get in the way," Dulcy said patiently. "Let's be logical about this. They were seen heading down the lake road in Leona's car."

"Where does the lake road lead?"

"Around the lake. As far as I know, most of the summer houses are closed for the winter. A few of the summer people come up for the holidays, but I don't remember if anyone did this year."

"Big help," Nick snapped.

"We've got two possibilities," Dulcy continued, ignoring his temper. "It could be either the Montebellos or the Barringtons. Try the Montebellos first. They're the second house past the schoolhouse. The Barringtons are farther in, maybe three miles from the Montebellos. You should be able to tell from the tire tracks."

"Why are you worried?" he said suddenly. "I thought Leona was a good buddy of yours."

"Leona is the sort of person who gives witches a bad name," Dulcy informed him. "Do you want me to meet you at the Barringtons'?"

"Stay put. I'll call you if I need help."

The moon was almost full, lending an eerie brightness to the snow-covered landscape. At least he didn't have to contend with another storm that night. All he had to deal with was a swindler-cum-witch run amok, who'd kidnapped the woman he loved. *Piece of cake,* he snarled to himself, skidding out of the driveway. *Goddamned piece of cake.*

"HOW LONG are you going to keep me here?" Sybil inquired in her most even tones. She was sitting by the fireplace, huddled there for warmth, her feet tucked up under her, the down coat wrapped around her. The sun had set long ago, but Leona had refused to turn on any lights, for fear it would signal their presence to any nosy passersby. Not that anyone passed by this deserted area even in the best of times. And surely everyone had something better to do on Christmas night.

"As long as I need to," Leona replied. "I really expected better of you, Sybil. Your professor was so enamored I would have thought he wouldn't have time to interfere with me. I must have miscalculated."

"You really did rip off the old ladies at the apartments?"

"Of course. You needn't be so disapproving, Sybil." Leona was sitting opposite her, the gun in one tiny little hand, a mug of instant coffee in the other. It was the first time Sybil had ever seen her drink coffee, but then, she'd never seen her hold a gun, either. It was a day for surprises. "I always left them enough to live on. None of them will want for anything. They just won't have enough to leave their children."

"Don't you think that's fairly rotten?"

"Not at all. The children never visit; they set their widowed mothers up in nursing homes and rest homes and retirement apartments and wait for them to die so they can cash in. Why should they get the money when they can't even come to see the old ladies?"

"Very touching, Leona," she said cynically. "But Mary Philbert's children come every weekend; they take her everywhere, even on their summer vacations. As a matter of fact, she used to wish they'd leave her alone. And you ripped her off, just like the others."

Leona shrugged her plump little shoulders. "What can I say? When it comes right down to it, I'm a rotten human being."

"You won't get an argument from me on that one," Sybil mumbled. "Are you going to kill me?"

"Heavens, no! I don't hold with physical violence. I'm simply going to keep you here until it's safe to let you go. When Nick starts looking for you he'll find a note at your house, telling him to sit tight and keep his mouth shut or they'll find your body in the spring."

"I thought you said you don't hold with physical violence," Sybil said, leaning back in the wicker chair. The mantel, like the mantels in half the summer cottages, was cluttered with golf tees, cross-country skiing wax, melted candles, sprung mousetraps and golf trophies. Old Mr. Barrington had won more than his share—there were cups and platters and even statues, all black and tarnished and forlorn-looking. Sybil eyed them wistfully.

"It's an empty threat," Leona said, and she wished she could believe her. "You see, my husband comes up for parole in a couple of days. We need everything peaceful and quiet until that goes through. Then I'll meet him in Canada and we'll live quite happily on the money I've been making."

"I thought your husband was dead."

"You also thought I was a nice person and your professor a danger. Let's face it, Sybil, you're not a great judge of character."

There was the quiet sound of teeth grinding, and then Sybil smiled. If there were only some way she could edge closer to the mantel and its nice heavy trophies. "So you're going to keep me here to keep Nick quiet until your husband gets out of jail. Then what will you do?"

"Tie you up, leave you and call Nick from the border. It's only an hour away, Sybil. You'll survive."

"What if you don't call him?"

"Then they really would find your body in the spring," she said in a comfortable tone of voice. "Be sensible for once in your life. Swindlers have a much lower law enforcement priority than murderers. I'll make sure your professor rescues you, whether you deserve it or not."

"I wish I could believe you."

"It doesn't matter whether you do or not," Leona murmured. "I have the gun."

"So you do." Sybil stretched her legs out in front of her, letting the coat slide down her lap. "I don't suppose you feel like letting me take a nap. I didn't get much sleep last night."

"I imagine you didn't," she said with a nasty smirk. "You can sleep right there in that chair. It's only eight o'clock—"

"We've been here six hours!"

"We're going to be here a lot longer than that before I'm through.... What was that?" She swiveled around at the muffled thud outside the door, the gun pointing away for a brief moment.

Sybil didn't dare hesitate. She leaped up, throwing her coat over Leona's tiny figure. She grabbed a large pewter platter from the Men's Handicap of 1978 and smashed it over Leona's head. She kept struggling, so the Men's Scotch Foursome cup followed suit, crumpling nicely. The gun went off, a bullet went whizzing through the coat to embed itself in the pine-paneled walls and a cloud of feathers filled the air. The Juniors' Handicap of 1941 was the last casualty, its cup parting company with the granite base, and Leona lay still beneath the coat and the feathers.

She heard someone at the door but ignored the sound as she moved toward Leona's motionless body. She knelt down, gingerly lifting the corner of the coat, steeling herself for a gory sight. Leona lay there peacefully enough, an imminent black eye purpling her skin, her plump hand clasped loosely around the little gun. Her breathing was even and steady. With a sigh of relief Sybil stood up, taking the gun with her, and headed for the door.

It wasn't an evil accomplice; it was Nick, looking terrified, furious and wonderfully worried about her. She was in his arms before he even charged through the door, hurling herself at him with enough force to knock him backward onto the snowy porch.

"Are you all right?" he demanded, his hands running over her body, searching for injuries.

"Fine. I knocked the old witch out."

"Good for you." He kissed her, hard, fast and deep on her trembling mouth. "Now if you'd just listened to me in the first place...."

"If you're going to say I told you so," Sybil warned, resting her head against his chest, "then the marriage is off. We'll just live in sin the rest of our lives."

"I won't say I told you so."

"Thanks."

"Not when you already know it."

"Nick ..."

"Is there a telephone in this place? We need to call the police, we need to call Dulcy...."

"How did you find me? Did Dulcy know that Leona had taken me?"

"Dulcy guessed. She called me in Newton and had me hightail it back here. I think I broke the speed record."

"I imagine you did. Thank God for Dulcy."

"What about me?"

She grinned up at him. "Oh, I've been thanking God for you for weeks now, whether I knew it or not."

"I'll make the appropriate response to that after we call the police," he said in a deep, sexy voice. "Where's the telephone?"

She led him past Leona's recumbent figure into the kitchen. "Is she okay?" Nick queried as Sybil began a tortuous leafing through the telephone directory.

"She's fine. I clubbed her as hard as I could, but only the good die young. You want to see if the Barringtons have anything alcoholic in their cupboards while I try to find the state police?"

"Can't you dial 911?"

"Not up in the boonies, you city slicker. Look over there." She flipped through the thin pages, deliberately ignoring the noise in the living room, raising her voice so Nick wouldn't hear. "Anything will do, even cooking sherry. I've never needed a drink so much in my entire—"

"What was that?" He whirled around, turning from the row of bottles.

"I don't know. Maybe—"

"Damn it, she's escaping!" Nick dove through the swinging kitchen door, with Sybil at his heels.

"Let her go, Nick," she called after him.

He stopped on the porch, staring into the moonlit landscape, listening as the sound of a car faded into the distance. Not the rough, sturdy sound of Leona's Pontiac. It was the elegant purr of a Jaguar disappearing into the night.

He turned to glare at the unrepentant Sybil. "She stole my car."

"I'm sorry about that."

"But you wanted her to escape, didn't you?"

She considered denying it, then dismissed the idea. "Yes."

"Why?"

"I don't know. Maybe as a Christmas present. So she's a slightly wicked old lady. I still didn't want to see her in jail."

"Even though she kidnapped you?"

"Even though she made a complete fool of me," she said, moving closer and wrapping her arms around his tall, stubborn body. "So I'm stupid and sentimental. Let someone else catch her—they will soon enough. I just don't want to be the one responsible."

He sighed. "I'll grant her one thing—at least she shot your damned leaking coat."

Sybil looked over his shoulder at the feathery mess. "You'll have to buy me a new one."

"You're ridiculous, you know that?" he said gruffly, bringing his arms up around her.

"I know," she said wearily. "Are you sure you want to marry me? Maybe you'll regret it."

"The only thing I regret," he said, his hands running down the length of the red velvet dress and cupping her hips against him, "is the years I spent without you."

"I won't be a yuppie wife," she warned.

"You'd be foolish to try. You're going to terrorize the stately environs of Harvard, you'll probably start a Cambridge branch of the Seekers of Enlightenment, I'll be stepping over pendulums and L-rods and springer spaniels and piles of books wherever we live, and my children will all be witches."

"Probably," she said, loving the sound of it.

"And I wouldn't have it any other way."

"Neither," she said, "would I." She reached up, feathering her lips across his. "Merry Christmas, Nick."

He pulled her closer, that demonic glint in his eyes promising wonderful things. "Merry Christmas, Sybil. Let's go home."

"Home," she murmured. "That sounds heavenly." She pulled away, scooped up her shredded coat and headed for the door. "The one thing that puzzles me in all this..."

"One thing?" He flicked off the light and shut the door behind them, stepping out into the chilly night air.

"How did you know where to find me?"

"Dulcy told me."

"But how did she know?"

"Someone saw you driving this way."

"Nick, we didn't pass anyone."

"Well, she just used common sense."

"Nonsense. She must have dowsed it."

"Don't be ridiculous, Sybil, she couldn't have—"

"She could have. After all, she's a white witch."

"I don't care if she's a purple witch. Besides, there are no such things as witches."

"Have yourself a merry little Christmas," Sybil sang. "Somehow I don't think our troubles will be out of sight."

He grinned at her from across the expanse of Leona's old blue Pontiac. "Honey, they're probably just beginning. Are you scared?"

She looked at him, her eyes clear and brown. "A little. What about you?"

"A little. Don't worry, if I get rowdy you can always have Dulcy find a spell for me."

"Or you can dose me with Hungarian love philtre."

"Or maybe," he said, "we can take care of it our-selves. Get in the car, Sybil, before I remember what hap-pened to my Jaguar."

"I never liked it anyway," she murmured, climbing in.

"Do we need to stop at Dulcy's on the way back?"

"Nope," Sybil said with a sigh. "She'll know every-thing's all right. After all, she's a witch."

"She is not."

"Is too."

"Not."

"Is . . ."

Have You Heard About...
Dowsing?

Dowsing is a technique older than recorded history. It's most widely used for finding water, but can also be used for finding oils, minerals, lost objects, missing persons and answers to questions both practical and ephemeral. Dowsers (also known as Diviners or Water Witches) often use devices such as pendulums, Y-rods, forked branches, L-shaped rods and any number of other helpful tools, or do it simply by instinct.

Are you a Dowser?

Find out more information by writing:

American Society of Dowsers, Inc.
Brainerd Street
Danville, VT 05828

Canadian Society of Questers
Suite 200-8566 Fraser Street
Vancouver, B.C. V5X 3Y3

British Society of Dowsers
Sycamore Cottage
Tamley Lane
Hastingleigh, Ashford
Kent, England
TN 25

AR177-A-1

ATTRACTIVE, SPACE SAVING BOOK RACK

Display your most prized novels on this handsome and sturdy book rack. The hand-rubbed walnut finish will blend into your library decor with quiet elegance, providing a practical organizer for your favorite hard-or soft-covered books.

Only $9.95

**Approximately
16" x 8"
when assembled**

Assembles in seconds!

To order, rush your name, address and zip code, along with a check or money order for $10.70 ($9.95 plus 75¢ postage and handling) (New York residents add appropriate sales tax), payable to *Harlequin Reader Service* to:

In the U.S.

Harlequin Reader Service
Book Rack Offer
901 Fuhrmann Blvd.
P.O. Box 1325
Buffalo, NY 14269-1325

Offer not available in Canada.

BKR-1

Take 4 best-selling love stories FREE
Plus get a FREE surprise gift!